Downfall by Degrees

Abdullah Hussein

Downfall by Degrees

and other stories

Edited and translated from the Urdu by
Muhammad Umar Memon

TSAR
Toronto
1987

To Asim and Anni Chan, with love

Copyright 1987 T S A R Publications
All rights reserved

Except for the purposes of review no part of this book may be reproduced, by any method, without the permission of the publisher.

ISBN 0-920661-02-5

Cover drawing by Tasaduq Sohail
Printed in Canada

T S A R Publications
PO Box 6996, Station A
Toronto, Ontario M5W 1X7 Canada

Contents

Translator's Preface and Acknowledgements 7

The Rose 13

The Exile 24

The Refugees 35

Downfall by Degrees 63

The Journey Back 128

Preface and Acknowledgements

The three short stories and two novelettes presented here in translation are quite different, in tone and texture, if not perhaps in their final concerns, from the fiction that appeared in the earlier volume *Night and Other Stories* (New Delhi: Orient Longman, 1984). Here, adolescent fervor, the burning impatience of youth, and raw emotion appear to have finally been tamed. We meet a more mature writer; his preeminent concern is now how to best capture the subtlest modulations of feelings, and capture them in a language as stark as he can possibly make it. His microscopic eye is trained, it would seem, on the slightest movement of minute crawling life in the subterranean rot, on the underside of pain, as it were. The tools to probe it, although stunningly simple, are applied with infallible certainty of touch. Overripe lyricism, which envelopes *Night and Other Stories* like a dense, obscuring mist, has given way, or nearly, and less of the syntactical gyration of the former volume intrudes the narrative flow; instead, the rhythms are free of dissonance and gentler, the style is taut and distilled. In contrast, again, to the previous work, the palpable tension generated by feelings of exile and nostalgia does not here lead to a violent end but to the maturer realization that exile and guilt allow no escape, that termination of life, often with explosive force, is hardly an option, let alone a viable option, and that, finally, it is in living through these predicaments that one approaches more nearly the proportions of true tragedy. The adolescents of *Night and Other Stories*—so full of themselves, indulgent, even self-destructive in the end—have at last come of age in their adult acceptance of "exile," of their status as permanent "refugees" in a world moving "by degrees" toward inevitable "downfall." In bearing their fate with proud but quiet dignity, the many characters of the present stories leave us with a more enduring impression of their doomed struggle.

The thematic preoccupation of Abdullah Hussein remains unchanged; he has been writing a single story all the time: emotional disorientation resulting from a harrowing sense of some real or imagined inadequacy, the unbridgeable gulf between longing and becoming. The sources of man's dissatisfaction are many, and most are found in his environment. But for the larger number of Hussein's characters, the malaise is produced, rather, in the interior landscape of the self, is inevitably pointed inward, and is therefore the more tragic. They cannot blame others for their existentialist condition; they are poised fatally against themselves.

Although doomed from the start, these characters ultimately reach a tenuous state of grace in the act of knowledge—a knowledge which, ironically enough, only deepens the sense of tragedy because it does not save, is not even meant to save, but only to enrich the pained consciousness in an abstract sort of way.

Thus, after ten years of being married to a man she respected but did not love, and all her thirty-two years of pining for the man she did love, Sarwat in the story "The Rose" finally gets what she wanted: a night of uninterrupted intimacy with Naim, her childhood love. But is she the happier for it? Has she been set free, as she thought she would be, after the delayed encounter of bodies? Hardly. The morning after she wakes up to the bitter truth: desires —fulfilled or unfulfilled—give us nothing; they only rob us. For once two hearts have lost their harmony, they drift apart, unlikely to come back together, even by a sacrifice of the flesh.

On the other hand, Naim is pleasantly surprised to discover that the woman he had all along considered utterly sexless and ignored had turned out to be so filled with sexual energy, "so... incandescent...so vibrant with life that she carried him to the summit of unimaginable bliss." By her true giving and spontaneity, she had awakened him to a new reality: "When passion has run its course, and the blood has chilled, love is what remains behind... like the fugitive scent of a rose" which, however intangible, "is still more real than its bloom."

But the knowledge comes—alas—too late to do either of them any good. As true exiles, the two must now drift inconsolably in their orbits of loneliness, equipped with a knowledge that does not redeem or soothe, but only picks away at the scab to expose the raw, throbbing wound.

Likewise, it takes a long time for the narrator of the story "The Exile" to realize—in a different time and place and quite by accident—the true reason for the self-imposed loneliness of the old head clerk with whom he had worked in an establishment some years ago. Yet in no way does this knowledge perform an act of salvation, either for the narrator, or for the old, wistful recluse. The fate of the latter is even worse: knowledge for him is the acceptance of the inescapability of alienation. A mild misanthrope, he comes to prefer the company of animals and birds, but is never quite able to transcend his subliminal longing for man.

For Aftab Umar of "The Refugees," on the other hand, it takes considerably longer—in fact thirty years, and then, only through the mediating innocence of his son—to begin to fathom the mystery of the terrible suicide of his father, who had thrown up a formidable wall around himself and lived behind it in a state of lethal solitude. Trained to be a minor civil servant, he rather wished to be a movie star—and loved horses.

"Downfall by Degrees," as poet-critic Muhammad Salim-ur-Rahman has aptly put it, "treats exile and alienation as a state of mind, as a destabilising mood.... It is not, as some readers have hastily concluded, an attempt at writing detective fiction. The narrator, a writer of fiction himself, tries to fathom what made an otherwise decent, unimposing civil servant kill his equally decent wife. Ostensibly he does this to help one of his closest friends, a distinguished lawyer, who is defending the husband. It is not idle curiosity that spurs the narrator to find out all he can about the husband and wife and establish a motive for murder. He realises, at a subliminal level, that in some way the case mirrors the inner, suppressed emotions of his lawyer friend. By wanting to defend the husband and discover a motive, the lawyer is in fact defending himself. He is on trial himself. The narrator, standing as a communicative barzakh between the two married pairs, manages ultimately to show, implicitly, that the murdered wife and her husband, who gets a life sentence, both faced up squarely to the emptiness and meaninglessness of their existence and acted without flinching from the consequences, while the successful lawyer and his wife, with the same emptiness in their lives, have lacked the courage to act, to make a choice and therefore, in spite of worldly glory, they are mere empty, defeated people" ("Modes of Survival," *Pakistan Times,* 24 November 1981, p. 4).

"The Journey Back" is a journey to nowhere, or perhaps to the dead center of a gnawing emptiness rarely encountered in contemporary Urdu fiction. Seemingly less subtle, even artless by comparison to other stories in the present collection, its narrative simplicity hides a more assured art. It is this simplicity in the end that invests the grim lives of the characters with a tragic destiny. "The Journey Back" explores, with brutal poignancy, the devastating effects of "alienation" on the lives of a group of semiliterate, lower-class Pakistani expatriates living their bleached-out, wraith-like, insubstantial existence in a ramshackle building in a Birmingham ghetto of Great Britain. Because they are illegal aliens in the country, they live out their days in cloistered isolation, in constant fear of deportation and the sundry humiliations their precarious status might expose them to. In the end, they are so dehumanized that they begin to fear even their own shadows.

None of the main characters comes out emotionally intact from the ordeal, not even when some of them have acquired legal residence in the country and made it in this affluent new world. Economic sufficiency—the temptress that lured them to their dank, chilly, sun-starved, British exile—has exacted a terrible price: it has robbed their lives of all meaning and joy. Indeed the effects of alienation are so pervasive that they reach even to some of the minor characters, among them the narrator's wife, whose presence is felt but fleetingly across the fictional space of the work. In spite of all the trappings of material comfort, she is at heart a very sad and lonely individual. Which makes her narrator-husband wonder: "I don't know what's eating her away. She has been unhappy since the day she set foot in this country. She has all the comforts anyone can ask for: her own house, a car, a TV which she watches all day long. Why, we have plenty. She lives a life of ease. The kids are in school. And yet, there's never been a glimmer of happiness on her face. I ask her, 'Don't you like it here?' And she tells me that it doesn't matter to her; she's happy wherever I am. Now what kind of an answer is that? What I can't figure out is, what is it that makes her unhappy?"

By contrast, the fate of some of the main characters is infinitely worse. Husain Shah and Irshad—uncle and nephew—are mutually eliminated, ostensibly, by a quarrel over money, but in reality by their jealousy over a white woman. Saqib—the delicate youth, radiant, if also naive and inexperienced, who inspired only the tenderest feelings of affection—is made permanently insane by a violent act of romantic love. When we next meet him, it is in a mental institution. Unable to feel or remember anything, he is now little more than a vegetable. And his vacant, glazed eyes mirror life's potential sadly gone to waste. But if he is the most thoroughly destroyed, a none too enviable fate awaits the narrator as he finds out that Saqib was after all innocent of the crime pinned on him. How this knowledge will poison the rest of his days and how he will deal with the nagging question—"What did Saqib do to deserve this?" —is anybody's guess.

Yet knowledge, though brutal in its exposition of alienation as an unalterable human condition, does not make these characters sluggish, unambitious or inactive. Bleak though their life may be, they still strive for perfection in their own small way, aware—always aware—that their longing for meaning might prove in the end to be no more than the desire for the unattainable. It is the unflinching application of the self to a courageous—but ultimately doomed—struggle that sets the tone of the present stories apart from the earlier collection, in which knowledge is another name for self-destruction.

While the simple grace of unadorned language of these stories—all of which appear in Hussein's Urdu collections *Nasheb* (Lahore: Qausain Publishers, 1981) and *Saat Rang* (New Delhi: Shaoor Publications, 1982)—has proved a boon for the translator, the final product has been made possible only through the editorial help of friends. Faruq Hassan of Dawson College, Montreal, Canada, read the drafts of "The Exile," "The Refugees" and "Downfall by Degrees" and offered valuable suggestions. And I'm grateful to him for his assistance. I would also like to thank Wayne R. Husted and Shelah Bloom. The former collaborated in the translation of the novelette "Downfall by Degrees," the latter in the translation of the novelette "The Journey Back."

—Muhammad Umar Memon

The Rose

"More?" the woman asked.
"No."
"Have another."
"No thanks."
"Just one more cup."
"Stop it," he said, feeling very irritated. "You know I don't drink much tea."
"No I don't."
"You don't what?"
"I don't know."
"What don't you know?"
"Anything about you."
"What!" He was stunned.

But he had known her for such a long time. In fact, he knew all her family—even her husband—so well that they considered him as one of their own...and from so far back he could hardly remember exactly when. Perhaps since the time when he and her older brother went to school together. One day they had fought over something and were both punished by the teacher: one had to do extra writing drills after school, the other to water the school plants. Later they returned home, school bags dangling from their necks, one walking behind the other, seemingly unaware of each other's presence. The next day they made up and became friends again. They were second graders then.

Or perhaps from earlier still: the day the strangers had just arrived in the house next door. He had spent practically the whole day glued to their doorway watching the spectacle: men, women and children scurrying in and out of the house, hauling in baggage, slamming doors and windows shut or open, and the clouds of dust swirling up from all their activity. He was so taken up with it that he had gone back home only once to grab a quick lunch, and then dashed back to his place in the doorway to resume watching. The children's mother once asked him where he lived, but he did not bother to reply. A while later when she invited him in, he didn't stir from his place or utter a word. The woman gave up and went inside. The next few days he contented himself merely with looking at the children from a distance, as if trying to get used to them being around...God knows from how far back!

"But you do," he said, emphatically. "You know me very well."

"No, I don't."

This was the very first time that she had talked with such headstrong defiance, such chilling certainty. He was absolutely stunned. He blinked his eyes a few times in utter disbelief and then just stared at her, as if he were trying to figure out who she really was.

The evening had crept into the room in the meantime, filling it with darkness. Neither stirred to turn on the lights. The china flickered before them in the faint, soft evening light. She was sitting bent over the china, twirling a spoon in the empty tea cup with one hand, the other lying curled up in her lap. Her head, with its thick, dark hair, was directly in front of him. There was not even a trace of mascara on her eyes and she was wearing no lipstick.

The thought that this could be happening after he had known this woman all these years pinched his heart with a sadness he could not understand.

"I am Naim," he said.

"Oh?" She lifted her face, full of mocking scorn.

"And you are Sarwat."

"Right again."

"So?"

"So what?"

He was stung by the cold indifference of her tone. A nameless, impotent anger began to curl its way up through his body and into his brain. The room was getting dark fast. Lights from a passing car shot in through the window, flashed on their faces, and disappeared.

"Get up and turn on the light!" he commanded.

"No."

"Do it!" he persisted.

"Darkness is better."

So unlike her! If he had half expected that she would act that way, he would not have let his temper get out of hand. As he was getting up to turn on the lights himself, his knee bumped the tea table and knocked it over. Suddenly his anger vanished. Something had calmed his nerves: perhaps it was the sight of the mess on the floor, or the sense of total independence emanating from her face as she sat quietly holding the spoon, or perhaps it was just the noise of the chinaware as it went crashing down in the darkness.

"This is all your fault," he said, feeling utterly exhausted.
"Things look," she began, "different in the darkness."
"How?"
"You cannot see...your mind moves faster."
"What's gotten into your head?"
"But there's an advantage," she went on, "Your eyes manage to get some rest."
"You've gone crazy."

Returning, he dropped down into his chair. This event was totally unexpected; it left him suddenly very tired. In spite of the passage of time, the presence of this woman—the mere thought of her being somewhere around—still inspired only the deepest sense of comfort in him; she was a haven where he felt perfectly safe and calm. And oddly, she inspired all that without possessing a trace of the seductiveness he seemed to find in all other women—whether close to him or not, with or without names. This infatuation with women had put him through much unnecessary pain. For much of his life he both feared and yet felt irresistibly drawn toward every woman that came his way. The resulting torment left him exhausted, and there were times when he felt he could not keep himself together any more. The sight of a young woman—the prettiest, most profound and complete creation of God—only made him flee her. Oh, yes, he knew years of that misery very well! And right up until he had finally married he knew, that no matter how much he ran around, the one place where he could find calm, care, and security, the place where he regained his insight, his ebbing confidence, and lived in unbounded freedom, was somewhere around this girl. That was how well he knew her!

"You're in a great mood today," he said. "Spoiling for a fight, aren't you...with everybody?"

"Not with everybody," she snapped, "just with *you*." She used the more formal *aap*, not the familiar *tum*.

"I can tell you've come here straight after a brawl with Mahmud."

"Mahmud is my husband."

"So?"

"What goes on between him and me is my personal business."

"I'm not part of your *personal* business?"

"No."

"W-w-what?"

"You are not part of my personal business."

"You've got to be joking."

"No, I'm not."

"Oh,..." he said, suppressing his anger. "How I wish it were true."

"But it *is* true. You have no part in anything that has to do with me."

"Then do me a favor, will you? Tell everybody else that."

"Why?"

"Because I'm pretty sick of trying to keep the peace between you and Mahmud all the time."

"Well you can blame yourself for it. After all, you created the mess."

"I created the mess?"

"You fixed my marriage with Mahmud—didn't you?"

"So I'm to blame for it—is that it?"

"At least you are responsible for it."

"So I'm to blame for it?" he repeated, genuinely shocked.

"I don't know. I don't know anything."

It was staggering, completely unexpected. The otherwise clear, incandescent region of the mind which might have registered the impact of what was happening—and so fast—suddenly went black. He stopped thinking about everything, concentrating on the floor, now littered with spilled milk, tea and sugar. Then getting up so effortlessly to pick up the scattered cups and saucers a little while later, setting them back upon the tray and straightening the overturned table, the tragedy of the soiled carpet and the shattered tea cup suddenly hit him with all its comic intensity. He could not believe that this woman—so fiercely independent now, unrestrained in her acts and words (come to think of it, when, in all those thirty years, had she ever looked any different)—had always seemed to him something like an empty tea cup—fragile, vulnerable, even dumb! And he thought he had known her for ages, the ages required to know somebody well! Ages—including childhood, when unaware of the passage of time one played with friends in far-flung spots nobody else knew existed, and played games so intimate that one even became familiar with the scent of the other's skin. The time that left its indelible imprint on all the subsequent stages of one's life, so that later even a casual walk through a spot vaguely resembling a place in childhood evoked warm memories of that rich time, of those places, names, voices, and sometimes, even an unfinished gesture, or a sudden gleam in someone's eye. Every moment in childhood lasted a whole lifetime. He knew her from back then!

"I'm fed up."
"With what?"
"Your foolish quarrels."
"Who asked you to—"
"To what?"
"—stick your nose into my affairs?"
"But I had to."
"Had to—how so?"
"How? Well...because...because I'm your...oh, well..."
"Yes, yes, go on, because you're my what?"
"Well, I mean a member of your family—or almost."
"But there are other members in my family."
"Then I suppose because I'm responsible for arranging a match for you."
"Who asked you to?"
"Who? Well...damn it, your family—who else?"
"But I didn't! Did I?"
"You...er-r-r, well, you...you knew about it all right."
"The important thing is, did you ask me?"
"What difference—"
"Does that make—right?"
"So what do you want me to do now?" he said in a dead voice.
"You just keep out of my affairs, that's all." She again used the polite but formal *aap*.

Even her curt, aggressive manner was new to him. They both went back a lot of years, and he could swear she had never, absolutely never, talked to anyone like this, at least not on a personal level.

"*Aap, aap...*" he said, "cut it out. Stop all this litany. Can't you talk to me in plain language?"

"Aap...that's the right word. Yes—*aap*."

"Ah-h-h-h!" he emitted a deep, tormented sound.

"All right, *tum*, if you insist," she smiled. "*Tum*—alright?"

This was all so strange, so unforeseen. For he remembered all that time very well. He had lost all sense of direction. In the evening he would wander around alone on deserted streets for hours, and then he would go over to her house and just slump down into a chair. Sometimes when the desire for company became very oppressive and she happened to be all alone in the house, he would lift his head up and say something to her—just anything, like: "Sarwat, do you have any idea where I was roaming around before I got here?" Or, "Come talk to me...I'm tired." Or, "Why are you always working—crazy?" And still working away in her slow, impersonal manner, she would make some gesture or merely utter something, putting him back into the state of peace he had been desperately seeking. And then there was that time later on, just after his marriage. He asked her, "Sarwat, how do you like Bilqees?" and she had replied, "Bhabi is nice. I like her a lot..." in a tone which he still remembered vividly, a tone which sent a chill over his body even now when he thought about it, not because it was tinged with envy or sadness, but because it sounded so impersonal, so metallic. It was so unexpected. And then there was also the time when his wife—the only person besides his mother he could get close to—had died. The incident had left him broken, lost. Sitting by her one day, the words just rolled out of his mouth, "Bibi, you tell me—why?" And she had replied, "Be patient!" Just about everyone had parroted those words to him—those words devoid of meaning and packed with utter indifference. They hurt a lot coming from her, too. Yes, these times and the many others before and after in which he had thought that they met as equals; they were still alive in his memory.

"These things you say, bibi, they're all so shocking."

"Bibi, bibi," she exploded, "*bibi?*"

"What?"

"Am I a sheep, goat, or what? Don't I have a name? Don't I—"

"Sarwat!"

"That's better. Sarwat...that's my name."

"Sarwat!"

"All my life you have never ever called me by my name, or acknowledged my existence, or considered me worth anything... anything at all..."

"Anything at all?" his mouth hung open in disbelief.

"You have gone on pronouncing my name—mechanically, that's all. But you've constantly ignored—"

"Ignored—what?"

"Me," she screamed. "Me!"

"I don't understand."

"You never gave it a thought, did you, that I, too, am a human being, like you, like everyone else. That I see, think, feel, and have an existence all my own. Just as you have, just as everybody else has."

"But Sarwat, I have always—"

"Cared for me? Right. Have been around me—always? Oh yes. Have been familiar and close? Yes, that is also correct. But totally indifferent all the same. How terribly indifferent—have you ever thought about it?"

"Wrong. Absolutely wrong. It's you who have been indifferent."

"My misfortune, Naim, is that you know me from a time when I was a mere toddler who ran about barefoot in the alleyways with nothing but a shirt on while you pulled my hair. Oh, yes—you were very familiar with me, but equally unmindful of me. You've always been. And if I've been indifferent, blame it on that familiarity which drew a curtain between us, making me too shy for words."

"That was your mistake."

"Mistake? More like my helplessness."

"I don't understand. You derive the wrong conclusion from our childhood friendship."

"So should I rather draw one from childhood enmity? Enmity means nothing. Enmity is foolishness. Friendship is what hurts. Look at me. Take me in—all of me. There, take a good look at me. You've never ever really looked at me. I am a woman, a person... has that never occurred to you?"

"I've never been unmindful of you."

"Oh, yes. You have always been mindful of me, but in exactly the same manner as you have been mindful of this chair, or that table, or that date palm over there. But have you ever considered me for what I truly am?"

"I have always considered you as Sarwat. Jawaid's sister. A very dear person. A reasonable, decent girl..."

"Do you even know what 'reasonable, decent girl' means," she said, throwing her hands up in the air indignantly. "Where we live, a 'reasonable, decent girl' is another name for a cow—a mere chattel, counting for nothing, always taken for granted, accepted, and ignored, yes always ignored."

"Aren't you overreacting...a bit? Think with a cool head..."

"After a lifetime of sheer torture, who can keep their head cool? One cannot even think. You men...you treat us so badly."

"We men?"

"Yes—you men."

"Oh, Sarwat," he said, feeling utterly tired, "am I really to blame for it?"

"And why not?" she said. "Mahmud was your friend. It was you who fixed my marriage with him. Couldn't you have asked at least?"

"Ask? But I did ask—your family."

"Family—who are they? They're just family."

"What do you mean?"

"The family wasn't important. You were."

"How?"

"For me. You mattered for me. They didn't."

"Sarwat..." Now he was truly rattled. "I don't understand what you mean."

He got his answer all right; not from her words, but from her bold, silent eyes.

He leaned back in the chair and began looking around, embarrassed.

She got up and began pacing around the room. Then she said, "Naim, women can be incredibly patient and modest. You cannot even imagine how much. In fact, up until recently I couldn't have dared to look you in the face and talk to you. But now, after everything I have been through, I have no energy left for patience or modesty. I'm already thirty-two years old, and I've seen life in most of its forms, however hidden or covered."

"Sarwat!"

"I'd thought of the world as being very large; its immensity, its problems would help me forget everything. What wouldn't a woman do to keep her head up? She will deceive everyone, even herself, right up to the end. Don't ever think that I'm blaming Mahmud for anything. My husband is a very nice person. He has never hurt me..."

He sprang to his feet, but sat back down just as suddenly.

She continued, still pacing, "It's been a full ten years since we got married but not once in all this time have I been able to talk with him openly. God knows I've tried. Every single day and every single night. Believe me, I have—"

"For God's sake shut up!"

"Every single night, in fact at every single instant, I've had this terrible feeling that somewhere along the line I've lost something —something that is essential for sincerity between two individuals. The loss has been gnawing away at my heart incessantly. Then, well, there comes a day when one begins to choke on one's breath, when one feels, inexorably, how futile it all is. How terribly futile and pointless it all is."

"Sarwat Begum," he interjected, "you cannot turn it all around now, can you?"

"True. But I can at least put an end to that pain."

"And just how do you propose to do that?"

"Naim," she said, "something is suffocating me. There is some unfinished business."

"How can I possibly help?"

"Set me free."

"How?" he shouted. "How?"

Then, the sight of her silent eyes, made bold by longing, and of her lamenting, despairing, but flagrant hands spread out in the air in eloquent entreaty immobilized him completely.

When it was past midnight, he awoke to the thought that love, too, came in different varieties. There was the love that robbed you. But no matter what sort it was, love was love; it had the power, at least, to distance a man from himself and carry him to something greater.

In the early part of night he had asked just one question, "Do you always sleep naked?" "Shh—" she had merely hissed, as one does to stop a child from being too inquisitive in sacred places or at funerals. That "Shh" turned out to be the only thing she uttered during the whole night. There are many kinds of women, he thought, feeling a bit surprised. Take this one: until this evening she had remained utterly sexless and unattractive. But then had turned out to be so spontaneous, so amazingly incandescent, so vibrant with life that she had carried him to the summit of unimaginable bliss instantly. When love and a woman come together, a miracle is born. One gets to experience a segment of life through this miracle. Be it sublime or low, it is momentous all the same, because of its truly exquisite power to transform and exalt man—even to immortality. And he was discovering all that only now—he who had thought that he knew all there was to know about man from birth to death, who had a taste of all life's highs and lows, its pains and comforts; he who had thought that nothing, absolutely nothing could surprise him any more. He was truly astonished to see how that same moment which he had experienced innumerable times with other women since puberty—the moment which had sometimes left him ashamed, sometimes full of anxiety, and sometimes simply satiated—how that moment, when love and a woman's perfect willingness blend, could suddenly both give man (in spite of its inherent poverty) the heady experience of power and introduce him to the heights of self-absorption where he could melt and permeate the whole universe. When passion has run its course, and the blood has chilled, *love* is what remains behind—like the memory of a good time, a memory more enduring and pleasant than the time itself. Or like the fugitive scent of a rose: no matter how intangible, it is still more real than its bloom...

He was discovering all that tonight. But that blissful moment had flitted away. His conqueror's body, now satiate and calm, lay stretched out on the bed as he stared vacantly at the ceiling. His eyes had adjusted to the darkness in the room. A lot was going through his mind, but every now and then he threw a distracted glance at the woman who was staring at the wall, her back turned toward him. Her long, dark body, which she had not even bothered to cover, was tremulous; she was continuously bursting into a series of gentle but deep, muffled and unfamiliar laughs—or perhaps they were sobs. Several times he felt the urge to get up and find out whether she was laughing or crying, but in spite of his best efforts he could not lift himself up, or even move a finger. He just lay there: his body victorious and calm; his heart full of death.

And so after thirty-two years of pleasant and unpleasant experiences she—who lay with her face to the wall—had finally learned that one didn't suffer from one's own fate or deeds in life, but from the chance of birth. Desires—fulfilled or unfulfilled—what did they give us? They only made us poorer. We had to suffer them equally. Once two hearts have gone out of harmony, they drift apart. Nothing can bring them back together, not even the sacrifice of body. Perhaps she was crying after all.

The next morning he found himself sitting across from her at the breakfast table. He stared at her continuously until her mother came in to clear the table. He tried to say something several times, but could not manage the right words. Finally, he uttered, "Sarwat!"

But she got up and said, "Let's go."

"Sarwat!"

"Let's go," she repeated. "Get up."

He said goodbye to her mother and followed her out of the house.

"There's been a letter from Jawaid," she informed him. "He's coming next week. This time he wants to take mother along. You know what that means? The house will be empty. Perhaps we'll lock it up…or rent it out…The sun is so cold this morning!"

"Sarwat!"

"There, look. Those girls have taken a nasty fall from the bicycle. Why must two girls ride on one bicycle?"

"Sarwat…"

"Shh—"

"Sarwat!"

"No, Naim, no!" she implored in a drained voice. "Please don't say another word."

He kept quiet, but went on staring at her.

"Shall we walk...or take the bus?"
"Whatever you like."
"Let's walk then. It isn't all that far."
"No, it isn't."
"Futile!"
"Huh?"
"Absolutely futile."
"What?"
"Futile? Stupid! Worthless!"
"No, it isn't! Sarwat, listen to me..."
"You men, how shabbily you treat us," she said, feeling miserable. "Well, there's my house."

He started and stopped short. When he proceeded toward the door, she turned quickly around and said in a resolute voice, "You can go now."

"Where?"
"Just go."
"But Sarwat..."
"No, Naim," she said, "you must go now."

Inside she found Mahmud slouched on the sofa reading the newspaper.

She sat down in a chair, and leaned her head over the back of it, closing her eyes.

A little later when she was fixing lunch and her husband sat close by, still buried in his newspaper, she smiled with some effort and asked, "What's the matter—you haven't gone to office today?"

The Exile

I stood upon a high place
And saw, below, many devils
Running, leaping
And carousing in sin.
One looked up, grinning,
And said, "Comrade! Brother!"
                STEPHEN CRANE

In those days each of us packed a lunch. During the noon break we'd get together and eat. Seven people, including me, worked in the office: three clerks, a dispatcher, a typist, a man who ran errands, and a head clerk at the top. At noon we would stop work, pull two tables together and set down our lunchboxes. Then all five of us would pull our chairs over to the tables, take a seat and start eating. Throughout the meal the office boy, who took care of our sundry needs and ran errands, would stand nearby, ready to serve us water. I still remember him vividly. From a mere clerk I have risen to the position of a deputy secretary and during this period I must have dealt with at least a couple of dozen office boys, but I can think of none who possessed a sharper intelligence. Our office boy had the uncanny ability to know, God knows how, exactly when during the meal each of us used to drink water. The typist, for instance, downed about half a glass after approximately every five mouthfuls; the dispatcher, on the other hand, drank a glass before the meal and a glass after; and so on and so forth. Without ever seeming to keep a close eye on us, the office boy would be ready beside us with a glass at our usual drinking time. He followed this routine with such unrelenting regularity that if anyone asked for water out of turn, the boy would just gawk at him and then look at the others one by one in sheer astonishment; the poor offender would be so embarrassed he'd immediately drop the whole matter. I was new in the office. As a rule, I never touched a drop of water during my meals. But the man, his abilities being truly remarkable, didn't take long to find that out. So, now, as long as I remained eating, he made sure to stay away from me. Did he work according to our habits? Or was it rather we who set our routines around his work pattern? I have never been quite able to figure that out.

    After we had eaten, he would close our lunchboxes and set them in a corner. Then he would wipe the tables with a rag and go out on the porch. There he would sit on a stool and eat his own lunch. He would chew each morsel long and hard and wipe his mouth with the same rag after each bite. In short, our office boy was quite a man.

There was another routine which invariably took place during our meal. I'd better mention that, too. This consisted of the following salvo of remarks:

"There, look!" someone would abruptly say. Everyone would look in the same direction out of the corner of his eye.

The rest would then start to snicker. Soon the chomp-chomp of jaws and the dull clinking of dishes would drown out the flurry of suppressed, mocking laughter.

"Come on, it won't hurt to ask him over once," somebody would suggest, as a joke.

"Yes, yes. We could do that—someday, maybe, not now."

"You can't be serious. He's rotten..."

"Of course we could invite him to join us. But then how are we going to get our daily fun. Think about it."

"What if he made it a habit to join us everyday? We wouldn't be able to get him off our backs."

"No, never." Someone would touch his ear lobes, as if dispelling a dreaded but likely prospect. "He spells trouble. Don't you see, he's dying to tag along. It's written all over the fool's face."

Again they would give the man a sidelong glance.

"Hee, hee, hee."

"The miserable wretch."

"Alright, tell me this," somebody would ask, looking perplexed. "What in the world is he going to do with his piles of money? He has nobody, nobody at all. Why, the stinking bastard doesn't even believe in spending money on his own food and drink."

"Oh well, some people are born that way. They just don't know how to enjoy."

"Look—"

"Ah-ha."

Once again the sound of dutifully masticating jaws and the glug-glug-glug of water being downed amid suppressed mocking sniggers would permeate the scene. And he'd be sitting there by a wall staring helplessly at us.

"Let's chip in and buy him a lunch. What do you say?" someone would propose.

"And he'll leave you a fortune in his will—is that it?"

"Ha ha ha!...Good God!"

"Oh, let him be. Look, look! Now's the time to see—"

"Hee, hee, hee!"

The butt of our mealtime exchange used to be none other than our head clerk. With some minor variations we invariably went through the above routine every day. Our conversation betrayed the peculiar mentality of our white-collar class who bend over backwards to find an element of the ridiculous in their superiors so as to vent their numerous frustrations. The sagging pouches below the eyes and the withered, ashen face belonged to our head clerk who had aged well before his time. The thick mop of snow-white hair gave his face a peculiar, somewhat disturbing look. He was a slim, slight man whose forehead, neck and arms were webbed with protruding blue veins. He was also a quiet man who seldom spoke, and when he did, his voice sounded like a resonance in a lofty dome. It gave the impression of an eerie unreality, seemed somehow borrowed rather than the speaker's own. Indeed you might even think it was so violently beaten it had been left only half-alive. It was hard to say exactly what was wrong. Too high? Too low? Or simply twisted out of shape? Whatever. At least one thing was sure: it just didn't go along with the man, his face, even the objects around him. Above all, it grated—in an absurd sort of way. Such, at any rate, was the effect of his voice and manner of speech. It was as if some thought came to him in waves, but never remained long enough for him to articulate it clearly. When he did try to express it, though—through a medley of pauses, reflections, intermittent droopings of the head and neck-scratchings—he never quite made it, managing to get out only a tiny fraction of what he'd wanted to say. The effort left him gasping for breath, his chest bellowing like an asthmatic. At such moments he invariably sank back in his chair, leaning hard against the back for support, and looked away from you. I got used to the eccentric man all right, but it took some time. When I was new to the office, though, I often wondered how there could exist men who had only to speak to you to make your blood freeze.

He never ate lunch. In fact, he had never been seen eating anything at all during office hours. As for outside the office, well, the question just didn't arise. Not a soul knew where he lived or what he did with his free time. All he ever consumed at lunch break was a cup of tea, which he'd ask the office boy to bring him exactly five minutes before the hour of twelve. He'd let the tea sit until thoroughly cooled. And then he'd sip it, in a manner rather like the way he talked, if perhaps a bit more unusual. For it revealed yet another peculiar aspect of his personality. The same routine would be played out every day without fail. As we ate our lunch, he'd sit with his cup of tea, his eager eyes greedily fastened upon us. He'd pick up the cup now and then, sniff the moist aroma, and put the cup back down. Or he would simply stare into the tea, as if watching his reflection, or barely touch the rim with his lips, or simply turn it around a few times before setting it back down untouched. He'd then go back to staring at us and our food with the same tormented look of depravation. At such times his face expressed the strange hunger and yearning which prompted, as well as explained, our lunchtime conversation. When we covered our faces to hide our laughter or momentarily withdrew our eyes from him to drink water, he would stealthily pick up the cup and take a quick gulp or two of the brew.

And yet the man also possessed a couple of uncommon virtues: self-reliance and a quiet dignity. These saved him, despite his glaring oddities and strange mannerisms, from looking like a total fool.

It is rather surprising that such qualities should be present in the sort of individual I have described. But the fact is that as long as he kept his eyes trained upon us from a distance, they never expressed anything other than helplessness, want and craving, each one of which, however, disappeared the moment he turned to his work. He would totally immerse himself in it, indeed he would become one with it. When he wrote with his pen, waving it now and then in the air, or tapping his forehead or the tabletop with its other end, he looked like the editor of some leading newspaper creating a great editorial. He would hand out his instructions without once taking his eyes off the papers, and hand them out in a voice that rang with ineluctable authority. The self-reliance with which he would turn down all our offers of assistance was truly remarkable. He had a gift for writing. From the stenographer to the secretary, none dared change a word or dispute a point once he had completed a draft. Through the cluttering maze of his table and numerous file cabinets, his slim, cadaverous—but above all self-absorbed—body glided with the agile, swift grace of a forest animal. Papers, files, and office furniture—this was his territory, his home ground, and the rapport he had developed with them was so natural and uninhibited it not only made for tremendous efficiency but also gave him an inner grace which both inspired respect and a sense of awe in all of us. These uncommon attributes of the man were in fact the reason for my unflagging interest in him. I was new to the office and still unaffected by the peculiar mentality of the white-collar worker—a mentality that undercuts the enjoyment of the wonder and novelty of experience.

I was soon obliged to leave that job. My desire to unravel the mystery of that man remained unfulfilled. And so it was that it became one more item in the catalogue of my purely intellectual frustrations with which every thinking being must wrestle from time to time.

But even in those few days of my employment something quite remarkable did happen. It helped me later—much later—in my effort to solve that mystery. It was the circumstance of my accompanying him to his house and spending an hour or so with him. It so happened that our office boy had taken a few days off and the head clerk unexpectedly had to take home an unusual number of files. Being a rather fragile man, he was unequal to carrying more than a few files. And so he ordered me—the junior-most member in the outfit—to carry the extra files for him.

His house was located in the back end of nowhere, so to speak. We had to go through the whole town to get to it. He walked briskly, and although I was young then, I soon found it difficult to keep up with him. By the time we arrived, I was quite simply out of breath and puffing. I put down the bundle of files on the staircase to catch my breath. What shocked me was that he hadn't tired at all, not even as much as he used to when he momentarily talked to anyone of us at the office.

He unlocked the door and we entered. Very softly, he pulled it shut and fastened the bolt. The first things that caught my eye were the pets that crowded the whole house from the entrance door to the courtyard and beyond it to the veranda and the stairs and porches. We were first greeted by a pair of medium-sized bulldogs. In a welcoming gesture they darted up and landed with their front paws on his thighs. Next, the parrot in the wire bird cage suspended from the veranda ceiling screeched an ardent "Welcome!" Whereupon, not be outdone, the mynah bird in the neighboring cage also warbled something which I couldn't quite make out. Meanwhile, a small white dog, his face buried under a thick mat of hair, rose yawning from a cot. Taking each step with exquisite grace and elegance, he walked over to his master and began rolling over his feet. There was a rather large cage in one corner of the veranda. It was crammed with scores of colorful tiny birds. They went wild the moment they spotted us. They began to fly about, falling all over and dashing against or dangling from the spiked walls of the cage, twittering and trilling boisterously. In the opposite corner was a slightly smaller cage with a mongoose in it. The mongoose suddenly lifted its snout and began to pace up and down excitedly. As we entered the room, a pair of cats, one black, the other white, jumped off a table and emitting happy meows, walked up to him and began rubbing themselves against his legs. He seemed to know intimately the nature and temperament of each of his pets. Some he fondled and patted, others he teased and spanked, still others he pressed between his legs or picked up lovingly in his arms. There were also those whom he only waved at from a distance. He reached the living room calling to them by their odd names.

"Have a seat," he said, without turning to look at me. Then he took a chair himself and straight away began poring over his files in quiet absorption. About half a dozen pets were stationed all around him on the floor and even on the chairs. All of this somehow didn't seem to bother him. He worked through it all with the same fierce concentration as when at the office. As usual, he punctuated his work by alternately tapping the table and his forehead with the end of his pen. Two things, however, put me slightly ill at ease. One was that he called out to his pets by their names every now and then and talked to them with the same natural ease with which one talks to human beings. He made solicitous inquiries about their well-being and scolded them for their slightest misdeeds. Once in a while he would also reach out his hand to pet one of them. The other thing was that by now he had become completely oblivious of my presence in his house.

Exasperated by it all, I decided to get the man to take notice of my presence. I got up. But he paid no attention. Finding nothing better to do, I began pacing up and down the room with my hands folded behind my back. The room was suprisingly bare of the usual living room furnishings, except for a dozen or so chairs and tables randomly placed. Three photographs, covered over with a layer of dust, hung from the western wall. I stole a sidelong glance at the owner of the house as I stealthily blew the dust off them. The first picture revealed a rosy-cheeked, bright-eyed, strapping youth, outfitted in a boy-scout uniform and laughing lightheartedly beside a mountain stream. His face was radiant with the sap of early youth, and stars gleamed in his eyes. His smile was so captivating that I found myself unable to take my eyes off him for a long while.

The next photograph presented a confident-looking young man in a black gown holding a diploma in his hand. His eyes burned with the strength of resolution and gave his entire face a look of granite determination. He was doubtless of the sort who reach out for the stars.

The third picture showed a few infantrymen in fighting gear. They stood by an army vehicle in the middle of nowhere. To the left and slightly apart from the group stood an aging man leaning over his rifle. He looked exhausted, his face worn by sheer boredom and misery. He bore a faint resemblance to the man who was now bent over his files, working away.

Surprisingly, the only inscriptions the pictures had were their dates. Thirteen years separated the second picture from the first, and six the third from the second. Suddenly through my musings, as I stood looking at the pictures, I sensed the head clerk's eyes silently intent upon me. But when I turned around to look at him I found him once again drooped over his files. I walked over to my chair and sank down into it. In spite of a shining clean floor and not a speck of dust on the furniture—or what went for it at any rate— the room was permeated by a strange mouldy smell one finds only in old monasteries or abandoned wells. From that smell, and the look of unfamiliarity in the eyes of his pets, I gathered that our head clerk was the sole occupant of this house and few outsiders had ever entered here.

Finally, after another half hour or so, the head clerk rubbed his hand on his forehead and got up. He had been through half a dozen files already and was folding them shut.

"Come, let's make some tea," he said on his way out of the living room.

On the veranda he stopped briefly to respond to something his parrot had squawked. I followed into the kitchen.

"Sit," he said.

This was absolutely the only spot in the whole house where the floor looked dirty. First he picked up a broom from a corner and swept the floor clean. And while he worked he kept up a steady barrage of gentle scoldings and instructions to his cats and dogs who had come trailing into the kitchen behind us. Then he turned on the stove, put the kettle on to boil and began taking down the tea cups from the cupboard. There was a small table in the dining room. On this he neatly laid out two cups, two spoons and a sugar pot. Since this room had only one chair, he went to the living room and quickly returned with another. When the water started boiling he carefully brewed the tea. After that he warmed some milk in a pan and emptied it into the creamer. Then he took his place at the table and poured the tea. All this while I had been watching him spellbound. He was just as fully absorbed in his household chores as when working at the office. The same conviction, deftness, and self-assurance, in fact, even the same professionalism and finesse informed his movements here at home as at the office. And here, too, among his cats, dogs, parrots and pots and pans—just as among the maze of chairs, tables and filing cabinets back at the office—he moved about with the ease and agile grace of a forest animal.

We weren't sitting opposite each other at the table. He had placed his chair so that he was facing westward, and I toward the north. We each drank our tea in silence.

After we had tea he took down an enormous mixing bowl from the shelf. Bread crumbs lay soaking in it. He put the bowl down for the three dogs. Then he poured out some milk in a smaller bowl for the cats and from a box took out a portion of what looked like a thick, gooey confection, the kind used by apothecaries. He divided whatever it was into two shares, giving the parrot one and mynah bird the other. Next he attended to his birds. He scattered bird feed, mostly millet, into their cage and refilled their cups with water. Following this he took the mongoose from its cage. On top of the cage was a small leather collar. This he fixed around the animal's neck and attached a narrow leash to it. Presently he made for the stairs, holding the end of the leash in his hand. The mongoose now walked beside him, now jumped onto his master's body and crawled up to settle on his shoulder. We walked up the stairs, one behind the other, and came out onto the porch.

Here a strange sight greeted me. There were pigeon coops all around, from floor to ceiling, piled one on top of the other. And as though this weren't enough, to accommodate more of them he had raised tall dovecotes that poked out into the sky through the unroofed portion of the porch. It was difficult to know what color the floor was, as it was literally covered with dried-up pigeon droppings. The pigeons were cooing and making riotous noises inside their houses. The whole area reeked of the peculiar odor that birds have. One by one he pulled the pigeon-hole covers up, allowing them to come fluttering out. Some, no sooner tumbled out than they perched themselves on his shoulders and head; some flew off to roost on the walls and dovecotes and a few remained on the floor and began to preen themselves. By the time he had finished, we were in the midst of a deluge of pigeons—about a hundred and fifty of them, of all manner and color. He filled some vessels with water and spread bird-feed on the floor. The pigeons, whether on roosts, walls or his shoulders, all swooped down to the grain. What a sight! A hundred and fifty pigeons of all different varieties and shades all at once pecking at the grain, while cooing or attacking each other with their beaks. And there he was, standing in their midst, oblivious to himself, why, even to the world around, a faint smile playing on his lips. The mongoose was still ensconced on his shoulder.

A long time passed; he didn't move or turn. I cleared my throat, but he didn't react at all. I cleared my throat a second time, and a third time still. My patience ran out. "May I go now?" I said.

He look up startled and just as suddenly turned his eyes away, as though shocked by the realization that I was even there.

"These pigeons,..." he said, quickly steadying himself, "do you like them?"

"Oh, yes."

He bent down to pick up a lovely pair with dark beige heads.

"These are for you," he held out the pair to me.

"Oh, no," I stammered, "I didn't mean that. I really didn't."

He gently let go of the pigeons, who immediately resumed picking at the grain.

"Why do you keep so many animals?" I asked.

"Animals?" he repeated absentmindedly. "Oh yes, animals. They are really nice."

"Nice?"

"Yes."

I laughed gently. He started and looked up. Suddenly I felt uncomfortable and blurted out in my confusion, "What do you get out of them?"

"What do I get out of them?" For the first time he laughed, a deep, short laugh. Then he bent down again, this time picking up a white pair. He brought the pigeons close to his face and said in a voice full of love, "You can call them to you, touch them, any time you want. Yes, any time—" He once again offered the pigeons to me: "Take them."

I remained silent.

"Come on, take them," he said, "or take any that you like. Or do you want the parrot, instead? Maybe the mynah? Or would you rather have the dog? The small one? You like him, don't you? Take him."

I hesitated and remained standing, rooted to the spot. For the first time he looked me straight in the eye and said in a gentle, urgent voice, "Please take them."

Before I could budge from my place, I noticed a strange change sweep over him. His glance wavered and, as it were, shattered. He quickly dropped the pair and somehow not bumping into anything, went hastily down the stairs. When I followed him into the living room, I found him hurriedly tying up the dozen or so files he had already gone over. He thrust the bundle out to me and explained through a few broken sentences, constantly rubbing his neck, that I was to take it home with me and bring it back to the office the next morning. Then he slumped into the chair and began to gasp. I tucked the bundle under my arm and left noiselessly.

Next morning he neither said nor did anything that might indicate our brief meeting the previous evening. At lunch break it was the same old ritual once again: the chomp-chomp of jaws, vigorously working away at the food, mocking remarks hissed in undertones, the twitter, the sound of water going down the gullet ...and the fellow once again sitting glued next to the wall, his eyes despondently fixed upon us.

A few days later I resigned that job in favor of one with vastly better prospects.

Several years passed and I forgot that incident, when something quite extraordinary happened and brought it all back. As luck would have it, I found myself in Tehran on some government business. Although I was not expected to stay there for more than a few days, I was obliged to bring my wife along at her insistence. One day while eating in a restaurant we saw a very old man. He was watching us with a strange, wistful look in his eyes. After a while, without caring to eat or drink anything at all, he suddenly got up and left the restaurant. But as he was going out, leaning on his walking stick, he kept turning around to look at us. We asked about him from the waiter with whom we had seen him exchange a few words. It turned out that the old man was originally a native of Lahore, Pakistan. He had come to Tehran in his youth and had never once returned to his country. He had married and settled down here. He was now believed to be among the wealthiest businessmen in the city.

Suddenly it all came back—the incident that had taken place during my early adulthood. And just as suddenly it was all so clear. The mystery had been solved, finally, almost in an instant. It was like being on your way to somewhere on a stormy night. All of a sudden you felt you saw some dark, dreadful figure. You took fright and stopped short. Then suddenly the lightning flashed. In its tremendous but brief illumination you found out that what had spooked you was just a harmless bush. The realization sets your heart at ease and you go on along your way.

The insight I now gained had been just as instantaneous. Apparently I had forgotten all about that baffling mystery; in reality, though, I had never quite left it behind me. It had remained buried in a relatively dark crevice of my mind and subconsciously had kept me restless and strung taut. Now, suddenly, it had been let out: resolved and all so simple.

I leaned back in my chair, stretched out my legs, and looked at my wife with a smile of deep contentment. She was still busy eating, quite unaware of the tremendous sense of release I had just experienced. In those few moments of vacuous calm I realized how it sometimes takes a lifetime to understand a simple matter. That realization left me full of wonder. The exile, however disillusioned by his people, is never quite able to escape his longing for them. How terribly strange it all is!

After we had paid the tab and left the restaurant, my wife still had no idea that on that day, for the first time ever, I was able decisively to leave behind that incident from my remote past. And I was leaving it behind in the restaurant where we had just had our meal, where a few diners still lingered on over their lunch, and from where our old compatriot had departed a little while ago—the old man who had come to me like a flash of lightning on a dark, stormy night. Nor did she know how simple it now was for me to leave the whole incident behind, once and for all.

The Refugees

I am a refugee from the world—
CHATEAUBRIAND

An event occurred thirty years ago and brutally took hold of Aftab's life. This is the story of that event. Events don't occur in a void, but are related to the great unknowns that flank them on either side. Human life, too, is a continuum. For although we can measure an individual life within a definite time span, we cannot separate it from the flow of time. And just as man's greatest asset is the duration that is his life, so the essence of a story is the event on which it is based. This story, too, derives its meaning from just two days in Aftab's life. That some thirty years separate those two days is quite another matter.

20 June 1940
It was well past the noon hour but the heat hadn't let up at all. The sky, a crisp bright blue in another season, was a blazing sheet of silver now. One couldn't even look up.

Shaikh Umar Daraz and his son had just performed the midday prayer in the mosque and gotten up from the prayer mat. On one side along the wall his boots lay on their sides, soles nestled against each other, with his khaki sun hat thrown over them. Shaikh Umar Daraz bent down, picked up his possessions, and started out. His son walked to the outer courtyard, where he had left his sandals, sat down at the edge and began slipping them on.

Before leaving the mosque, Shaikh Umar Daraz wet his large square handkerchief under the tap, wrung it out thoroughly and threw it over his head. Over the handkerchief he fixed his sun hat rather carefully. The white kerchief was about the size of a small towel and conveniently came down over the nape of his neck and ears, though on the forehead it sort of flapped an inch or so above the eyes. If you looked at it casually, you might even think the hat had a fringe stuck to it.

Shaikh Umar Daraz's skin was a healthy pink. His face reminded one of those sepia photographs in which British colonial officers sporting knickerbockers or breeches, their heads covered with handkerchiefs and hats in a similar fashion, were photographed against a background of tropical jungles or sun-scorched deserts. Even the expression on his face was the same—as if he didn't belong to his immediate world and lived comfortably away from it, like those colonial officers.

Of the travels of his youth just these two mementos remained with Shaikh Umar Daraz: the fringed sun hat, and that faraway look in his eyes. Below his face he was just an ordinary man: clad in a white shalwar-qamis suit and a pair of boots. Occasionally during winters, though, he would slip on a pair of khaki breeches and full boots. But then, instead of mounting a horse, he would hop on his bicycle and ride to work, or, if it were evening, stroll down to his grainfields, ostensibly to inspect them, all the way twirling his walking stick with a flourish.

As father and son stepped out of the mosque compound, a gust of hot wind slapped their faces. "Aftab," Shaikh Umar Daraz said, "you go on home. I'm going out to the fields. I'll be along soon."

"Now?" The boy was surprised.

"Yes. I have something to take care of."

"I'll come along."

"No. You go on home. The wind is awfully hot."

"I'll fetch a towel," the boy insisted. "Please let me come along."

Shaikh Umar Daraz looked around uncertainly for a moment, then decided it was all right for the boy to come along. "But make sure you wet the towel well," he shouted at the boy who in the meanwhile had sprinted off to the house.

Minutes later the boy returned, his head and face covered with a wet towel. The two started off. The dry, white walls in the alleys shimmered in the sun. The hot wind would gust in, hit the walls and bounce back like a ball of fire. The pair quickened their pace and soon came out of the complex of alleyways. A single thought occupied their minds: to get out of the city as fast as they could and hit the blacktop highway where you at least had some large shady trees. Within about ten minutes they had walked to the city's edge.

A hot, shimmering desolation enveloped the city. Although it was a district headquarters, the city was marked by a simple peasant ambience. Only the presence of a bazaar, a hospital, the Friday congregational mosque and 'idgah, a district court, a cinema, a horse-show ground, an assembly place, an intermediate college, and two high schools set it apart from a qasba-town. A twenty minute walk in any direction from the centre of the town and one would be out of the city limits and in countryside of open spaces and farmland.

Coming to the Grand Trunk Road, the father and son felt a bit relieved. Tahli and sharin trees bordering the highway provided a welcome refuge from the heat and glare. Their dense shade somehow filtered out the heat from the scorching summer wind. They had barely walked a few paces down the highway when a tonga-carriage came up from behind and stopped beside them. "Come Shaikh-ji, hop in," the coachman said slapping the front seat to wipe it clean of dust. "You're headed to your fields, I guess?"

"Yes, Qurban," Shaikh Umar Daraz said. "But you go on. It isn't much of a walk...really."

"All the same, hop in. The carriage is all yours." Qurban climbed down from the tonga and respectfully stood beside it.

There were two other passengers in the tonga already: a peasant, setttled in the front seat, and his wife, all bundled up in a white flowing sheet, behind him. Shaikh Umar Daraz climbed up and occupied part of the front seat, and a happy Aftab jumped into the rear next to the woman. The woman flinched, squirmed to the corner of the seat, leaving some empty space between the boy and herself. Qurban, balancing himself with one foot on the foot-rest and the other planted firmly on the floor of the cab, urged the animal to move again.

"Shaikh-ji is our provider," Qurban said, seemingly to the peasant. "We live by his kindness."

Here and there the sun had burned holes into the highway and a thick, molten tar oozed from them. Every now and then the wheels of the tonga would land in one of these potholes, come out laced with the tar, and leave a long, tacky black trail behind them.

"Shaikh-ji works as Head Clerk to the Deputy Sahib," Qurban proudly enlightened the peasant.

Duly impressed, the peasant looked at the strange man sitting next to him, gathered his sarong respectfully and shrank to the corner of the seat.

"It's a scorcher, Shaikh-ji," Qurban continued. "The poor animal, it can't speak, but it feels the heat all right. He's dearer to me than my own children. But what can I do, I have to fill my stomach somehow."

Shaikh Umar Daraz nodded and said, "That's true, Qurban."

About a quarter of a mile down the highway, Qurban stopped the carriage. Shaikh Umar Daraz and his boy got down. From this point, the way to their cropland was mostly narrow dirt trails snaking through the fields.

The older man patted the horse's back and said, "You've got a fine animal, Qurban." He kept looking at the gorgeous animal, while caressing its body.

"If I'd my way, Shaikh-ji, I would never let him off my front steps," Qurban proudly said, "but I have to fill my stomach somehow."

Qurban raised his hand to his forehead to say goodbye and made a clucking sound to urge the animal on.

"Father, do you own this tonga?" Aftab asked.

Shaikh Umar Daraz laughed. "Qurban was just being nice. You see, I had him released from police custody the other day."

"Had he beaten up someone?"

"No. He was talking to his horse...the idiot!"

"Talking to his horse?"

"Yes. He was telling the horse to go on undaunted just as Hitler did." Shaikh Umar Daraz laughed again.

"And the cops got him for that?...Just that?"

"Yes. You see, the war is on. And Hitler is our enemy."

"Father, do you think we will win the war?"

"Who knows? Things don't look good."

They would stop briefly under an acacia or an ancient peepul along the trail to shield themselves against the relentless sun and then they would start on again. The last wheat had almost all been gathered and the parched fields, scarred and crusted by the sun, rolled out to infinity. The gusts of scorching wind would blow away the few remaining dried wheat stalks lying randomly in the stark fields. The monotony of the sun-drenched white landscape was broken only by the solitary green of an occasional hayfield, which also served as a reminder that the area was not a wasteland after all. The farmers had now begun to gaze at the sky in hopes of rain clouds.

On summer afternoons, Aftab found two sounds very comforting: the screeching of a kite flying high in the sky and the soft, sonorous cooing of a mourning dove. The later invariably made him want to withdraw to a quiet corner and listen to it uninterruptedly. For the dove's music was permeated with the dead stillness of the lazy summer afternoons and soothed him in the gentlest of ways. On the other hand, the screech of the high-soaring kite always filled his youthful imagination with distant thoughts.

"Father," the boy said, "why do you finish the du'a so quickly?"

"Do I? Whatever do you mean?"

"You barely raise and join your hands and run them quickly over your face."

"That's already long enough."
"What do you ask God for in so short a time?"
"Forgiveness."
"For what?"
"Sins."
"You commit sins?"
"Oh, come on now. I don't on purpose, but sometimes maybe I do without wanting to. Just happens..."
"And you don't know about it?"
"Sometimes I don't, but sometimes I do."
"How can that be?"
"Oh, well, man is an erring being."
"Does mother also commit sins?"
"Maybe. But surely less frequently than I do."
"When she prays, she prays for a long time."
"That's her habit."
"Is it a good habit to pray?"

After a prolonged silence Shaikh Umar Daraz said in a feeble voice, "Perhaps."

The boy continued, "You only pray for forgiveness?"
"Yes."
"And mother, what does she ask God for?"
"That, you must ask her." Shaikh Umar Daraz looked at his son and smiled. "Young man, you do like to badger me with questions. You'll make a good lawyer when you grow up."

That made the boy's thoughts take off on a different tangent: What would he want to be when he grew up?

"Father, you had run off to Bombay—is that right?"
"When?" Shaikh Umar Daraz flinched and looked at his son.
"When you were young," the boy looked up at his father triumphantly. "Mother told me all about it."

A smile quivered on the older man's lips. "Yes," he said, "I did."
"You were very young then?" Aftab asked.
"I was a young adult then."
"How old is a young adult?"
"About twenty, twenty-two years."
"And just a plain young man?"
"I'd say about eighteen, maybe twenty."
"So is a twenty year old a young adult or just a young man?"
"Damn it, you'll surely become a lawyer," Shaikh Umar Daraz said as he smiled again.

"You had run off to become a movie actor?"

Suddenly, for the first time, the older man's color changed. It was as if his son had pierced the thin, invisible membrane on the other side of which he lived in his world of terrible solitude. But this was not a color of worry; if anything, it betrayed a distant emotion that had surprised him with its sudden, inexorable closeness.

The boy, finding no answer, lifted his face to his father, but the shimmering sun flooded his eyes.

"Mother told me," the boy said, "that you'd gone off to become a movie star."

"That's true."

"So did you?"

"Well, yes. I did work in a movie."

"Did it show in our hometown?"

"Oh well, in those days only a couple of big cities had movie theatres."

"What did you play?"

"A soldier."

"Like a police constable?"

"No. An army soldier."

"So did you fight in a war?"

"A big one. Between the British and the Muslims."

"Where?"

"Up in the hills...in the deserts..."

"Are there hills in a desert?"

"In some, yes. This sort of terrain is ideal for battles. I had a white stallion."

Suddenly the boy had the feeling that his father was now not just answering his questions, but also taking a lively interest in the conversation which he had deftly veered toward things closer to his heart. And that made the boy very happy. This strange, wordless communication dispensed with even the need to know on whose side the father had fought. The boy knew, as certainly as his own being, that his father had opted for the role of a British cavalry man.

Finally the boy asked "Who won?"

"We did, of course. But the Muslims, too, put up a good fight. It was a fascinating script. The movie cost hundreds of thousands of rupees. That's like millions today. Our costumes came straight from England. A hundred and twenty horses were bought. They were later sold back, though. But those were gorgeous animals. Each had its separate groom. The white charger I was given was a real thoroughbred. I never saw a nobler animal. The first time I ever rode him, he bore me with such spontaneity and ease, as though we had known each other for a lifetime. I had him for a whole month. For the whole of that month nobody else ever dared touch him. For a full thirty days..." Shaikh Umar Daraz suddenly stopped, as if savoring a fond memory. "For a full thirty days I alone owned that animal."

Aftab's mind had stopped straying. He had been imagining the whole scene.

"Did they use rifles in the battle?" Aftab asked with visible impatience.

"Yes. We started out with guns. Then when the armies began to fight hand-to-hand we threw away our rifles and drew our swords."

The boy didn't realize that sometime during the conversation both he and his father had stopped walking. With the montage of desert scenes, of hilly tracks, of the fierce battle between the British cavalry and the brave Muslims running, inexorably, through his mind, Aftab involuntarily raised the branch in his hands and wielded it a couple of times in the air like an accomplished swordsman. Shaikh Umar Daraz stretched his hand and took the shisham branch from Aftab's hand. The boy lifted his head and looked straight into his father's eyes, even though the shimmering sky still dazzled him. Before him was the same bright face with its sharp, sculptured features, but flushed with the heat of some uncontrollable inner excitement. It was as if the thin shisham branch had changed, the moment it came into the older man's hand, into a sharp-edged sword, its point having pierced the membrane separating the two.

Shaikh Umar Daraz was standing right beside a dead, stunted, leafless acacia. A few round, dried-out limbs poked randomly into the air.

"Imagine it to be a horse," Shaikh Umar Daraz suddenly leapt into the air and landed straight on one of the limbs, mounting it as if it were some charger. He raised his left hand in the air to take hold of the imaginary reins, and with the other started whirling the "sword" all around him with dazzling agility, his eyes shining with awesome brilliance. He seemed to be in the thick of battle, cutting down enemy soldiers by the dozen. "And now my horse is wounded...it falls," he shouted as he quickly dismounted, but the frenzied movement of his arms continued unabated.

That was the most bizarre scene. In the dead stillness of a sunswept afternoon, in the middle of a parched field, a man wearing a fringed sun hat, his arms and legs outstretched, was brandishing a thin shisham branch with painful concentration, kicking up storms of blinding dust. A couple of fields away a few village brats, driving their buffalo home, momentarily stopped to watch this comic sight. But for the little boy, who stood close to the sword-swishing man, the scene was all too sublime; it certainly wasn't ridiculous. Oblivious to himself, and with total absorption and wonderment, the boy watched his father who, standing beside his dying horse, attacked the enemy soldiers to the right and left of him, in back and in front of him, making short work of them with his shining sword. His eyes glowed with animal fierceness and his body moved with uncommon alacrity, as the sword swished and struck the air.

The towel had rolled down Aftab's head and was dangling from one shoulder. In that instant the boy was impervious to everything: to the incandescent, blinding glare, to the scorching heat. Pure human emotion and animal passion had come together in that instant—an instant in which every boy comes to recognize, unmistakably, his father in the man before him, regardless whether the two are joined by blood. What is important, what counts, is the man's ability to capture fully the boy's attention.

But those moments flew away as fast as they had come.

Shaikh Umar Daraz abruptly stopped thrashing his sword about, thrust the slim shisham switch back into his son's hands, and laughed gently. He had broken into a fine sweat, and beads of perspiration rolled down his face. He picked up the sun hat which had fallen on the ground with one hand and with the other dried his face on the handkerchief. Then he carefully spread the kerchief back on his head, over which he fixed his hat, and started to walk on again. The shisham branch had turned back into a mere switch in Aftab's hands. Its thinner, flayed end had even broken off. Within those few short moments the boy had stolen a fleeting view of a wondrous, expansive world where the days didn't burn, nor did the nights strangle. His heart was suddenly like a bird—soaring uninhibited into unchartered space.

In a corner of ten acres of irrigated land stood a well shaded by tall, dense trees. Aftab had already counted all of those trees many times over. He know trees didn't grow so fast as to increase their number in a matter of days, but he still would count them each time he came to their cropland. There were eighteen dharaik trees, four big sharins, a single one of jaman, and two tahlis. So dense was their shade that the sun never managed to penetrate all the way down to the ground underneath.

Father and son sat down on a cot lying in the shade and each drank a cup of refreshing salted buttermilk. Then Aftab got up to go through his ritual. He would come to a tree, touch the trunk, count it, and then move on to the next one and repeat the routine. Generally he would thread his way through the grove, passing by the left of one tree and the right of the next one. This made his trail a winding, snake-like one, which pleased him very much. Sometimes he would turn around after he had come to the last tree and loop his way back to the first, but without breaking the count. Then when he had returned to the first tree, he would divide fifty by two. This made him feel that he had completed a round, that the count was what it should be, but, more importantly, that the invisible circle he had drawn around the trees would somehow protect and keep them green.

In the meantime the share-cropper had come out of the hut, holding a hubble-bubble in his hand, and sat down near the cot on the bare ground. He began to tell them about the crops.

Shaikh Umar Daraz's face once again looked normal. He was lying on the cot, his head propped up on the pillow of his folded hands, gazing into the trees above. From his manner of responding, it was obvious that he was only half listening to the man. The share-cropper had become used to it. Unbothered, he went on talking to the older man.

That peaceful look of mild self-absorption on his father's face generated a feeling of strength and fondness in the boy's heart. It was as if a gentle secret had come to be lodged there. Kneeling on the ground and resting his elbows on the thick, low wall, he leaned over the well and peered deep into the cavity—way down to the mercury platter of water—to catch a reflection of his head. A few yellowed dharaik leaves floated on the surface. Soon the peculiar smell of the water—musty, cool, aged, but above all, permeated by a sense of a certain past time (his grandfather had built this well)—began to rise up to his nostrils. Nothing, absolutely nothing, ever smelled like that. The boy, as if to retrieve that certain, long lost time from the bowels of the earth, emitted a medley of sounds, some shrill, some heavy and hoarse, and listened to the well return them only as a volley of deep and muffled echoes.

It was not an electric well; a pair of oxen pulled the rope that raised the water bucket to the ground level where it was emptied into the irrigation ditch. If he came at irrigation time, Aftab would himself drive the oxen, until his head began to reel. This afternoon, all was quiet at the well and the oxen quietly grazed on the fodder in one corner in the shade. Aftab got up from the well and walked over to the oxen. The cool, comforting smell of the well, which recalled his grandfather's image for him, still lingered in him. He also carried another presence within him, that of his old father, which now began to grow like a tiny drop of ink spreading out on a blotter. For the first time, the boy, barely ten years, felt the passage of ancestral time through his being. And it filled his heart with a certain uncanny satisfaction.

The boy's eyes fell on a puppy dog which had sneaked up on him from behind and was now standing at his feet. It was a pup the color of gold, and so tiny that it wobbled all over even as it stood. When the boy bent over to pick it up, it shrank back, yapping shrilly, and tumbled off to the wall and disappeared behind it. The boy followed the pup. Behind the wall he noticed the dog belonging to their share-cropper lying with her young in a hollow. The dog knew the boy. She cocked her ears once, and finding that her pup was safe, went on leisurely suckling her litter with her full teats sagging to one side. Only last week the boy had seen the dog with her ballooned stomach swaying from side to side, but it never occurred to him that she was about to give birth. He came to the hollow, squatted down at the edge and stared enraptured at the pups. He could see only four pups: three were black and white, busy attacking the dog's full teats with their eyes closed shut, and the fourth, this gold-colored one, that had just returned from its adventures outside the hollow and looked more outgoing than the rest. It had abandoned the teats and was struggling to climb up the dog's stomach. The share-cropper's son, seeing the boy's utter fascination, grabbed the gold-colored pup and stuffed it in the boy's hands. The pup began to yelp. The dog raised her head and growled a bit, then quieted down. The boy, holding the pup against his chest, came to his father and asked, "May I take it home?"

With half-opened eyes Shaikh Umar Daraz looked at the pup that was still making faint noises and said, "He's so tiny. He needs his mother's milk. Wait till he's grown a bit."

The boy, still holding the puppy, returned to the hollow. Shaikh Umar Daraz dozed off for a while. His hands were still folded under his head. The share-cropper went on rambling between puffs of his hubble-bubble. The boy again sat back on his heels at the ege of the hollow and, supporting his chin on his hands with his elbows on his knees, returned to staring at the gold-colored pup in quiet ecstasy.

On the way back many thoughts occured to Aftab, among them to remind his father that the latter had skipped his afternoon prayer. But that was nothing new. Shaikh Umar Daraz offered his prayers only when the fancy struck him; other times he'd be content with just being by himself, happily self-absorbed. The strange thing, though, was that whenever he put off his ritual prayers, he never felt the slightest remorse. On the other hand, if Aftab's mother ever forgot to pray at the prescribed time, she'd be so upset that just about everybody would know about the incident. Only much later, after he had grown up, had the boy come to know that the state of being at prayer was the state of being happily self-preoccupied.

The sun had begun its descent and the temperature had dropped some. As they passed by the green hayfields, a gust of fresh cool air would sweep over them. Many times during the walk home the thought occurred to Aftab to ask if that movie also had some pretty English memsahibs. He couldn't bring himself to, though. He was strangely aware that that incident, which only he know about, had entered his heart surreptitiously, like a secret, and that he was never to let anyone in on it. If ever he broached it with anyone, the sense of a certain wholeness would be shattered forever. Many times he looked at his father to find his face still permeated by the same softness and serenity.

On their return trek through open spaces along shaded paths, it didn't feel so uncomfortably hot, but the moment they entered the city, broiling heat and eddies of hot grit and stinging dust struck them with oppressive force. After the paralyzing midday heat, the city was returning to normal activity. People—freshly bathed, neatly combed and clad in gauzy malmal kurtas—had sauntered out of their houses and were now milling around in alleyways or crowding up storefronts. Circular Road was again busy with tonga traffic. An old, beat-up rickety bus zoomed past them, kicking up clouds of dust and sending a few bicyclists in front scrambling off to the sides. Dust particles, fired by the day's heat, cut into Aftab's body. A water carrier was squirting water along the edge of the street.

Shaikh Umar Daraz bought Aftab an ice from a vendor and said gently, "Your mother doesn't like dogs. She thinks dogs are unclean. Don't tell her anything about the pup. I'll talk to her about it myself." Then, after a pause, he added, "Let's go visit Chaudhri Nazir."

They turned into an alley, abandoning the path leading home.

Chaudhri Nazir, Shaikh Umar Daraz's childhood friend, emerged from the house wearing only an undershirt and a white sheet wrapped around his lower body. Aftab always found the man a bit too intimidating: not only was he the vice-rincipal of one of the two local high schools, but he also had this habit of talking to children with an air of unnerving seriousness. With Shaikh Umar Daraz, though, he appeared altogether relaxed, even informal, and addressed him as Shaikh-ji, sometimes as just Umar. With him he wouldn't mind even laughing heartily, slapping him on the hand every now and then with great informal joy.

Chaudhri Sahib led them into the small outer sitting room and later served them a sweet iced drink. A while later he started to pull energetically at the cord of the hand-operated ceiling fan and talk somewhat secretively but in a loud voice, his bespectacled face thrust slightly forward. This feeling of closeness and informality was reserved only for Shaikh Umar Daraz. Only with Chaudhri Sahib did the boy find his otherwise reticent father talk a lot, be perfectly at ease, and sometimes even break into gales of laughter.

By now Aftab was quite beside himself with the heat. The cool drink brought rivers of sweat gushing out of his body. Suddenly he wanted to leave this horribly stuffy room, dash off home, peel the clothes off his scalding body and throw himself under the streaming tap.

"Jot down the file number," Shaikh Umar Daraz said to Chaudhri Sahib. "Who knows, I might forget it."

The Chaudhri looked unbelievingly at Shaikh Umar Daraz. "Umar," he said, "you have never forgotten anything in your whole life; how will you forget my file number?"

"All the same, write it down," Shaikh Umar Daraz laughed gently. "It might just come in handy."

The Chaudhri suddenly became silent and gave the other man's face a deep, probing look. Shaikh Umar Daraz quickly turned his face around to look out through the open door. The Chaudhri extended his arm, put his hand over his friend's and said in a concerned voice, "You're all right, Umar, aren't you?"

"I'm fine," Shaikh Umar Daraz laughed. "I'm just fine."

The heat was now stinging Aftab and he was beginning to lose patience with Chaudhri Sahib, who was needlessly prolonging the conversation, asking after his father's health over and over again. Finally, when the two got up and started out for home, Aftab's heart began to pound fitfully, as if Chaudhri Nazir's silent fear had somehow crawled into the boy's heart where it was generating numerous other fears, large and small. Suddenly the boy felt he no longer wanted to go back home. Mother would be sitting on the wooden prayer platform, he imagined, and Bedi would be filling the earthen water jars under the tap. But these thoughts failed to ease his heart. His mother's voice kept hammering away at him. "Your father would have been a magistrate today," she often said, "if only he hadn't wasted his time in his youth." Adding a little later, "He has a brilliant mind. He just doesn't pay attention. We don't even make a penny from the land; the sharecroppers eat up everything."

His mother was a wonderful woman—forbearing and affable— and he loved her very much. Right now, though, the heat emitted by the closed alleyways was so oppressive that the boy was overwhelmed by the desire to get out of the steaming city once again with his father, walk down the shaded highway, then along the cool, comforting hayfields, till they returned to the well. Abruptly an irrepressible desire arose in the boy's heart to shout and ask, "Father, why did you come back from Bombay?" But when he lifted his face, the stern look of his father unnerved him.

At home it was exactly as he had imagined: in the small, brick courtyard, his mother was sitting on the low, wooden prayer platform, telling her beads in quiet absorption as her body swayed gently from side to side; and Bedi, done with sprinkling water over the bricks from which arose a soothing, moist, warm aroma, was now filling the water pots at the tap. Aftab went straight to his mother and sat down beside her on the platform. She patted him affectionately on the head and pressed him to her side. Shaikh Umar Daraz entered and greeted, "Assalamu alikum!" It was an old habit. Every time he entered the house he would say those words, even if no one were around. His wife threw a casual glance at him and greeted him with a slight nod of the head, still preoccupied with her beads. Shaikh Umar Daraz stood awhile in the middle of the courtyard, looking around blankly, and then quietly repaired to the sitting room.

The moment he was gone, Aftab hurriedly peeled off all his clothes and made a dash for the tap. The cold crisp water streamed over his body and tickled it. The boy began to shiver and scream with delight. The girl laughed at his ecstatic squeals and worked the hand pump harder. A couple of minutes later Aftab's body stopped shivering. He wet his head under the spout, sucked into the streaming water to catch a few cold gulps and choked over them, then stuck his head under the stream and with his eyes closed began to enjoy the cool sensation of the refreshing water flowing over his body. The dark, uneasy feeling that had earlier gripped him at Chaudhri Sahib's had now completely disappeared, and he was feeling nicely hungry. He knew that after he had dried and changed, his mother would get up from the platform and bake fresh chapatis and they would all eat a hearty meal right here in the courtyard. He was happy.

Daylight was fast ebbing away in the sitting room. Shaikh Umar Daraz, a creature of habit, would always leave the sitting room door and windows open in the evening. Today, he didn't though. In the stuffy, closed room he sat sunk in his rattan chair. Today, in fact, he hadn't done anything according to his habit: he had neither taken off his sun hat and set it on the table, nor removed his boots, nor even turned on the table fan in the corner. Fat drops of sweat oozed out from under the hat's fringe and flowed down over his forehead to the web of his thick, bushy eyebrows where they hung poised. For some time he sat motionless and quiet, as if exhausted from his long daytime trek through the summer heat, then, as one suddenly remembers something, he removed the hat with both his hands and set it carefully down on the table. He dried the sweat off his skull and forehead with the handkerchief and then let it hang from the chair arm. Then, instead of bowing down to remove his boots, he got up from the chair, walked over to the door opening into the house, closed the door and latched it noiselessly. He opened the wardrobe, took out his double-barrelled shotgun and stuffed a pair of cartridges in the chambers. He put the rifle butt on the ground and lowered his ear directly over the round, dark barrels, as if straining to catch some elusive sound. Then he extended his arm, stuck his fingers into the trigger guard and pulled both triggers down forcefully.

20 June 1970

A little before noon a tallish man got down from the train at the railroad station, accompanied by a boy of about nine or ten. In facial features and gait, the boy bore a striking resemblance to the older man. They were father and son. The former, Aftab Umar, was a lawyer who practised in Lahore. He had come to this city with a single purpose in mind.

The sun was spewing fire overhead and the gusting wind rose in blazing fire balls as it bounced off the scorched brick platform. To escape the sun, Aftab Umar snapped open his umbrella and quickened his pace along the platform, carefully keeping both himself and the boy in the shade of the umbrella. Coming to the long roofed porch of the platform he stopped, threw his attaché case on the bench, yanked out a handkerchief from his pants pocket and began drying his face and neck with it. Then he extended his arm to do the same for his son, who flinched, jerked his face away, quickly pulled out his own handkerchief and used it instead to dry himself. Both unfolded their handkerchiefs, examined the lines left on them by sweat and dirt, and stuffed them back into their pockets. Aftab squinted in the glare at the platform.

"When I left here," he said, "the station didn't have this platform."

"Didn't the train stop here?"

"It did. But the platform wasn't here."

"Where did the train stop then?"

"On the bare ground."

The boy, a bit confused, looked at the platform and asked, "So when was the platform built?"

"A few years ago."

"You never saw it before?"

"No."

Twenty years ago a single peepul tree stood outside the station building—everything else was the sun above and the raw earth below. Now the space directly opposite the terminal was paved and lined by tall shishams. Standing under their shade on the ground covered with pollen-packed tiny white flowers were many tongas, too many to count. A half dozen private cars were parked in the small parking area reserved for automobiles. The cars, all except one, were being loaded and people, those who had just disembarked from the train as well as those who had come to receive them, stood near them talking animatedly, laughing, fanning themselves with a magazine or newspaper. Next to the area for car parking was a stand for scooters and bicycles. All these developments had fundamentally altered the look of the railway station Aftab once knew.

All at once a number of coachmen swarmed up to Aftab and the boy, each trying to offer his tonga for hire. Aftab looked intently at their faces, but failed to recognize a single one. Finally he got into a tonga and said to the coachman, "Take us to a good hotel."

"Rivaz Hotel is the best. Very clean and quite close to the court-house. Gulnaz isn't bad, either, but it's got a bad name. Respectable people stay away from it. Sir, you look as though you don't live here—right?"

The street was still the same—broken and riddled with potholes —but many new shops had sprung up on either side. It was almost noon and, despite the hot wind which had started blowing, all you saw around you was a surging sea of heads. Automobiles, scooters, tongas and bicycles crowded the street. Aftab took out his sunglasses, put them on and stared at every passing face from behind the cool lenses. He strained to recognize a single familiar face, but in the twenty-minute ride found none and began to doubt if he had spent the first twenty years of his life here. Twenty years ago, when he had left here, he had just finished his BA in the newly-opened college. He knew hundreds of people. Where had they all run off to? he wondered. It seemed as though the entire population of the city of his time had been physically lifted and settled elsewhere, making room for a population of strangers.

Aftab was familiar with the Rivaz Hotel. But it was not the old, smallish, bungalow-style building he expected to see; a box-shaped, off-white, four-storey tall monster with cement floral vines crawling along the windows greeted him instead.

A gust of mouldy smell, characteristic of entombed places, struck Aftab's nose as he opened the door to his third-floor room. He quickly flung the window open. The rooms had all been built disregarding the prevailing air currents. In this season of hellish heat, Aftab marvelled at this architectural travesty. The hotel attendant, trailing behind them, had in the meantime checked out the light switch by flipping it on and off a few times and was now dutifully trying to get the ceiling fan to work. A couple of wires had perhaps come off loose in the fan's regulator, which was covered with fly-specks.

"Would you like me to bring up the meal, sir?" the attendant asked.

"We'll eat downstairs in the hall...after a while," Aftab said. "Could you bring us some ice water for now?"

"Right away, sir."

"I think I'll take a bath." Aftab said to his son as he took off his shirt.

"Daddy, let me take a bath first."

"Tell you what. Let's slip on our shorts and take a bath together."

Aftab opened the attaché case and took out a towel, soap bar, comb, talcum powder, two clean boxer shorts, a big and a small one, and piled them all up on the bed. The room was furnished along modern lines. Two single beds with a side table wedged in between lay against a wall. The sheets were clean and a crisp white. The bathroom boasted of a shower, but the pressure was too weak to pump the water high enough for the shower to work properly. Water flowed down in a faint stream from the shower head and was collected below in a bucket with an enameled mug set close beside it. Aftab gazed wide-eyed at everything, hoping to find at least one familiar object. He stepped back into the room and sat down on the bed. His son stood in the middle of the room with only his boxer shorts on, cooling himself under the ceiling fan.

"Daddy, where was your house?"

"There—" Aftab pointed in a direction.

"Who lives in it now?"

"God knows. I sold it before I left."

The attendant returned with a jug of iced water. It was an iron jug and its handle was riddled with reddish-gold welding marks. Both had a glass each and stepped into the bathroom.

The marble chip floor of the dining room was messy with dried up gravy spots. Even though curtains had been lowered over the doors and windows, it didn't much help against the attacks of pesky flies. They swarmed on tables, chairs, plates, on people's arms and incessantly working jaws—just about everywhere. Gingerly, like an actor on his first appearance on an unfamiliar stage, Aftab entered the half-lit dining room. He had briefly hesitated at the door and looked cautiously around, as if startled—becoming aware, suddenly, of an awesome loneliness crawling into the dead center of his heart.

They walked over to an empty table and sat down opposite each other. Quite unconsciously Aftab found himself concentrating only on the middle-aged faces in the hall, as if hoping to retrieve in them a reflection of himself. Finding not even one that looked even vaguely familiar, he felt, instead of disappointment, a tremendous sense of relief, as if some crushing load had been finally lifted off his heart.

"Daddy, aren't you going to tell me the story? Remember, you promised?" the boy reminded Aftab over the food.

"Not now."

"When?"

"When we go out for a stroll."

"At four o'clock?"

"Yes, about that time. After the sun's gone down a bit."

After they had returned from the dining room the boy lay down on the bed and read his comic book for a while, then turned over and fell asleep. Aftab also tried to sleep, but couldn't. He got up and walked over to the window. Opening out before him was a view of the city's busiest square at the busiest time of the day. People were returning from work; young men and women from schools and colleges. There was a messy traffic jam. Seemingly, the passage of twenty years had left the square's appearance intact. The same businesses were still around: three shoe shops, including Bata, a tailor's shop, a dentist's clinic, a stationery store, and the cigarette-and-pan stall. The atmosphere in these stores hadn't changed either, nor had the ambience of the streets where girls, crammed into tongas, most of them without their veils, were on their way home from school. Aftab had heard that an all girls' college had been opened there. This was his hometown. He had passed through this square countless times on his way to and from school, and then later as a college student. Hundreds of times in these very streets, he and his friend Mustafa had chased after the perky Government School girls who were always bundled up in their black burqas. A quarter of a mile down the street into the inner city was the house where he was born. Even today, if he climbed down the three flights of stairs of the hotel and took himself to the square, he could walk blindfolded to his house or, for that matter, in any direction, as though he had never left here. Between him and his city there were just these forty-five stairs.

All at once he was overwhelmed by just such a desire: to climb down the flight of stairs to the square, remove his sunglasses, look up old acquaintances among the milling crowd, shake hands with them, talk to them, and then push on to his house, or to Mustafa's. Mustafa's father might still be alive, he thought.

Aftab took off his sunglasses for a second. The glare stung his eyes. The traffic was thinning out in the square and the shops were closing one by one for the noon break. Within an hour the square will be deserted, he thought.

Nothing, absolutely nothing in the city, now belonged to him. He was nineteen years old when he had gotten his BA and landed a job in the Government Secretariat at Lahore. A year later, during his mother's sudden—and fatal—illness, he had briefly returned to his hometown to dispose of everything, house and all, and permanently settled down in Lahore in a new house outside the city in the Model Town suburb. He was still living in that house. After getting a law degree he had given up his old job and set up his own practice. Every year he would promise himself a visit to his hometown and childhood friends, some of whom dropped by now and then to visit with him or to ask a favor. They had all been married and raised children. Mustafa had died in action in the 1965 Indo-Pakistani war and Aftab hadn't been able even to go visit his survivors and console them; managing, instead, a letter of condolence. When Iqbal, another friend, fell seriously ill, he had him brought to Lahore and admitted to Mayo Hospital. But in the past twenty years he hadn't once been able to travel these seventy miles to his hometown. How on earth could he now go and stand in the square? Standing in his hotel suite, the thought that he was now gone from this city for good hit Aftab with a chilling finality.

"Daddy—" his son's groggy voice called at him.

Aftab turned around. "You're up?"

"Imran's daddy has bought a brand new chair."

"Oh. What kind of chair?"

"A swivel chair."

"Is that so?"

The thought of visiting his hometown had emerged so suddenly, so unexpectedly. Not even a whole day had passed. Faruq, his son, was playing with his friend Imran in their backyard. Aftab, too, had come out in the yard after his shower and was now seated comfortably in a chair studying a brief. Nasrin, his wife, was sitting in the chair opposite him browsing through a magazine. Aftab removed his feet from his slippers and slowly put them on the ground, letting the cool grass tickle his soles. Once during his work he casually lifted his head and his eyes fell directly on his son. And the whole matter gelled in that single instant.

All his thoughts became ineluctably focused on that frozen instant of time. In that instant much went swirling through his mind: It was 19 June today; tomorrow it will be the 20th. Faruq, his son, was ten years old, while he himself was reaching his fortieth year. Exactly 30 years ago he was ten and his own father, forty. These uncanny resemblances, these striking harmonies became concentrated, inexorably, in that whirling instant which swept over him like a magic spell. Aftab became oblivious to the brief of the case due to start the next day lying open in his lap, his wife sitting opposite him, everything. He felt as if that instant was whirling round a pivot which drew him irresistibly toward it. Slowly it dawned on him that the pivot was none other than his hometown.

Then and there, sitting immobile in the grip of that spell, Aftab decided that it was time he visited his hometown. He told his wife about his decision. She could understand his desire, but not why he should insist on dragging Faruq along in the miserable heat. But she didn't fuss over it, thinking that, after all, his parents were buried there and that he had never once gone back.

Aftab sent for his assistant and gave him instructions about the court hearings scheduled for the next day, June 20th. He talked Faruq into accompanying him with a promise of showing him around his hometown and telling him a fascinating story once they got there.

That night he couldn't sleep a wink. His thoughts remained fixed on that instant, where time seemed to have hit a dead end and halted. As the night progressed the thought that that instant was steeped in a mystery became a conviction. That mystery had, in fact, kept a part of his mind paralyzed for thirty years. Perhaps the time had come to solve it!

"I tried it out myself," Faruq said.

"Hmmm."

"I mean the chair."

"You did?" Aftab said absentmindedly. "You said it's a swivel chair?"

"Yes. It goes round and round," Faruq explained, tracing circles in the air with his hand. "Yes, daddy, it does—round and round!"

"Hmmm."

"What time is it?"

"Four o'clock."

"Let's go." Faruq was impatient for the "fascinating" story his father had promised to tell.

"All right," Aftab said, "let's go."

It was getting on toward late afternoon but the city still hadn't fully snapped back into action; here and there, though, some tentative signs of life had begun to show: water was being sprinkled in places and shops were again opening, but it would be a while before the customers showed up. The only people who were there now were shopkeepers' acquaintances and friends who regularly dropped in for an idle evening chat.

Carefully huddled under the shade of the umbrella both Aftab and Faruq walked into the bazaar. Aftab stared at some faces and for the first time recognized a few, vaguely though, just as one does trees and dwellings. What he thought he recognized were the timeless, anonymous faces of shopkeepers whom he had seen all his life glued to their storefronts. Some had visibly aged, with a pronounced grey showing in their beards, while the others looked strangely unaffected by time. None of them, however, paid any attention to Aftab. He walked through the bazaar unnoticed, hidden behind the anonymity of dark sunglasses and an umbrella. At the spot in the road where they had to take a turn toward Circular Road, Tunda—who sold spicy grilled shish kabobs—was just setting up. On the front of his box-shaped stall lay the flat, rectangular open barbecue grill which he had filled with charcoal, but hadn't got it going yet. Instead, he was scrubbing the dozen or so skewers with a piece of dirty rag. An old, beat-up small fan was set beside the grill which he used to blow on the coals with. Perhaps it was the same fan, Aftab imagined, which Tunda had used twenty years ago. Shortly smoke will bellow out of the grill, he thought, carrying the appetizing aroma of roasting spiced meat, and bring otherwise perfectly satiated people scrambling out to Tunda's stall. Already before the time for the sunset prayer a crowd could be seen milling around his stall and wouldn't begin to thin out until it was time for the night prayer. Then, as the cry of the muezzin arose from the neighborhood mosque, Tunda would wash the skewers in the large empty bowl in which he kept the spiced ground meat for the kabobs and carefully put them away. Then he would empty the grill in the gutter, where a few coals, still red-hot under a layer of ashes, would die out hissing loudly and sending up clouds of smoke, put the grill back into the stall, lock up the stall and make for home. Although Tunda's left hand was intact, his right had been amputated just below the elbow. In spite of the handicap, he did all his work alone. From the time Aftab was a mere child, he had always found Tunda perched on the platform of his stall, no bigger than a chicken coop, working away using one hand with a deftness and speed that defied description. Tunda was famous throughout the city for his delicious kabobs.

Suppose he were to take off his sunglasses, Aftab toyed with the idea, and install himself in front of Tunda and accost him, would he, Tunda, recognize him? Surely he would. Had he not, after all, from childhood right up to his late teens found himself twice a week standing in the crowd at Tunda's stall waiting for his turn to buy a few sizzling-hot, crackling kabobs smeared with peppery-hot onion sauce, which Tunda would wrap for him in a piece of newspaper, before dashing home with his mouth watering?

Passing by the stall Aftab turned his head to look behind. Tunda was still busy scouring the skewers.

By now the two had crossed the bazaar and reached Circular Road. The traffic was sparse, mostly tongas and bicycles; the irritating dust had not yet begun to rise. They walked on Circular Road for a while and then, instead of following the curve, walked straight up and got on the path connecting the city's center with the Grand Trunk Road. This barely half a mile long stretch stood in Aftab's memory as a dusty, unpaved path which looked deserted even in day time. Not so now. It had been paved and an assortment of big and small factories had sprung up along both sides, with large bungalows wedged in between them. A completely new neighborhood! Pools of stinking water, covered with mosquitoes, had formed next to the factories and residential houses. Aftab hurriedly strode out of the area.

The moment they got on the Grand Trunk Road, Aftab felt as though time had suddenly reversed itself and then stopped, preserving unchanged in its core a pristine vision of the world as he once knew it. And, today, still very much the child he once was, he had returned to play in that world.

The open fields, the land, were still the same: ancient and familiar. The same shisham trees lined the road and swayed in the wind and provided, with their shade, a refuge from the scalding winds.

Aftab snapped shut the umbrella, removed his sunglasses and put them back into his pocket. The glare no longer hurt his eyes. Off the road the landscape was dotted with the same old fields. Wheat had already been harvested and the parched fields looked mournfully sad in their stark nakedness, their surface riddled with dark rodent holes where freshely dug-up dirt was piled in tiny hills. Dry wheat chaff lay strewn all around the fields. These mouse holes, Aftab remembered, used to scare the daylights out of him because as a boy he had always thought they harbored vipers. Today he knew they were just mouse holes. He still couldn't look at them without fear. He told his son to give them good clearance. Walking by a hayfield he bent down a little, broke a long green leaf and began to chew on it.

That dead, ancient tree was still there in the field. Aftab stood a few feet from it and gawked at it; he couldn't believe his eyes. All along he had been thinking that when he got there chances were the tree wouldn't be there; and even if it were, he would have to look around quite a bit to find it—he was obsessed by the desire to return to it once again and narrate the whole story to Faruq right by it—but as soon as he had crossed over the tall hedge of bushes, what do you know, the tree stood right in front of him, immobile as a statue. Aftab took a few slow steps over to the tree, and then extended his hands gingerly to touch a twisted, black branch, as if afraid that the merest touch would send the whole tree crashing down. But the tree stood firm. And although every single fiber in that tree had been dead and dry for a long time, its stiffness, its mournful spread and the tremendous force with which its roots gripped the earth had not changed at all. Even the line left behind by the stripped bark was in its place. It was as if the tree had become frozen in the moment of its death and become a permanent mark on the earth's topography. The single thing that didn't fit in Aftab's memory of the tree was this new, awesome-looking shisham that had sprung up a few yards from it. After the incident thirty years ago, Aftab had stopped coming to their land. Later his mother had rented it out. And though he did come here once or twice as a young man, it was by chance; and then again he didn't walk but bicycled down to it on the paved highway recently built by the District Board, the highway which passed by their well and went to Ahmad Pur Sharif.

Aftab lifted his head and looked into the dense shisham foliage above.

"Daddy, I'm tired," Faruq said.

Aftab wiped his son's sweaty face with his handkerchief and said, "We're almost there." He ran his fingers through Faruq's hair. "There, you can almost see it."

"Where?"

"That grove of trees...you see it?" Aftab pointed in a direction.

"Yes."

"There's a well under those trees," he said. "Around the well are many fields. Well, that used to be our land."

"But Daddy, I'm really tired," Faruq said, whimpering a little.

"It's cool and shady down there," Aftab said. "Come on, it isn't all that far—really."

"Unh-nh-nh!" the boy whined. "The sun's killing me. I don't want to go there." He flopped down under the shisham.

Aftab looked ardently at, and let his eyes linger awhile on, the familiar, dark, dense foliage of the grove a quarter of a mile down the trail and felt its comforting cool touch on his sunburnt cheeks. The touch seemed so familiar, so recent he thought he was in the grove only a fortnight ago, catching his breath awhile in its shade. His throat was badly parched and a desperate longing arose in his heart to gulp down a bowlful of that refreshing salted buttermilk. Who might be living here now?—he wondered, with a trace of confusion and anguish.

"Daddy, let's go back home."

That sensation of comforting shade suddenly vanished. Aftab walked over to his son and sat down beside him leaning aginst the shisham trunk. Then he said, "Son, let's rest awhile here and then we'll go."

"Daddy, when will you tell me the story?" the boy said in an exasperated voice, tired of waiting.

Aftab lifted his eyes and looked far into the bright sun. Way down, the dead tree stood still in its stark nakedness, mutilated, terribly mangled—like a frightening nightmare. Aftab put his sunglasses back on and started to tell his son the story...that story.

In a soft and collected voice he recounted for his son the event that had occurred thirty years ago and had paralyzed his life since. The entire incident was fresh in his memory, and yet he couldn't begin relating it without a certain diffidence. He was having difficulty talking about it; he felt as if something was buried deep inside the earth and he had to actually dig and pry it out of there. For a while he talked haltingly, as if trying to press disjointed events into a rational order but finding them too stubborn to connect; later his voice grew more confident and coherent as randomness coalesced into order, and each insipid detail became vibrant with life. His words formed into slithering links which closed in on him like a chain. He was now speaking with flow and smoothness, the words flying out of his mouth like birds following the track of sound which terminated in a frozen moment of time.

In that sun-soaked, broiling afternoon, sitting under that intruding shisham, Aftab saw the dark, long tunnel of his life recede to reveal a tiny point of light at the other end. The speck of light gradually moved toward him and stopped right before his eyes, causing everything and every moment to ripple over Aftab's skin with remarkable tactile sensation. It felt as though the past thirty years had been suddenly divested of all meaning—that not only time and life but even man's own body had no significance at all before his inexorable memory—a memory that integrated one generation into the other and gave the world its sole meaning.

Aftab raised his head to look at his enraptured son and ran his fingers into his hair, as if transmitting through touch the end of the chain. He had hit the end of his story.

In relating that incident, Aftab had made one change: he never did reveal that the man with whom he had gone out on a stroll through the fields exactly thirty years ago, the man who had on returning from the stroll shot himself without uttering a word, was in fact his own father. He didn't have the courage to let his son in on the secret; instead, he told him that the man was a neighbor of theirs.

The story told, both got up and started back. In spite of the blazing sun, Aftab neither popped open the umbrella nor put the sunglasses back over his eyes, but kept walking into the sun, impervious to its searing heat and blinding glare. A crushing load was suddenly off his heart and his body felt strangely unstrung and weightless—weightless, but strong. And although his mind was empty of thought, his body vibrated with the feeling that this city of his childhood was still very much his own. These fields, these trees, these streets now alive with traffic, tongas and automobiles that zoomed past kicking up clouds of dust, the bazaars full of popsicle vendors and sellers of fragrant motiya garlands, the alleyways where women sat on their house fronts or doorways fanning themselves as they chatted with their neighbors, mouths thrown open from the deep heat, the children who tumbled and rolled and capered about in the dust as they played unbothered by the heat, the houses from which rose the sound of metal bowls striking against earthen water jars, or the pungent aroma of frying or sauteed onion or garlic spreading everywhere around—all these places and sights and smells Aftab felt, through an unbroken continuous sensation, to be his own. He had left his hometown for good twenty years ago, but throughout that time and at no place—Lahore where he had settled down, the cities where he was obliged to spend some time on business, and those other places which he had merely passed through—nowhere, absolutely nowhere had he experienced the state he was in now, the state in which one becomes oblivious even to one's body. Although for thirty years his heart had remained numb, his body had shivered every instant with a nameless fear, as if somebody would sneak up on him from behind and grab him. Only now his body had stopped trembling and become light, every muscle in it perfectly unstrung, relaxed and calm, he not even aware that he had a body. Only the heart was the seat of every sensation and knowledge. For the first time in his life, Aftab found out what exactly the two words "My hometown" meant, which he had so often heard people say.

    Sitting across a table from each other in the small front garden of the hotel Aftab and Faruq were sipping Coke from chilled bottles. Condensation formed into droplets in the smudge marks left by their fingerprints and trickled down, cutting crooked pathways into the frosted surface. It was getting on toward evening. Beyond the three-foot-high garden wall, a second wave of traffic had started to funnel down the street. The time for the last evening trains was approaching and the anxious coachmen were crying "Station! Anyone for the station!" People, freshly bathed, neatly combed and wearing fine malmal shirts, had come out of their houses for the evening stroll. Faruq got up, walked over to the chair near the wall,

reading his comic book. A little later, Aftab too got up, grabbed his

Coke, walked over to his son and slumped down in the chair next to him.

"So, did you like the story?" he asked.

Faruq inattentively mumbled something and went on reading the comic in the fading daylight. A naked lightbulb burned in the hotel veranda, its light too far and too dim to do him any good. After a while, Faruq got tired, stopped reading, looked up and suddenly asked, "Daddy, are you going to write this story?"

Aftab thought for a while and then said, "I might."

"Daddy, you could become the world's greatest lawyer if you didn't write stories."

"Oh!" Aftab broke into laughter. "Whoever told you that?"

"Mommy."

"Really? What does she say?"

"Just that if Daddy didn't waste his time writing stories he could become the biggest lawyer."

Aftab laughed again and became silent. After a while he said, "Faruq," he put his elbows down on the table, "shall I write this story? What do you say?"

Again the boy emitted a faint, uninterested sound and began looking at the street.

Aftab continued, "Tell me one thing."

"What?"

"Why did the man kill himself?"

"I don't know why."

"Come on. Think about it." Aftab insisted. "Only when you tell me that will I write the story."

"Why?"

"Because I myself don't understand why the man shot himself."

The boy stared unbelievingly at his father, then turned around to look at the street, as if thinking. Both remained silent for a while. Aftab's heart pounded violently. He shifted his weight on his elbows and lowered himself over the table. The same old fear his body knew so well began to return.

Suddenly Faruq turned around to look at Aftab. There was a strange glint in the boy's eyes.

"Perhaps he loved horses," the boy said.

The fog began to lift from in front of Aftab's eyes and narrowed into a tiny bright dot of uncommon intensity. The dot slowly expanded into a large pool of light in the middle of which Aftab saw a shimmering white stallion galloping away. The sun poured over its body with such brilliance that the eye skidded off and could not behold it. Every muscle in the horse's taut body was so firm, so prominent as though it had been carved out of granite. A rider was firmly mounted on the horse's back, confidently holding the reins. The rider was outfitted in the white uniform of a British soldier, with a sun hat stuck on his head. He held a bared sword pointing to the sky. With each gallop, the horse and the rider soared into space in such unison that it seemed they were a single body which would jump across the length of the earth in one gigantic bound. In the ebbing light, still leaning on his elbows, Aftab stared at this scintillating picture of perfect beauty and harmony, until the fog rose again and obscured his eyes. The scene disappeared as fast as it had appeared, but it left in its narrow wake the knowledge that that was the finest moment of his father's life.

It was getting dark. The momentary brightness was gone. In the crowding darkness something quite new had emerged. It was as though that swift-footed bright moment had left its dark shadow behind. Something was found, but something was lost too; something was revealed, but something had also become forever hidden: "This city," Aftab found himself thinking, "this city where my father had lived his whole life had finally lost its appeal to him. And here I am; I left it for good, only to return and be fully alive again. Anyway, what does it all mean?"

The confusion that had been gnawing at his heart had certainly been removed. Or perhaps it hadn't been. If there was anything he knew with certainty, it was this: he belonged here...

It was night now. Street lights had come up. Faruq, his legs still resting on the low wall, was again browsing through his comic in the dim light of the electric pole in front.

"Daddy," Faruq said suddenly, "I'll go to America when I grow up."

Startled, Aftab looked at his son. The boy's eyes were sparkling. Aftab stared at him for the longest time, then, somewhat casually, said, "Is that so?"

"When I grow up I'll become a doctor. And then I'll go to America."

In the comic book that lay open in the boy's lap, a gigantic black man was crossing the street with his giant-size strides, while a string of cars funnelled through his wide-apart legs. Faruq turned his face to look at the street again, his eyes still gleaming with an illicit, faraway look.

A little later Aftab got up from the chair and looked at his son, as if contemplating whether to say something, but then said nothing.

He left the boy in the garden and went into the hotel. In the hall he stopped and looked around for a few moments and then slowly began to climb up the stairs.

A few minutes later, Faruq too decided to return. When he opened the door, it was dark inside. He jumped up and turned on the light. His father, still in his day clothes, his feet in socks and shoes, was lying stretched out on the bed. His arms were gently folded over his chest and his face was drenched in sweat. It was terribly hot and stuffy inside the room.

"Daddy, shall I turn on the fan?" Faruq asked.

Aftab remained immobile. Faruq walked over to him and called out gently, "Daddy!"

Aftab opened his eyes and stared at the ceiling, as if trying to recognize it. "You may, if you like," he said in a faint voice.

"Daddy, I'm hungry."

Aftab got up. He went into the bathroom, washed his face with cold water and dried it on a towel. Then, taking the boy along, he walked out of the room.

"Daddy, when will we go back home?"

"Early in the morning."

The two began climbing down the stairs to the dining hall.

Downfall by Degrees

Just about every month I go to Lahore to visit Ayaz. The last time around Ayaz mentioned an incident in passing which reminded me of a time many years ago. I have returned from Lahore only yesterday, and every detail of that incident—so interwoven within the fabric of Ayaz's life and mine that it cannot possibly be viewed independently—is still vividly before me.

Ayaz Baig has been my friend since childhood. In the period I speak of he was a promising young lawyer in Lahore. Recently he had fought two famous court cases. The first was a murder trial in which the son of an important landowner had shot and killed a peasant during a dispute. The second case had political overtones and involved kidnapping, bribery and violence. Because both cases figured prominent people, the newspapers really played them up. For weeks page after page was covered with the court proceedings. Although Ayaz had won one case and lost the other, his growing popularity stemmed ultimately from his humanitarianism. In both cases he had fought for the weak and powerless party. In those days the young intellectuals of the city saw Ayaz as a man up in arms against all forms of oppression, exploitation and highhandedness. His enemies, on the other hand, felt that his humanitarianism had a motive: he was aspiring for political power and tactfully paving the way for it. Ayaz had never given me the slightest indication of nourishing any political aspirations, still I knew that if and when the door to politics opened to him, he would plunge into it with the same zest that characterized most of his other activities in life. We both came from the same town. We grew up in the same neighborhood, went to the same primary and high school and later to the same college. Ayaz's career as a student just bumped along. Up to the fifth grade he was the class's biggest underachiever. He couldn't read, write, spell or remember his multiplication tables. He was notorious for neglecting his homework. Constant punishment was his fate in class. But the moment we hit fifth grade and went on to the high school, it seemed as though Ayaz took off. Whereas earlier he had been falling behind in class, he had now in one year's time caught up with the straight-A students. A complete change came over him. And we saw it. His clothes became cleaner and tidier, his hair looked neatly combed and his shoes brightly shined. We were only ten or twelve years old then—a time when only sheer physical force matters to a boy—even so, Ayaz's sudden transformation could not fail to amaze us all. He kept up the same pace for the next three years.

We must have been in the ninth grade when Ayaz's father suddenly died. This forced Ayaz's older brother Iftikhar, who had just graduated from school and entered college, to quit his studies and take over their father's retail cloth business. Their father never let his sons have anything to do with the store; he would never even let them hang around it for any length of time. Instead, he had wanted them to get a decent education fit for a civil service job. Therefore, when Iftikhar took over the store he was a complete novice and their income steadily declined. In the meantime another change came over Ayaz. He began to neglect his studies and his position in class gradually slipped, which worried his teachers.

I vividly remember that summer as I spent the entire vacation with Iftikhar and Ayaz in their store. Every morning Ayaz went to the store with his brother. I, too, would think up some excuse to come to the store, then we'd spend the entire time chatting. Ever so often a villager on his way back from selling his wares or standing trial at the court would wander into the empty store and buy a few yards of calico or coarse cotton. I remember that whole summer as one image, distilled from its myriad scenes. It is the image of that little cloth shop, its shelves gradually emptying of its bolts of cloth and no one coming in, just we three boys sitting on the floral spread covering the floor endlessly talking. When the afternoon heat grew unbearable, Iftikhar would get up, crank out the store's awning, lie down with his head on a pillow and a handkerchief over his face, and drowsily shoo away the pesky flies. I'd open my books and try to catch up on my school work.

Right next to their store was a small shop where you could borrow magazines and novels for a fee. Ayaz would bum some novel from this shop, come back and lie around reading it. That summer Ayaz read a couple of cheap, mushy romances like *Saudai* and *Harjai* from cover to cover half a dozen times.

A great deal of time has since passed but to this day I remember some of the episodes in those novels which Ayaz had read aloud to us. When I had some difficulty with my school work, I'd ask Ayaz for help. Most of the time he'd give the correct answer without even bothering to look at my book or notes, then go back to reading his novel. He didn't even open a textbook during the whole vacation, as if it didn't matter.

When school reopened he thought up a splendid ruse: he told all his teachers how the day before he had left all his notebooks at his brother's store and how later someone had just taken off with them. The teachers sent him off to the principal. Until that time one was sent to the principal for offenses such as picking fights or creating trouble, this was absolutely the first time that anyone had been sent on account of school work. Our eyes were glued to the principal's office and exaggerated ideas ran through our little brains. The opinion of the more knowledgeable boys was that Ayaz would be kicked out of school. When, however, Ayaz emerged from the principal's office, his face betrayed no sign of punishment. He slipped into his seat and the lesson resumed. After school we asked him about his fate at the principal's, and he told us that he was neither spanked nor scolded, instead the principal patiently explained to him that if he paid more attention to his school work, he could easily become the school's star student, and so on. Ayaz, however, did not change his ways. Worse still, he even started skipping school now. In the evening he delivered clothes for his mother who had taken up sewing for the neighborhood. During the day he would hang around the store with his brother.

Well, he passed all right, but just barely—at the bottom of his class.

Two months into the tenth grade, just after summer vacation, and we were in for another big surprise: Ayaz had begun to attend school regularly again and he also did all his homework. During vacation I often went over to their store but would never find Ayaz there; instead I'd find him in the small, front room of their house, studying. He hardly ever went out now and seemed to have altogether lost interest in playing and other such things. Often I would sit there with him for hours on end trying to talk to him but he'd just grunt something and stay absorbed in his work. By then his brother had gained some experience in running the store, which, consequently, began to show a small profit. For the entire year Ayaz remained immersed in his studies and passed high school in the first division. In fact, he was the class's salutatorian. Among the images from that last year of school that are still fresh in my mind, is that of the small living room of Ayaz's house out of which we both emerged and did our high school.

In college Ayaz took up science and I opted for the humanities. The very first day of college heralded his progress and my decline.

We were a fairly prosperous landowning family. Sometime in the past our great-great-grandfather had bought up a lot of land outside the city limits. It had now been settled. Also, over the years the city continued to grow until it now reached halfway to our land. Originally agricultural, our property developed into urban and then into residential land. Its value increased tenfold in a few short years. My father sold some land close to the city's edge and continued to farm the rest. When I started college I naturally fell in with the group mostly made up of kids from landowning families in nearby villages. These young men wanted nothing to do with education. They knew they would ultimately revert to their leisurely feudal life of fun and pleasures. So why get involved in education or go for a low-paying job in the civil service? They came to soak into the refined life of a city student for a few years. Their interest in college rarely went beyond its opportunities for sports and athletics, elections and party politics.

We were in our second year of college when a fight broke out between two rival groups over the student union elections. Three students were expelled of which, as luck would have it, I was one. That more or less ended my student career. I started helping my father take care of the land. After a couple of years, he turned over everything to me and retired. He spent half the day in the mosque and the other half over at Uncle Rashid's brokerage shop or talking with mother about my marriage.

Meanwhile, Ayaz passed his Intermediate with highest honours, got a scholarship and went off to Lahore. Whenever he was back I would go and see him; on long vacations he would come over at least once a week to see me. But our visits were growing shorter and shorter. For one thing, he had gone away from town and, for another, my preoccupations expanded and with new preoccupations came new friends. We were both aware that our lives now moved along different paths, and that things would never be the same again between us. In spite of this, whenever we met, the enthusiasm and camaraderie of our childhood friendship would surge out from within us and we felt nothing could ever destroy that friendship.

The day after the B Sc results came out, I was passing through the market when my eyes fell on a newspaper the front page of which carried three photographs, one of them Ayaz's. I bought the newspaper and found out that he had gotten a gold medal for his performance in the B Sc exam. I went straight to his house.

Ayaz's mother, her exuberance uncontainable, was entertaining a few relatives and a bunch of the neighborhood women. Ayaz was sitting in the living room with three of his maternal cousins and a couple of friends. His brother Iftikhar had closed the shop and was passing out sweets to the guests. I congratulated Ayaz's mother and brother and scolded Ayaz for not telling me the good news.

"But I just got back from Lahore," he explained.

I sat down and had some sweets. After half an hour of idle chatter Ayaz blurted out, "Let's get out of here."

So we ambled out. When we reached the market, I asked, "Want to take a walk through my fields?"

"Sure. Why not?" said Ayaz happily.

I felt as though he just wanted to get away from it all—the pressing crowd at home and the excitement. He had suddenly grown quiet while we were still at his house. It had seemed as though he had already put his stunning success behind him and had turned his thoughts elsewhere.

We wandered in the fields for a long time until, finally, we came to the dera and sat down. Ayaz spoke little that day but I remember one thing he did say, "I'm going to enter Law College."

What? There we were assuming that after such a tremendous achievement Ayaz was certain to get a scholarship for an M Sc and later go abroad for a Ph D on a government grant. After he returned he could easily get a civil service job where he could rise to the top without any effort, recommendations or the usual headaches. This business about studying law took me by complete surprise.

"Will you get a scholarship?" I asked.

"Probably not for studying law."

"Then?"

"I'll get by somehow."

"But Ayaz," I couldn't help but ask, "what rhyme or reason is there in studying law after all this hard work in the sciences?"

"Who said anything about hard work?" he laughed. "What's the big deal about a gold medal? Just use your brains a little...that's all. What will I do with a science degree anyway? Teach in a college, or slave away in some laboratory for the next thirty years—like a bullock, with blinders pulled over my eyes and no mind to what's going on around me? Is that it? Oh, no. I want to get involved in the real world." He stretched out his arms and continued, "I want to get out where the action is. Where a man really talks to a man. Where there's friendship and enmity, profit and loss. Where there are fights with or without reason. The bargaining for life and death. That's where it's really at!"

What he said struck me as odd but true. None of our group had ever said anything quite like this. We were the sort who never had any clear plans; we rolled whichever way our parents or conditions shoved us. Whatever offered itself, we grabbed, or were grabbed by it, and time wore on. When one path ended we took the next that was open. Ayaz was the first person who knew exactly what he wanted to do and broke away from the prescribed path. I remember feeling a twinge of envy at that.

"Alright. It may work out in our favor," I said as I laughed. "You might come in handy."

That same year Ayaz entered law college. I can't remember now whether he got a scholarship, but Iftikhar's business was doing well and I knew he was sending Ayaz spending money now and then.

At Lahore Ayaz was put up at a distant maternal uncle's in the Krishan Nagar neighborhood. His room was so small he could barely fit his cot into it. There was only one other item: a small table loaded with books wedged into a corner. There were more books on the floor, on the windowsill, on the bed, in just about every conceivable place. His clothes were hung on the walls and on a nail in the back of the door. He'd do all his studying on the cot. That's how I remember his room from the time I stayed overnight with him when once I had to go to Lahore on business. Both of us had to sleep on the living room floor. We turned off the light and talked late into the night. Ayaz was in his second year of law college. He told me that he had been elected as secretary of the student union and was also the editor of the college magazine. He was complaining that he had taken on so many responsibilities that they were cutting into his studies, but I was certain that if Ayaz hadn't taken on all this extra work, he'd never have been satisfied with himself.

During the next few years my father died and my mother had me married. The pressure of these two events produced a change in me. I suddenly developed the urge to read and to write. Early one morning, Ayaz, back home on vacation, came over to my house looking for me and found me out at our dera where I was having some work done. In his hand was a literary magazine in which I had published a short story. He was flipping through the pages striking them with his hand and showing surprise, uncertainty and happiness all at once. He just couldn't believe that I had taken to writing fiction without telling him and was producing work that was even appearing in print.

I explained that so far this was the first and only story I had written, which surprised him even more. We stood there for a long time looking at each other and laughing.

"How did you get hold of this magazine?" I asked.

"I read it regularly," Ayaz explained. "I brought it back with me from Lahore but I only got around to reading it today."

I had written the story under a slightly different name, so I asked him how he knew it was my story.

"How? Isn't this is the story about our town?" he laughed. "All of our bazaars and alleys are in it. How could I not recognize it. I can even recognize myself in it!"

That day heralded a new friendship between Ayaz and me. Whenever he came home he dropped by to see me almost every day. Back in Lahore he would not fail to write me every few weeks. It was as if he saw a new person in me who besides being a childhood chum was his companion as a young adult. Now he'd discuss everything with me which perhaps he had discussed only with his Lahore friends till now: literature, conditions at home and abroad, the complicated, twisted affairs of men and women from which his restless mind constantly drew sustenance. Sometimes I thought he had become bored with our town, as there was perhaps nothing there to hold his interest, that his thoughts had moved far beyond the confines of our small town, or that he came to see me only to escape his feeling of confinement. Needless to say, this gave me a certain sense of worth and secret happiness.

Ayaz passed his LLB with distinction. He was offered a position with a famous law firm in Lahore but he turned it down, preferring to return to his hometown. When I asked him why, he explained, "True, there's no money here, but I cannot think of a better place than the village for someone just starting off. There's a whole spectrum of human conflicts here and you come to know the mentality, the precise manner in which the minds of the petty government clerks work. Why should I become the assistant to a barrister in the High Court and slave away for him? Why not set up my own office in the District Court...beneath the peepal tree?" he laughed. "Why shouldn't I do my own work?"

That left us, his friends and his family, little say in his affairs. We were reduced to silent spectators. Ayaz practiced in anonymity for the next few years in his hometown, working under a tree, just as he had described it to me the first time, down to the last detail.

The city had two prominent lawyers who worked from offices in their manors. The other lawyers, however, made do with the court compound where they had set up their moveable, make-shift offices under the numerous ancient, shady banyans and peepals. During the previous few years the population of budding lawyers had outstripped the population of available clerks—the so-called munshis. As a result, one clerk was obliged to serve two or three lawyers, even working as their broker. Most of these munshis, though, made more money than the young lawyers just starting off or, for that matter, the unsuccessful older ones.

Ayaz, too, set up his office under a peepal near the office of a district court magistrate and got the part-time help of an experienced munshi. When his practice picked up after a year and a half, he replaced the munshi with a young scrivener. In the law business this was an unprecedented act. For one thing, a scrivener was always considered to be a far lower status than a munshi (the latter was addressed as "Mr. Lawyer" by the illiterate village people) and any scrivener aspiring to the rank of munshi came up against enormous roadblocks. For another, the lawyers themselves supported this ranking system, although it didn't affect them one way or the other. But these people, steeped in age-old traditions of their occupation, saw their security in slavishly preserving those traditions. (This is evident from the barest glance at the comical jargon of law or from hearing a lawyer indulge in casuistry. Then it is hard to escape the conclusion that what matters most to them is not how best to serve justice but rather preside over the law itself.)

Ayaz, however, managed even then to deviate from these small traditions of his profession without transgressing the legal boundaries. His opinion: better to train a new man for the job than rely on the services of some experienced but sly munshi.

Those days I was having a new house built for myself on a piece of our property outside the city limits. I spent most of my time on the site but when I'd have to go to court on account of a friend or an acquaintance, I'd make it a point to see Ayaz. His chair was almost always empty, as he was in court all day. At such times I'd ensconce myself in his chair and make small talk with his clerk. After wrapping up one case, Ayaz would come back and chat for five or ten minutes, then rush off to another case. If I needed any of his help in some matter, he'd come personally. I knew a couple of other lawyers there as well. Whenever I'd run into them, they'd invariably say, "Chaudhry, your types are born to live in luxury. Your baron fathers have left enough money to last you three generations. Look at us. We have to hustle around in the petty courts just to get by."

But not even in jest had Ayaz ever spoken to me in that vein. He was free of jealously or envy. One look at him and you knew he was destined for higher places, that his eyes were trained on summits beyond the sight of ordinary mortals.

Every once in a while on a Sunday he'd take his files out to my dera, always remembering to bring a fresh issue of some literary magazine along. There, perched on the cot, he'd work all day long, leaving me to read the magazine. We would take a break to eat, talk or roam in the fields. He loved to talk about writers, both modern and classical. This was one subject on which he intently listened to my views, even preferred them to his own. The look of concentration on his face at such times was a source of constant marvel; I could never cease to wonder that a man could live all at once in so many different worlds: of home, neighborhood, relatives, his childhood and adolescence out of which he grew to manhood; and the world of work which ran solely on incisive intelligence and unshakable confidence; and a third one yet, of literature, on whose threshold he stood diffidently looking in. He told me that while at Lahore he had written several articles for the law college magazine, but lacked the time to indulge his muse now. I often thought that if he hadn't become a lawyer, he certainly would have been a brilliant writer.

Ayaz had been living in the same house with his mother and kid sister Salma. Iftikhar had gotten married and after a year had moved to a place of his own above the cloth shop.

Inside our town's Company Gardens was a small, exclusive club where government officials and lawyers got together in the evening to play tennis, table tennis or cards. Rumor had it that there was also drinking and gambling. Ayaz never joined that club. Whenever I visited him in the evening, I found him buried in work behind a paper-strewn table in his small living room. A couple of times he had casually mentioned how he wanted to have a house built for himself outside the city. And I had offered to give him a piece of land at no cost. But he had laughed it off, saying, "No time for these things now."

His success was phenomenal: within two years not only his relatives but also all his associates in the profession felt that at his present pace he'd soon outdistance every other lawyer. During that time I observed the other lawyers' attitude toward him gradually change; no doubt he was someone to reckon with. There was also a rumor going around then that he would be offered the position of civil judge in the government.

But at that point Ayaz unexpectedly changed course. He told me he was going to England to study for a Barrister-at-Law degree.

"Outside of my family you're the first person I've told this to," he said. "So keep it to yourself. I haven't told mother about it yet.

She looks a bit troubled these days. I have a distant relative in England, my father's cousin or something. I've been corresponding with him for some time now. He's made all the necessary arrangements for my admission and all."

Of the few scenes from my life that are etched on my mind, this is one: It is August. Ayaz, holding a leather attaché case, is standing in his doorway ready to leave. His mother is clinging to him, crying her heart out and repeatedly going over his head, face and chest with her fingers in a desperate attempt to preserve the whole of her son in her touch. The residents of the lane have come out of their houses; men standing outside Ayaz's house to send him off, the women and children framed in their doorways silently watching the scene. Iftikhar picks up Ayaz's attaché case and we all start walking out of the lane, but Ayaz's mother follows us out and begins to wail with her hands flung out to the sky. Ayaz tries to console her with the promise to return within three years.

We had sent him off as we would someone going on a long trip; alone the old lady knew, perhaps intuitively, that her son was leaving town for good.

Ayaz returned from England after five long years, but not to his hometown. He stayed on in Lahore and sent for his mother and siblings. When the latter returned from visiting him, Iftikhar told me that in Lahore the family stayed at their Krishan Nagar relative, but Ayaz didn't join them there, preferring to stay at a friend's mansion. Iftikhar, though, brought back a letter for me from Ayaz, asking me how I was doing and urging that I come and see him in Lahore.

The first two years of his stay in England Ayaz had kept up a steady correspondence with me. His letters were always full of new and exotic things. For someone like me who had never left his hometown for more than a day at a time, they provided excitement and adventure. I'd find myself eagerly awaiting Ayaz's letters and would pore over every one of them many times before reading it aloud to my friends. For days we would talk about them. Even though my friends and I were long past being mere teenagers and just about all of us were family men, the fascination and appeal of Englishwomen titillated our thoughts. Ayaz, though, had never written about any relationships with Englishwomen; we saw them everywhere in his letters all the same.

Once my friend Salim, a really scrawny, diminutive man who desperately wanted to build up his body, spotted an ad for some wonder pills in an old issue of an English magazine. The ad guaranteed that the pills would help one become robust and muscular all around. Salim nagged me that I write to Ayaz for the pills. Finally, I did, uncertain that he would go through all that trouble for a friend of mine. What do you know, within two months I got a neat little packet from Ayaz. (By the way, the pills didn't help Salim a bit, rather, they made him terribly ill.)

Then Ayaz's letters stopped coming. In the last one, though, he did mention about having some financial problems, but reiterated his resolve to do whatever it took to finish his education. To his mother, though, he continued writing every two weeks, sending me every now and then his good wishes through her.

So it was with mixed feelings that I went to see him in Lahore. I was expecting to see him drastically changed. After all he hadn't cared to return to his hometown, preferring to settle down in Lahore, instead. When, however, I met him, all those doubts evaporated. He embraced me with the same old warmth and affection. On this visit I had brought along my oldest son Kamal who was then six. Ayaz held him in his lap for a long time and talked to him with genuine affection. As for the changes, well, I did notice a few, the obvious ones: Ayaz was clad in an expensive-looking dark-colored suit and his black shoes shined so brightly you could see your face in them. He also used a lot of English words now, sometimes whole sentences. He seemed much more refined in his mannerisms, but, still, he was the same old Ayaz. Which set me completely at ease within a few minutes.

He introduced me to his friend Azhar. Both had studied for a Bar-at-Law degree in England and had now returned together. Azhar was not entirely unknown to me. Ayaz had frequently spoken about him in his letters from England, especially in the ones in which he recounted some humorous incidents of his first few days in England in which Azhar figured rather prominently. Ayaz brought up again those incidents and the three of us had a good laugh.

Ayaz told me that he was going to join the law firm headed by Azhar's father, Shaikh Mazhar-ud-Din. The elderly gentleman was an established attorney and hailed from a respectable family. Some of his relatives held high government and political posts. They lived in a stately old mansion in the city. Ayaz was putting up in an annex of this mansion these days.

"I feel I've known you for a long time," Azhar said to me. "Now my family is eager to meet you."

Ayaz just sat and smiled on. I looked over at him quizzically. He got up and went over to the bookshelf, picked up a book and showed me the dust-jacket. It was a copy of my most recent collection of short stories. I felt a strange satisfaction in seeing my book in Ayaz's hand.

"How did you get hold of that?" I asked.

"This is the first Urdu book I've bought in five years," he chuckled. "What wonderful stories you've written. I read them all in one night. I was familiar with only four, the rest must have been written after I left."

"Yes," I agreed.

"You've really become a famous man, eh?"

I burst out laughing. "Nobody gives a damn about writers here and you know it."

Ayaz suddenly became silent. "Yes," he said after a pause. "But one day they'll have to look the writer right in the eye. There's no getting away from it."

There was a strange glint in his eyes as he said this. The slight change present in his tone disappeared momentarily, revealing the same old voice—optimistic, undaunted, and slightly tremulous—which I used to hear when he practiced law in our hometown and dropped by my place on a Sunday for a stroll through the fields where we talked about poets and prose writers. That voice, it made the intervening five years disappear and, with it, whatever was still left of my uneasiness.

Ayaz mentioned that my best stories were those I had written about our hometown, especially the ones which dealt with my childhood and adolescent years. That sounded a bit naive to me and I smiled. Many, many years later, though, I realized how right he was.

He also mentioned having written during his stay in England a few articles for some law journals, one of which had become quite popular and was also widely excerpted.

We had lunch at Azhar's. I also met Azhar's sister Nasim who later became Ayaz's wife. She was a very bright and attractive woman who taught English at a local college. She, too, had spent a year in England getting her degree, I found out talking to her, and it was there that she had first met Ayaz. When it was evening I said goodbye with a promise to return soon.

Every four or five weeks I would now routinely visit Ayaz in Lahore. After a year he was married to Nasim. The couple lived in the annex of Nasim's parental home for a few months following their wedding and then moved into a rented house in a new development complex in the suburbs. Ayaz practiced law in partnership with Azhar and the latter's father for two years and then took another big step: he ended the partnership and set up his own practice. Now when I'd visit him, he'd often insist that I stay overnight. "We have a lot of room now," he'd tell me, "and, besides, you're the only friend I have to whom I can tell everything."

That was true, to an extent. The people Ayaz was acquainted with were all connected with his profession. He saw them all day long in various courts, barrooms, or wherever. Other than that he didn't have any time for socializing. At home he would work until eleven or twelve o'clock every night on his briefs for the cases next day. Sundays he and Nasim would go over to her parents' estate and normally have lunch there. If I happened to be in town, I'd go with them. Most of the conversation at Ayaz's in-laws centered around family or law. In the afternoon we'd take Ayaz's used Ford for a leisurely drive back. Then, after a short rest, Ayaz and I would go out for a long walk—the only time when we could really get a chance to talk with each other. Every once in a while I would accept his invitation to stay overnight, but then I'd invariably end up talking late into the evening with Nasim while Ayaz worked away in his study. Over breakfast I'd talk to Nasim a bit in Ayaz's absence and then leave. We always laughed about how Ayaz always insisted that I stay and how he would then immerse himself in his routine as though I wasn't even there.

"Just your presence is enough for Ayaz," Nasim told me once. "Having you around means a lot to him. He feels as though a member of his own family were here."

Nasim was brought up in an environment radically different from Ayaz's or mine. I remember when I first brought my wife over to meet them—they'd just settled in their new place—she went into something of a shock seeing Nasim address Ayaz with the intimate *tum*, rather than with the more formal *aap*. Nasim moved in a mixed circle and felt as much at ease with men as with women—a delightful blend of informality and polite restraint which belonged to the women of a certain class and, thus, made them ever so attractive to men of other, especially the lower, classes. She didn't have any of Ayaz's penetrating intelligence—the sort that allows you to unravel the most twisted problems with relative ease—and she knew that. She had accepted that fact as naturally as she had her place with respect to the males of her family, like her father and brother. But this acceptance was altogether without any sense of inferiority. To Ayaz, who remained entrenched in his own class but had no qualms about breaking its conventions whenever he could, this aspect of Nasim's personality perhaps made her all the more attractive. Where she was a challenge for him, she was also the bedrock of his confidence, though her own life was as much filled with common dissatisfactions as anyone else's. If she could have had her way, she'd never have left the annex of her father's mansion that was as large as a medium-sized house.

"Why did he have to give up the practice with my family?" she complained to me several times. "It was a considerable practice. Everyone was doing fine and would have continued to. We all tried to reason with him but God knows what got into his head. He kept saying, 'It was interfering with my independence.' Although no one held him back, ever. Now you see where it's gotten us. At least then we used to have some time for socializing, now we don't even have enough to scratch our heads."

Even after the wedding, Nasim's life continued to revolve round her old friends and family. In four years she had two boys, which circumstance forced her to resign her position at the college. Most of the time she took the boys over to her mother's as soon as Ayaz had left for court, returning an hour or two before he was due back.

"Daddy offered to buy me a new car," she told me once, "but Ayaz turned him down. Who knows why? There must be something off in his thinking. I'm getting frazzled taking buses and taxis all the time."

Nasim's contact with Ayaz's family was practically non-existent. Wives couldn't have asked for more, but for Nasim, with whom one would think such minor things carried no weight at all, this affair could well have been the source of persistent unhappiness.

Ayaz's mother was continually ill, and Iftikhar had given up the flat above his store and moved back home with his wife and children to take care of her. Salma, Ayaz's sister, was with her husband, an employee in the Excise Department in Jhelum. As for Ayaz, he would drop by Sundays every few months to visit his mother for a couple of hours. On each visit he would insist that the old lady move to Lahore, that Nasim, too, wanted her there so that she could be properly looked after and treated for her ailment. But I had the nagging suspicion that his offer lacked conviction, that it was a mere put on. Only once, at 'Id, did Iftikhar, his family and the old lady go to stay at Ayaz's as this was the 'Id Ayaz had decided to celebrate at home and not at his in-laws. Ayaz's mother had returned from the trip full of praises and good wishes for her daughter-in-law. Nasim had from time to time confided in me that she really wanted Ayaz's mother to stay with them, even if for a few months, but the old lady was adamant: they'd only take her out of her husband's house feet first. Anyway, one thing was for sure, Nasim hadn't visited our city even once.

After four or five years of independent practice, another change began to show in Ayaz's lifestyle. His life, up to now, had taken many directions, but not randomly; indeed each seemed premeditated and carefully planned. This time, however, it somehow seemed different. One could not say whether the changes were of his own volition or whether in response to force of circumstance. He was going on thirty-six and though still sound of body, his face had begun to show the effects of his long labors. It's possible that one morning he went to the mirror to shave with something on his mind and stood there totally amazed, thinking, "I seem to know this face from somewhere." But, considering his nature, a more plausible reason might be that he was beginning to tire of his cheerless daily routine, uncertain about his next move as he had already achieved what he had set out for. Surely, he had already acquired at his relatively young age what a successful man works all his life for. He had bought the mansion he was renting and had furnished it with all conceivable modern amenities. He had bought a new car for himself and given the old one to Nasim. A cook, an errand boy, a nursemaid, and a gardener worked for them. His practice was simply flourishing and he had started to work considerably less at home. In the office he had employed two junior associates, both intelligent and industrious. They prepared Ayaz's briefs and settled the preliminary dispositions in the lower courts, leaving Ayaz with only the Session or High Court cases. He now had considerably more free time to spend at home. They had two darling boys and they lived together in perfect harmony, full of happiness and free of want. It wouldn't be inaccurate to say that by that time Ayaz had reached all his objectives. Little did I know then that the most important phase of his life, far from ending, was in fact about to begin.

Ayaz and Nasim began to socialize. There was no dearth of people desirous to be included in their circle of friends. Two or three times a week the couple would have a few friends over or go out. Both were very discriminating about selecting their friends. Most of Ayaz's friends were drawn from his own profession: barristers and lawyers of his own age with whom he had worked side by side for years, and a couple of younger colleagues whom he had included only because they had impressed him by their intelligence and zeal. As time wore on people from different professions, a few of them at any rate, were also allowed in. For some time now Ayaz had taken to writing on international law and similar subjects. His articles appeared in English language newspapers. So his select group expanded; now, among them, one could also see the sort of people who represented a mix of journalism and teaching on the one hand and literature and politics on the other.

Although Ayaz and Nasim's attitude toward me had not changed, a distance of twenty years allows me to admit that back then I did feel a twinge of jealousy seeing them surrounded by their friends: Ayaz laughing and jocular, Nasim confident and gracious as she entertained, enchanting her guests with her grace and elegance. With the passage of time all such uncomfortable feelings disappeared.

It is hard to know exactly when in his life a man ends one phase and enters another. A retrospective glance across the intervening twenty years exposes an altogether trivial incident which may be viewed as a milestone in Ayaz's life.

Summer. A Sunday. I had come to see Ayaz. As usual Ayaz and Nasim were expected at her parents', but it was so hot out that they decided to stay home instead. We had dinner and stayed on at the table under the ceiling fan chatting. Finally, when we got up, Ayaz said to me, "I want to show you something."

A few minutes later he emerged from his study with a sheaf of typed pages which he stuffed in my hand, saying, "Here, I wrote this. Mind looking it over?"

I took the pages and returned to my room. Ayaz had never shown me his writing before, nor had I really ever wanted to read any of it. First, because they were mostly on purely legal matters; second, because I had no stomach for the ponderous legalese in which they were invariably written, riddled with citations, articles and sub-articles. But this was something different. I started reading and couldn't put it down. The article focused on the question of human rights, and though it was well argued and legally styled, it didn't at all seem legalistic. In simple unadorned prose Ayaz had explained how and why the laws upholding human rights applied indiscriminately to all countries. This article was so tactfully written that in spite of its characteristically stark prose one could not accuse the writer of sedition. Still, it was late 1958 and a delicate time in our country.

Later in the afternoon over tea, I pointed out the possible dangers I saw in the article.

"This is *the* time for this sort of writing," Ayaz said excitedly. "Precisely why I didn't write it earlier. But don't worry, I haven't attacked any government agency or its policies up front. However, if people want to read between the lines, let them. That's precisely what I'd wanted. Anyway, I'd very much want you to translate it into Urdu."

I looked at Nasim, hoping she'd try to stop him from taking such a hazardous step, but she remained silent.

I sweated over that translation for three days. A fortnight later the article appeared simultaneously in both English and Urdu newspapers. The joyous pride I felt seeing it can only be compared with that which I had felt upon seeing my first short story in print. I saved clippings from both newspapers. I still have them.

At our next meeting Ayaz told me that he had been summoned, quite unexpectedly, by the Chief Secretary. And a few days later, he was invited to a reception at Government House where the Governor, whom he had never met before, addressed him as an old friend and casually mentioned a thing or two. He was never berated or asked to cease his activities but the hint was dropped that the government expected the country's intelligent men to expend their talent in positive undertakings. Ayaz got the cue all right. He forthwith stopped writing for newspapers, for a time at least (or the newspapers kept away from him).

Precisely at this point his work underwent a dramatic change.

I remember one time I went to see Ayaz. I caught him in the midst of a discussion with his father-in-law about this very change. The discussion exploded into a veritable argument. Ayaz's practice was fast deteriorating. His junior partners, loyal to him beyond reproach, were trying their best to keep the practice afloat, but there was no denying that Ayaz's income was dwindling as his partiality for the underprivileged was fast turning into a full-blown passion.

"But Daddy!" I heard Nasim shout at her father, "this is a matter of principle for Ayaz."

"Principle! Principle!" the old man fumed. "What do you people know about principles? We, too, have served this country. Indeed the people who created it have all come from our profession. For God's sake all you ever learned is training. What about mental discipline? Whatever you do, do it with decorum. A little discretion wouldn't hurt. Why do you go marching off to court like an alderman to defend every Tom, Dick and Harry who wanders into your office? Are you out to get a vote or something?"

"Anyway, Daddy, please don't interfere in Ayaz's work," an angry Nasim cut her father off curtly.

This was the first time I had seen Nasim side with Ayaz in an argument with her father. In the ensuing months even I wondered if Ayaz's discipline hadn't lost out to his passion. In quick succession he fought several cases for measly fees and won them. Once he told me he had received a message from the Governor.

"Guess what it was?" he grinned.

"I give up. What?" I asked.

"I've been offered the position of Assistant Advocate General."

"Well?" I was expectantly tense.

"Ha!" he exclaimed. "They've fooled you. Brother, this is an out-and-out bribery. You think I'll let those bastards trap me? Never!"

Ayaz was not himself those days, even I felt that. He looked more like a stranger. To me he was a man who built his life around the primacy of reason and never let his emotions get in his way. This was the first time his heart took precedence over his mind, although this doesn't mean he had lost his former mental agility, rather, whatever direction he had taken, his mind was racing on ahead faster and more efficiently than before. It seemed as though his mind had halted for a split second at some nameless place, took a confused, frightened look around, and then shot off in a completely new direction.

During that trying period, when just about everyone avoided Ayaz, his friend Azhar and his father-in-law included, Nasim proved to be his greatest ally; steadfast and unwavering she stood by his side. She never argued with him. For the first time she seemed his companion in every sense of the word. I still feel it was largely her supportive attitude that gradually put some order back in his life.

After a tumultuous year Ayaz settled back as if his disposition had ultimately rejected this unnatural pace and returned to its original ordered and disciplined rigour, or as if he had finally found his direction. His passion hadn't subsided, only it had become more controlled and enduring. He had divided his practice into two neat spheres. In one he took and fought cases any lawyer would and made good money. In the other he used whatever time he could spare to take on a case of his liking without regard to any economic reward. His relationship with his in-laws, too, had improved, which made Nasim very happy, as happy perhaps as I had seen her only in the first few months of her marriage. Shortly afterwards Ayaz fought the two notorious cases I mentioned earlier. All at once he was the talk of the town, his fame no longer confined to the legal circle.

Till now I've only mentioned those different forms which Ayaz's life assumed from time to time. Often I have even characterized them as "changes." But as I reflect on it, there was nothing new about those forms as one is born with them and assumes them—according to a preconceived plan, as it were—at different stages in his life. Rarely, if ever, does an event—or an incident—radically transform a man's personality, or affect, decisively, all its subsequent forms. Still, some men, or at least some forms, obviously do carry within them the potential for complete change and the change inevitably does come about. Inwardly some such incident occurred in Ayaz's life.

That incident is a complete story in its own right. And, without relating it, I can scarcely describe my friend's life. I must also relate it because this was the first occasion that I was completely involved in an episode which concerned Ayaz's life.

It was winter. I had gone to Lahore to see Ayaz for the first time in two months. It was a Sunday evening and a few of his friends had gathered at his house (the very people who had avoided him for some time but were now swarming back to him). We gossiped, had supper, and then gathered around the fireplace, where we munched pinenuts and walnuts between sips of coffee. Ayaz, I noticed, was keeping unusually quiet. The conversation went along the usual course: law, politics, journalism, and the general state of the country, with a lively joke in between. Ayaz, who normally led the conversation as he played the host, seemed somewhat preoccupied that day. Finally, after the guests had left, Ayaz came back and sat down in front of the fireplace again. He stretched his legs, propped his chin up with both his fists and stared into the crackling fire. His forehead was creased. I talked with Nasim for a while. Finally I couldn't stand it any longer.

"What's wrong?" I asked him. "You're awfully quiet today."

Ayaz started at me, then instead of answering he laughed gently and returned to silence as if hesitant to speak.

"Ayaz is stuck on a case," Nasim explained.

"Stuck?" I repeated, quite surprised. Law was his forte. I had seen him sweat while preparing a brief, but be so worried on account of it—never. "What kind of case?" I asked.

"A murder case," she said.

This was nothing new for Ayaz. He handled murder cases all the time. But he was trying to avoid talking about this one. As I chatted with Nasim, he arose and began pacing the room, lost in deep thought, his forehead lined with concentration, his hands jammed into his pants pockets. I quietly watched him. After a while he sat back down.

"Is it a tough case?" I asked with a smile.

Ayaz smiled faintly in response. "No, not really tough," he said. "It's just different."

"Tell me about it."

"When I was in England I used to see a lot of such cases," he said. "Over here, though, murder is committed with very simple motives: old feuds, property disputes or, at best, adultery." After a brief pause he added, "You could say adultery is involved in this one, too—in a manner of speaking."

"Let's hear it."

"Well, there is this educated young civil servant who has murdered his wife on suspicion of adultery. I'm defending him. The accused has confessed, there are witnesses, et cetera. The crime is indisputable, I will not plead his innocence. The case can only be defended on the grounds of diminished responsibility."

"Then what's the problem?" I asked.

"Problem? It is imperative to establish the evidence of adultery."

"And there's none?"

"Not a clue, yet."

"What does the accused say?"

"Right now he's pretty mixed up. Earlier, though, he did maintain that he found his wife and her lover together and attacked them. But it appears the paramour wasn't even there. It looks more like he killed her on the mere suspicion of adultery. The man's extremely intelligent, but in a state of shock since the incident. We'll have to keep him from testifying. The prosecution can and probably will insist that he take the stand, but I think we can block their motion. Now if that happens, there's only one way out."

"What's that?"

"Plead insanity."

"What's stopping you?"

"For one thing, it would both complicate and somewhat weaken our case; for another, we'll have to depend on whatever the doctors' reports say."

"Hmm." I thought for a bit and then added, "You've got a problem."

"Any court in Europe or America would have no difficulty accepting a plea of insanity, or even temporary insanity on the mere suspicion of adultery," Ayaz said. "Over here, although the legal system runs along British lines, the courts still lack those refinements. Anyway, there are other ways of handling it. Right now I'm not certain which way to take." He was quiet for a few moments. "Well, what's bothering me..." and he emphasized the word, "is that the man's not guilty."

"Wh—at?"

"He's not guilty!" Ayaz said with finality, spreading his arms confidently as though that were enough by way of proof. "The man is innocent!"

"How do you know?"

"I don't really know how, but I do," he said. "That's all I know. I just feel it. The man is innocent. Now it's just a matter of proving it."

I was profoundly shocked. His was a trained lawyer's mind where conjecture had no place. For him, anything that couldn't be proven didn't exist. (To accept even those things that didn't have to be proven he would find some proof for anyway. Sometimes I wondered if God's existence didn't reside in his mind in the form of a proof.) Till now Ayaz had never said anything which fell outside the sphere of evidence and proof, nor had he ever tried to prove anything by disregarding the events and circumstances. That's what made him a first-rate lawyer. But today he had broken his own principles and was saying so casually, almost carelessly, "Now it's just a matter of proving it." This was the first time ever that he had abandoned the terra firma of hard facts for the mire of conjecture which swallows you without your being aware of it.

I just gawked at him. He went back to staring into the flames. Meanwhile Nasim had quietly gotten up and gone to another room where she could be heard humming. My curiosity was piqued. I wanted all the details of the case from start to finish. Who was this man who had killed his wife, had confessed his crime and yet had managed to convince a staunch rationalist like Ayaz of his innocence? Ayaz looked across at me. I could tell from his look that he had read my thoughts.

"You're a writer," he said, "you claim to know people's innermost thoughts. Tell me, what do you make of it?"

"When did I claim any such thing?" I laughed. "This case is quite interesting, though. Tell me the whole story and maybe then I'll be able to say something."

He kept looking at me for a few moments, as if trying to come to a decision. He pressed his lips hard for a bit, glanced at the flames and gave an affirming nod; then he looked at me and said, "All right, then listen."

Now when I think about it, I realize that it was in those few moments that Ayaz had decided to bring me in on the case. Here are the details as he related them.

Zafar came from a village. He was quick in school. He attended high school and college in a nearby city. After BA he landed a job as food inspector, but kept studying for the PCS exam, which he passed after two years. After his initial training he was posted to several cities and townships as a magistrate. One of these townships was Qusur. It was here that he met the family of his future wife, Kausar, in connection with some claim suit. They were refugees from Delhi who had settled in Qusur in 1947. At that time Kausar was in her early teens. When Zafar was posted in Qusur, Kausar was in her last year of BA at a college in Lahore. Zafar and Kausar were married after she finished college.

Following his term of service in one or two other cities, Zafar was appointed to the Secretariat in Lahore. At the time of the incident they had been married five years and had lived a little more than a year in Lahore. They had two children. The family lived in half of an old, rented mansion near Chauburji. It was here one evening around nine or ten o'clock that Zafar strangled Kausar. For the next couple of hours Zafar didn't budge from the house, then he woke his children, put them on his scooter, the four-year old boy behind him, the toddler on his lap, and drove one-handed to a friend's house. It must have been some time after midnight when this friend finally contacted the police.

After relating these few bare details, Ayaz stared at me blankly as though he had nothing more to add. All he said was, "If you want, you can look at the brief."

So this was how I came to be involved in the case. I studied the brief and all other relevant documents. Aside from the circumstances of the murder itself, the investigation conducted by Ayaz's assistants did not go beyond a few details about the couple's life. A few professors at the college, and friends and their families had been contacted for information about the murdered woman's student days. Around Qusur a few acquaintances of the deceased and her family had also been questioned. One of the statements came from an influential man who pointed to some compromising aspects of the victim's character. The case for the defense could have been based to a great extent on just this statement but it was later discovered that this man had a standing feud with the victim's maternal uncle. So his testimony had to be discarded.

Another statement made a casual reference to an alleged affair with a male lecturer at the college but a subsequent intensive investigation yielded nothing further. There were also references to a few other events, mostly insignificant, based on rumor and conjecture which a run-of-the-mill lawyer wouldn't have hesitated to introduce as circumstantial evidence to strengthen his case but which carried no weight with a man of Ayaz's sophistication. So, up to now the case for the defense was built solely on some of the incidents of Zafar's life and preeminently his character. It wasn't difficult for even a layman like myself to sense that this pile of circumstances, incidents, facts and figures lying before me didn't point to any definite direction or yield a conclusive proof.

I spent a couple of days with Ayaz and then returned home. But I felt restless. Barely a few days had passed when I decided to go back to Lahore. Even at that time there were hundreds of similar cases in the dockets throughout the country but this particular case had captivated me almost entirely. And although I was not involved in it mentally, quite as Ayaz was, it still had gripped me so compellingly that it was impossible to break away. I explained the situation to my wife and the very next day went back to Lahore.

"Can I meet Zafar?" I asked Ayaz during one of our conversations.

"I very much doubt that," Ayaz replied. "Only his lawyers or his immediate family are allowed to see him."

At least three different versions of Zafar's statements were on record. The first contained an unequivocal accusation of infidelity on the part of Kausar, and it appeared that Zafar had finally caught her at it. But the police investigation revealed that her alleged lover, a college professor, had at the time been out of the country for a year—a finding that damaged Zafar's position considerably. Then there was this statement which the accused had made at the stand. He had stated in it that for the previous few months his wife's behavior made it evident that she was carrying on with another man. She often disappeared from the house and every few days took the children over to her mother's for a whole fortnight or so. One time when Zafar went to Qusur to bring her back he found out that she had left the children in her mother's care and herself gone off somewhere else. Even her mother couldn't say where. After a few days when she returned she absolutely refused to talk about the matter. (This was confirmed by their maidservant whom Ayaz had intended to use as a witness.) In a third version, which was formed much later during Zafar's conversations with his lawyers, he had revealed that Kausar had been depriving him of his conjugal rights for a year. He had also accused his mother-in-law of being an accomplice in what he described as a "shabby intrigue."

Basically there was no contradiction in Zafar's statements. What impelled him to commit his crime was his wife's unfaithfulness. The bottom line, though, was: how was one to produce before the court the proof backing up this accusation?

Nasim prepared a room for me. I had packed a suitcase with my things and come intent upon a lengthy stay. Ayaz and Nasim were simply euphoric. Ever since they had moved in this house they had been pestering me to spend a few days with them, but circumstances had never permitted me to stay with them more than a day or half at any one time. Little did I know that I would end up staying with them for quite a while in connection with an event which would come to have, in my opinion at least, a particular importance in our lives.

Early during my stay I noticed something unexpectedly new in Nasim. Like myself, she, too, had ceased being a mere spectator and was beginning to take a keen interest in the case. But while Ayaz's attitude toward the case was professional and mine mostly inquisitive, hers betrayed ambivalence for quite a while. Being a wife, naturally her loyalties were with her husband and, as a result, her sympathies with Zafar. On the other hand, she had the visceral feeling that any man who could murder his wife forthwith forfeited any claim to sympathy.

Often after supper we would talk about the case among other things, the conversation being mostly between Nasim and myself. Ayaz, although no longer quite as contemplative or worried as before, was still tight-lipped about it. After staying a few days I decided to go on a trip.

I had been thinking for the previous few days how to get a handle on the case. No matter how resourceful a lawyer is, he only collects the most obvious facts and details pertaining to an event, adducing proofs therefrom, according to his ability and understanding of law, to put up a good defense. It is a rare lawyer indeed who by disposition is compelled to examine the subtleties inherent in the background of a case or become embroiled in the personal lives of the people involved. The lives of others are like twilight bogs that require time and persistent effort to work through.

To the extent that Ayaz had invited me in I was, of course, involved in the case. Personally, however, I was interested rather in its dramatic element. I had already obtained the details of the crime and its perpetrator from Ayaz's office, and it was useless to pursue them further.

I reflected for a couple of days and concluded that the real course of action did not begin with the crime and end at Zafar but the other way around. Zafar's personality ought to be my starting point. Who was this man? What kind of temperament did he have? Did this sort of crime come naturally to him or was it just a solitary impulsive act? It was ironic that the man whose personality I was trying to put together from bits and pieces gathered from here and there was locked up in a prison a short distance away and I was powerless to see him.

The only way to achieve my objectives was to go out and get the information myself, I concluded. I packed a few things in a small travel bag and set out. First I spent a few days in each of the three or four cities where Zafar had worked as a food inspector and later as magistrate. Because this was delicate work and also I didn't want to attract attention to myself, I abandoned my city clothes for a peasant's garb. Though I regularly wore this sort of clothing around the house, I never wore it on trips. For the first few days my new outfit made me feel like an impostor, but the feeling soon wore off.

I hadn't set out with any specific plan in mind, so I played it by ear. Mostly I gathered information from civil offices and circuit courts, limiting my contact to only the people at the lower levels. I knew how to deal with these people due to the nature of my work at home. To start a conversation, in many places I presented myself as a peasant from a nearby village asking how I could get in touch with Zafar Ali Chauhan the magistrate. People gawked at me and said that Chauhan Sahib had been transferred to Sialkot some time ago. Nothing except a brief preliminary report had until then come out in the newspapers concerning the murder, so most people were unaware of the incident. In Sialkot I was told that Chauhan Sahib had moved to Chichawatni. Some of the people who had been exposed to the ways of the court system asked a few questions of their own before answering. Who was I? Where was I from? Why was I asking all these questions? And so on. So much of their time had been spent fleecing people that whenever they spotted a stranger their first thought was what to squeeze out of him. I had to feed these people a different line. For instance, on one occasion I had said that some time ago the Magistrate Sahib (meaning Zafar) had come to our village to attend the wedding of one of my relatives and had told me to look him up if ever I needed his help. But my lie backfired. Everyone knew that Chauhan Sahib never accepted any social invitations nor could he be talked into doing favors. To get out of that lie, I had to fabricate quite a few more. I had never done this sort of thing before, and doing it now made me feel pretty bad. But the feeling subsided after a few days. In fact, I began to enjoy this detective work. It seems that inside every writer is a liar and a detective; that's why he can dish out fabrications to people as hard facts, and perhaps because of this a writer's work is fraught with danger: when he can't find the truth, he's reduced to being a lying detective. The thought of the world already saturated with this sort of dangerous people made my heart race.

As a food inspector Zafar would rent a small dingy rooming place somewhere in the market area of whatever city he happened to be posted in; but as a magistrate he found lodgings in a regular house in one of the city's respectable neighborhoods or else in bungalows in the Civil Lines. I got a little information from the shopkeepers and servants in the vicinity of his residences, but I wasn't getting any closer to the man I was searching for. When I returned to Lahore after eleven days of intensive work, I hadn't added anything to the information already on hand. The kind of man I came to know was Zafar Ali Chauhan the government officer: so impeccable in his honesty that when he worked in the Food Department, notorious for its graft, people swore by him. As a magistrate, on the other hand, he was famous as a hard-working, intelligent and principled officer. All his former subordinates and domestics had been very happy with him and his wife. I myself even heard the older servants utter a few prayers for him. Zafar's wife was well known for her piety. She never turned anyone away from her home empty handed, I was told; she was generous to a fault and never talked down to anyone. Zafar thought the world of her and they loved each other very much. Zafar brought the best recommendations to each successive transfer. There was one thing, though, that struck me as somewhat odd: they almost never did any socializing. In this respect Zafar was the same, before marriage, and after. He never joined a club or organization. Prominent men and their wives of whichever city he had been transferred to would pay them a social call every once in a while, but Zafar and Kausar never returned the visit. Except for official banquets Zafar never went out, nor had he struck up any friendships with any of his colleagues. He never even participated in sports. He spent his entire time away from the office at home. He brought his office work with him, read a couple of Urdu and English newspapers and every once in a while took his wife and kids out for a walk. Soon after supper the family retired early.

"So what's new?" Ayaz said. "We already know all that."

"I'm going to Zafar's hometown," I answered, as though that was the only "new" thing I had brought along from this trip.

Ever since my return I had been feeling that I had run aground: I had gone searching for someone but had been sidetracked. During those eleven days, though, I had never for a minute thought that I wasn't getting anywhere. And that was suprising. When I was knocking around those cities, I was so caught up in my work that I had lost touch with everything else, as though my actions had no other purpose than to keep me preoccupied. Now I felt like a total idiot. Ayaz's friendly jibes made me feel even worse. He certainly was in a jocular mood that day.

"When did I ever tell you to go off snooping around like some detective? All I wanted you to do was just to listen to what I had to say, familiarize yourself with the details of the case, and maybe then say something that we mortals may have missed," he laughed, "or else write a story about it."

"I'm going to his hometown," I repeated.

Ayaz seriously tried to talk me out of it. "The case is in court now. It's between the court, us and the police. No outsider can butt in with his own investigation. The first thing you know you'll be grabbed by the police."

I spent the entire evening in a state of depression. I really wanted to shrug off this feeling, talk and relax from the accumulated weariness of my journey, but the incident was weighing rather heavily on my mind. Ayaz was jabbering on. It seemed he had finally put the case behind him. Then again, looking at his booming practice, it was unlikely that he would allow a case to preoccupy him for more than a few days.

Anyway, Nasim and Ayaz were filling me in on a scandal involving a woman and a famous politician from our district. The scandal had surfaced only a few days ago, in the form of a case, which Azhar, Nasim's brother, was handling. I went through the motions of listening, even smiled some, but my thoughts were elsewhere. Why, really, had Ayaz taken this case? I had never thought about it before but now, when all sorts of crazy ideas were going through my head, I was wondering: just why? What was so special about it that Ayaz was prompted to take it? Those days he was taking either simple cases that produced fat fees or those that didn't bring a penny but he fought on some moral consideration alone. The present case had nothing to do with either. Nor was this the sort of case that if won would add to his popularity. That he had taken it was surely puzzling, but even more so the fact that he had let it dominate his thinking for so long.

After dinner I felt more like myself. We remained at the table talking for a while. An enthusiastic Nasim badgered me with questions about my trip. She wanted to know what prompted me to set out for the first time in my life on a business I had no previous experience in. How did I accomplish it? And how does it feel to be doing something that one only reads about? Nasim had the uncanny ability to captivate everyone, no matter what the conversation, no matter what the circumstances. So for the first time I gave her a detailed account of my experiences during the previous eleven days. She sat wide-eyed, listening to my story and Ayaz laughed at my so-called exploits. Whenever I referred to the present case I felt that Nasim's sympathies had now shifted completely to Zafar and she no longer blamed him for his wife's murder. It was as if she had finally resolved her earlier mental conflict. My story told, I felt pleasantly light. We said goodnight and went to bed.

In the morning before leaving for his office Ayaz completely stunned me with a question. "You're certain you want to go to Zafar's hometown?" he asked as though he already half agreed with my plans.

"Yes."

"In that case I'll give you a couple of letters to take with you."

I told him I'd come and pick them up from his office as I wanted to return home some time that day.

I went to Ayaz's office that afternoon. He was out. I picked up the two letters from his clerk and set off for the bus terminal. I was surprised by Ayaz's sudden change of mind, but the desire to get to Zafar's hometown as soon as possible simply overshadowed my feeling of surprise. I spent the night at my house. A few matters needed attention and I spent the whole next day taking care of them. The following morning I boarded the train to Zafar's hometown.

I disembarked at the Gujrat terminal and reached his village after an hour and a half trip by tonga. One of the letters in my possession was handwritten in Urdu and, as it was meant to be my letter of introduction, addressed to Zafar's father. The other was a typed and sealed document which said in convoluted legal jargon that I had Ayaz's permission to gather information about the case. (I was to keep this letter with me and use it as a last resort. Luckily, I never had to.) Zafar's father, a certain Miyan Muhammad, sent for his son-in-law, the headmaster of the local school, to read the letter for him. That done, he invited me to stay in his home. For a while he and I sat on a cot in the sun chatting, then he got up to busy himself in the usual hospitalities.

I've noticed that most of the people in our country who rise to prominence in government service, commercial trade, education or the arts hail invariably from small towns and villages of the hinterlands, and only a small minority (save the leaders and high officers in the political and military establishments) from urban centers and suburban villages. Although the essential environments of the center and the periphery are the exact opposite of each other, still the two regions do share a few characteristics that make their inhabitants aggressively ambitious and pushy.

Zafar's hometown, a village to be exact, was located on the Grand Trunk Road near a small city. The environment of such satellite villages that grow, as it were, in the backyard of a city is different from that of the far-flung villages. Here, the city exerts a certain influence on the populace's daily activities; as a result, the common farmer appears to be fairly prosperous and closer to urban culture. Because politically they are considered quite important, one frequently finds schools and clinics here.

Zafar had graduated from his village's secondary school. His father was just a common farmer. At one time their family had owned enough land to make them middle-class landowners. For generations his ancestors had only had single heirs, so their property remained for the most part intact. But this state of affairs ended with Zafar's grandfather Miyan Ahmad, who had four sons and three daughters. He was forced to sell part of his land to cover the expenses of his daughters' weddings. The remaining land was parcelled out among his four sons. Miyan Muhammad was the youngest. All his older brothers had gotten married and already fathered two or three sons each. The new crop of boys threw themselves headlong into farming almost as soon as they came of age. Finding their land too small to support their growing needs, they began to contract out. Slowly their enterprise grew and they branched out into other areas. The sons of one brother started a flour mill, the sons of another set up an oil press, and those of the third started growing vegetables on a large scale. They also bought a used tractor for their own needs and also rented it out to others. In this way the families of the three older brothers grew to be quite prosperous.

Miyan Muhammad had only one son and, as luck would have it, he turned out to be a real bookworm. Miyan Muhammad tried in vain to involve his son with the farm after the latter had passed his secondary school, but Zafar insisted on leaving the village and continuing his education in the city. Then when Zafar graduated from high school and entered college, Miyan Muhammad gave up all hope of being a landowner and instead tied his hopes to Zafar's education. When Zafar got his BA and became a food inspector, Miyan Muhammad was truly happy for the first time in his life. Zafar's cousins started treating him as an equal. Zafar was the first person in his family who had gone this far in education and then landed a government job. But when he became a magistrate, it was as if Miyan Muhammad's world had changed completely. He catapulted from the lowest to the highest position in his family, indeed among all his relatives.

Only two government agencies exerted any influence in village areas: the Department of Finance and the Department of Police. Two other men from Zafar's village had reached high government positions. One worked for the railway, the other for the Customs Department. Neither job bestowed much status, though their occupants were the only ones in the village with brick houses. (After the murder Miyan Muhammad had contacted them and had them use their influence with the police, but it didn't work.) By contrast, becoming a magistrate—in other words, having the power to lock up people—was something like being part of the government itself.

"Miyan-ji, your son is the *government* now," people coming to congratulate the elderly gentleman would say. "He can let anyone go that he wants or throw whomever he wishes into jail."

Miyan Muhammad's older brother who up to then wouldn't give him the time of day, now started coming over in the evening and hanging around the house. Zafar's cousin, though older, began to treat him with deference. Every single member of the clan was proud of him, and rightly so. So Miyan Muhammad stood head and shoulders above even the most important village administrators. He had his daughter married to the son of the village revenue officer, who was his kinsman. Miyan Muhammad's son-in-law finished high school and along with being a landholder became the school's headmaster. Zafar was the only person in the whole rural area—a fairly extensive area including numerous villages—to have risen to the position of magistrate. The biggest of the landowners were more than willing to marry their daughters to him, but Miyan Muhammad had long had his eyes set on one of his nieces. When Zafar went off and married an outsider, it was the first real shock he had given his family. When they found out that she came from a refugee family, they felt downright slighted. But Zafar's status was such that no one dared say anything to him. When the time came, Miyan Muhammad put all the hurts behind and had his son married with great pride, pomp and ceremony.

After their marriage, the couple came to Zafar's village, stayed for three days and then went on to Qusur. Those three days was the only time in Kausar's married life that she ever spent at her in-laws'. At that time Miyan Muhammad had not yet built the two-room brick extension to his house, so he put up his son and daughter-in-law at one of his older brother's.

Miyan Muhammad gave me all these details that very night. I was sitting on a cot huddled in a blanket. It was bitter cold outside. There was a frost on the fields. I remember the potato crop was ruined that year. On the opposite cot sat Miyan Muhammad, also wrapped in a blanket. The hubble-bubble between us had long gone out but his fist remained wrapped around the mouthpiece.

In the space of a few short years the man before me had soared to the heights and then plummeted right back to earth. Presently he was meticulously going over each incident of his son's life as though Zafar's fate was in my hands and his salvation depended on those details. A long time passed without my asking a single question. Meanwhile his son-in-law came, sat with us for a while, and then hearing the sound of a young woman crying inside the house immediately got up and left. The crying stopped a little later.

Miyan Muhammad didn't bat an eyelid and continued to talk as before. His eyesight was failing and he was left alone. For the first time since I got involved in this affair I felt a twinge of regret as I sat before this poor old codger. I resolved to get out of there as soon as possible.

I only stayed another day there. I didn't speak with anyone else in that village and spent the whole next day in the city nearby. I could find nothing new or extraordinary about Zafar. It seems as though all he ever cared for or did was work, this being as true of his school days as his adult years as a professional. I went to his former high school, talked with his teachers, then went over to the college campus. Some of his former professors were still there, as well as some of his old classmates who had become lecturers. I had a long discussion with them. The professors knew about the incident and expressed great regret over it. They remembered Zafar quite well as he had been one of the school's most brilliant students in his time. I wandered around the whole campus trying to find even the slightest trace of Zafar's presence: a photograph, an award, a trophy—or even just his name. It seemed he had left no trace of himself except in the memories of a few professors. In the main hall, the common room, the library, where photographs of all the old athletes and members of the debating team hung, there was no picture of Zafar. Wandering through these buildings I could not escape the strange feeling that if I were in Zafar's shoes, a person searching for my trail too would have left quite as disappointed. Time—how deftly it sweeps away the vestiges of our life!

As I was returning from the college something Ayaz had said hit like a ray of light in the darkness around me: "...or write a story about it." Yes, why not? Perhaps in the process, I'd come upon something I had overlooked. I had the tonga-carriage stop at a place and bought a fat notebook. That night at Miyan Muhammad's house I sat down by the light of a lantern with the notebook open before me, but I couldn't write a single word. The next morning I left for home.

For the whole day I brooded over what to write, where to start and which way to go. Till then all I had to do was let my imagination construct the situation, which was fairly easy. If a detail turned out to be particularly difficult or unwieldy, I'd change it, or delete a word if it didn't fit—all lay within my power. Now when I was confronted with a real-life situation, I was finding out how difficult it was to write about a concrete event...as it happened. My words had failed me; even the structure of my writing had become random and shaggy. For the first time ever I realized I had absolutely no control over real events. None of my old devices could possibly deal with them. I needed a new approach. What would it be?

That night as I sat down with the notebook before me I hadn't the faintest idea what I was going to write. I sat there blankly for some time, then compulsively picked up the pen and scribbled on the first page, "My Diary." For a long time I stared at the two words. In them I saw my way out. It was as if through the turmoil of the day I had quite unconsciously reached a decision: I was going to start afresh, just as countless children sit up in bed at night to express themselves and write "My dear Diary..."

That was the first day of my diary, and I've been faithfully keeping it for twenty years now. The first page of volume one is open before me today. It has caused a strange feeling to sweep over me —the sort of feeling that washes over you when you look at a snapshot taken in your youth. I never knew, not until I looked at this page, just how much my handwriting had changed in the intervening twenty years. On the whole, the style is still the same and even now one looking at it would invariably recognize it to be mine, though only I can see that the balance, the vigor in the way the words are written out, in the neatness of lines, in the care exhibited in placing the *madah* over *alif*s and *shaddah* over doubled consonants, and in the flourish and the vertical stroke of the letter *alif*— are all absent in my handwriting today.

What follows is written on that page:

"For the better part of the day I roamed around the high school and college. I was exhausted by the time I left. Before I returned I went outside the buildings on campus and sat down awhile by the hockey field. The breeze came in faint, cold gusts, but the sun was bright and warm. A bunch of students were sitting in the middle of that field, soaking up the sun, peeling and eating oranges as they talked in high-pitched voices and laughed. Zafar never participated in any games, was never first in any exam, had never won any awards, nor stood for any elections. Granted, he was always among the top few students, but a small comfort for one searching into someone's past.

"A few of the students had stretched out on the ground for a catnap, the remainder of the group had lit cigarettes and were talking in quiet tones. Thinking that most of the toil in the world was destined to be spent in such anonymous places that might well never have existed I felt a twinge of regret. Slowly, however, a certain image of a man began to form itself in my mind—the image of a man who had built his life according to his innate strength and ability, who was only interested in his work, had never wasted his time, and who recognized that he would never quite reach the top but knew he'd come close to it and was satisfied with just that. That man was now an influential magistrate. But the atmosphere in which he had grown up was characterized by life's utmost simplicity: a couple of loaves of bread, a change or two of clothing and a woman counted for all of life's needs. On the balance, Zafar had gotten far more than he would ever need and desired nothing more. But for his wife, a woman educated in the metropolitan city of Lahore, this was clearly not enough. So she had looked for and found a way to escape the unmitigated drabness of her life, though this way was certain to be a temporary one. One commonly sees that women, however dissatisfied with their lives, almost never even think of giving up a comfortable and influential life, unless it be for one with a promise of still greater comfort and influence. Obviously, if Zafar hadn't come from a village and had the *savoir-faire* of a city man, he could easily have brought his wife back into line. But he was a different sort of person, who when he saw that..."

Here the entry ends. I vividly remember that, as I was happily writing along, all at once I felt as though reality had slipped from my grip and I had, imperceptibly as it were, backslided into my old writing style. Zafar had stopped being an individual and became, instead, one of my fictional characters, the knots of whose personality I was trying to unravel through sheer imaginative power. My imagination had seized the quintessential event; it was like an automatic toy in my hands which I had wound up and was smugly watching it go through its gyrations. Through a circuitous route I had arrived at the point where it was proven that Zafar was the sort of person whose nature didn't preclude murder. But wasn't this the very starting point of our investigation? My pen froze. Once again I realized the inadequacy of creative imagination vis-à-vis life's palpable situations. That Zafar had committed murder was indisputable; why he had committed it was also known; what one needed was the proof of his innocence without questioning the crime itself. I couldn't whimsically turn the tide of events as and how I pleased. The reality of the gulf that had all along existed between my life and my creative work became all the more clear to me at that point. An assortment of devices is available to any writer; he uses them to avoid confronting reality. His explanations apply more to the changing surfaces of reality whose true nature cannot be seen through the obscuring mist of rhetoric. Literature is surely a house of deception.

No one has the heart to let his life's work go down the drain. I read my work over and over again as though it were some intricate puzzle whose solution lay concealed in one of its words. I didn't find it, but in the process of reading it over and over again, two things did dawn on me which brought me a few steps forward in my investigation. I felt, as I was reading my analysis of Zafar's personality for the seventh time, as though Ayaz were standing in his place. At first I thought that this, too, was one of those ideas which often rattled through my head. But with the passage of time, instead of disappearing, the feeling grew more insistent. Finally, I put the diary away and began to think about Ayaz. Undoubtedly there were more than just a few similarities in Zafar and Ayaz's past. Their early life and their development read like a piece from a single story: impoverished family, uneducated surroundings, impediments, gifted intelligence, success through unremitting work, the rise from the lower to upper class, leaving the parental home, marriage outside the clan, wives almost cut off from their in-laws, and so on and so forth. The more I thought about it, the greater my amazement grew. How staggeringly similar their lives were! I remembered how at one point I had wondered about Ayaz taking this case and giving it altogether so much importance when it involved neither large fees nor even some principle. Certainly our sympathies were with Zafar. Finally, I too had come round to the idea that although Zafar had committed murder, he was nevertheless blameless. But this was a proposition a writer like myself could afford to make. For a diehard legal mind like Ayaz's to say that "Zafar is innocent, it's just a matter of proving it," was a momentous thing. Wasn't it, perhaps—I thought—that Ayaz saw himself in Zafar and was thus moved to save him at all costs? Had the mission to save Zafar become an emotional need for him? The mission of that entire class with which their two pasts were inextricably tied? The mission to preserve the right of an indigent boy to attempt to rise above his class? Suppose Ayaz were unable to save Zafar—what then?

The extraordinary similarity between their two lives was pointing in a direction that made my heart stop for a moment. This was a ludicrous idea, I thought. Such coincidences occur only in the minds of writers. Real life follows its own unpredictable course. Now the reader might feel that the idea which helped me dispel that line of thought is ridiculous, all the same I was absolutely convinced of what seemed its incontrovertible truth at that time. Ayaz's and Zafar's lives were certainly similar, but there was also one glaring difference: Ayaz had always come out on top. I repeated these words to myself several times. Ayaz had always come out on top: in his education, in his work, in his profession, but he had never felt satisfied enough to lay back and take it easy, to become oblivious to everything else. He had no illusions about life. No matter what his achievement, he was prone to find yet another objective to strive for. His was not a life of anonymity, but of limelight and centerstage.

The other thing that occurred to me that night concerned Kausar. When, after reading through my diary numerous times, I finally put it down, the image of a woman suddenly began to materialize from my subconscious. This was the first time that she had appeared to me, not as Zafar's wife but as an individual in her own right. I say "appeared to me" and I use the expression advisedly. Her appearance was truly unusual. She had taken form in my imagination, then suddenly she was standing before me. It was well past midnight. Everyone else in the house was asleep. I was sitting alone in my study. And then, in an overwhelming moment of silence, I felt her presence as though some actual flesh-and-blood person were there in the room with me. The feeling remained for only a fleeting moment. I am no feeble-hearted person, but as soon as I realized that this woman was dead and I had never seen her alive, I became downright terrified. I involuntarily spun around, looked behind me and everywhere else in the room, and then I got up and paced around for a bit before sitting back down. Never before had any of my imaginings taken on such a concrete form. Her visage kept floating in my imagination for some time as if she were saying, "Come to me, look for me. I am Kausar..."

That night I realized I had unwittingly stepped into dangerous territory. If there was a clue to the incident, it was not in Zafar, nor did it seem to be in Zafar's circumstances; rather, it was in this woman who was dead now, who before being murdered was a vital being, who had an identity and who now appeared before me in the form of a mysterious, bewitching succubus, beckoning me like the women who in the dead of night go out to the deserted country roads beyond the city and lure unsuspecting wayfarers.

I arrived in Lahore at the end of two days with a firm resolution. I didn't tell Ayaz about my diary, though I did tell him briefly what knowledge of Zafar I had been able to dig up. As far as I was concerned, this was more or less useless. My search was focused on one thing alone. All the same, I had to fill him in on my trip. As I talked I looked at him more intently than ever before but found him totally expressionless. His attitude was completely professional. Finally I told him what was on my mind.

"Meeting Kausar's family wouldn't be easy," Ayaz said.

"Why?"

"Well, we have the right to do it but the prosecution can object, especially if a third party started interviewing them. The prosecution might accuse us of influencing witnesses."

"How can we go about it?"

"But we have everything on Zafar's wife. Haven't you seen it?"

"I have," I said, "but I can't be sure I remember."

"Come to my office and have a look."

"But Ayaz," I finally blurted out, "I need to talk with somebody who was close to her. Her mother's still around."

"I wouldn't advise it," Ayaz retorted. "Her mother wouldn't even appear as a witness for the prosecution."

"But isn't it true that Kausar loved her mother more than anyone else in the family?"

"That's what one hears."

"Then why doesn't she appear as a witness for the prosecution?"

"I don't know. At one time we even considered having her take the stand but couldn't track her down. At any rate, if she wouldn't cooperate with the prosecution, how far do you think you'll get with her?"

It was obvious from Ayaz's tone that he didn't want me to get involved in the case any more than I already was. I remained silent but I was so far into it that I couldn't possibly leave it without seeing it to the very end. I spent the next two days in mounting restlessness. Finally I decided to see the maidservant who had worked for Zafar and Kausar during the last days before the murder incident. But then I changed my mind. The truth is, Kausar and her mother had overwhelmed me so completely that I could scarcely think of anything else. Half-heartedly I dragged myself to Ayaz's office and browsed through his files on Kausar. Whatever I was able to glean from them I set forth below:

Kausar's parents were big landowners in a small town near Delhi. Her father was the only member of his family who had made it to college and it was some time since he had turned over the business to his brothers and settled in the city. His only surviving children—a son named Qaisar and the youngest daughter Kausar —had something of a quarter-century difference between their ages. The children in between had all died in infancy. Qaisar got a college education and after hanging around the house unemployed for a few years had set out to see the world. At the time of India's partition, it had been eight years since the last report about him had reached the family. According to this report, he had settled on some island around Java and Sumatra. The next report came from a man returning with a group from the Indonesian archipelago during the Second World War. He mentioned that he had bumped into Qaisar on a small island. Qaisar was married to a native woman, had a whole batch of kids, and had gone native, wearing a sarong and living in a thatched hut. He seemed quite content, even happy.

In 1946, Kausar's father started making arrangements to go to Indonesia and personally bring his son back. But he was an old man. He took ill and in the space of a few weeks passed away. Kausar was then eleven years old. The family had by then given up all hope of Qaisar ever coming back. 1947 saw the family deeply divided. Kausar's paternal uncles refused to leave their village and country. So her maternal uncle, the biggest landholder in the district, took along his sister and niece and migrated to Pakistan. Their first stop was Lahore. After a few days a refugee from their hometown in India informed them of a large manor house in Qusur abandoned by migrating Hindus which they might be able to claim in lieu of the property they had abandoned in India. Within the space of one night the entire family occupied it. In time their claim was accepted and the manor house became theirs. Kausar's uncle was allotted some irrigated and a good deal of unirrigated land. As for Kausar's mother, her claim dragged through the courts for many years because legally her son was the sole heir and there was no proof of whether he was dead or alive. (It was in connection with this very claim case that Zafar had first met her family.) In the end the old lady was allotted a part of her claim. Of course it wasn't anything like old times, but Kausar's uncle had fallen into enough property to promise them a comfortable existence. Kausar attended the local school at Qusur, then went away to Lahore for college, and married as soon as she graduated. Her life since I have already related. There was just one other thing, an affair from her college days, but after a little reflection I thought it irrelevant and put it out of my mind.

Since I last spoke with Ayaz, I had been losing hope of ever getting to the bottom of the case. At the same time, I was also growing more certain that the only person who could give me, voluntarily or otherwise, any information on the victim was her mother. But how could I meet her? I just couldn't think of a way.

Then on the third day Ayaz unexpectedly came to my rescue. He had returned from the office that evening and looked like one who had a lot on his mind. After supper he said, "Shall we take a stroll?"

We went out. After walking awhile in silence, Ayaz said, "There just might be a way to meet Kausar's mother."

Stunned, I could only stare at him. He had a strange look on his face, as though he was speaking against his better judgement but wanted to do it all the same.

"How?" I asked.

"There's a hakim here in the city who's also a bit of a spiritual teacher and healer. Kausar's mother is a great believer in him. Earlier on she would herself come to see him but after her health deteriorated it's the hakim who goes to see her in Qusur."

"You think he could put me in contact with her?"

"Our information is that Kausar's mother is both his patient and his disciple."

"What would I tell him?" I asked like a fool.

"Why ask me?" Ayaz laughed. "You've become the expert at this sort of thing." Then he suddenly shook his finger at me and said in a serious tone, "But I'm warning you. If you go and see her, I know nothing about it."

I just gawked at him, as if in a daze. He continued. "If it damages the case in any way, don't come running up to me for help. I will have nothing to do with you. Think it over before you do anything."

In other words Ayaz was saying that although until now we had more or less shared in the case, from this point on I was entirely on my own. My heart skipped a beat, which had nothing to do with the particulars of the case, rather it came from that momentary feeling that hits us when someone tells us, "Now you're on your own."

For some moments I stared at Ayaz. His face still had an anguished look, as though he was torn between doing his damndest to stop me, while at the same time urging me on.

"Alright," I said, nodding.

As we started back, Ayaz's face began to brighten. That evening I realized without a shadow of a doubt how deep the roots of this case had worked their way into Ayaz.

Pir Bakhsh Shah was a spare, thin man who sported a completely grey beard. He was soft spoken and affable. He practiced medicine from a room in his house located in an old, run-down bylane in the inner city. Here he was called "Shah-ji" rather than "Hakim-ji." For two days I mulled over how to get to him and what to say once I got there. Finally, early one morning I set out, feeling that the easiest way would be to present myself as a patient.

In a large room the hakim was sitting on the floor with his back against the wall. The room seemed like any ordinary clinic save that it was crammed full of men and women, most of them quite old. I sat and watched the hakim go about his business, all the while trying in vain to tell apart his patients from his disciples among the crowd. Some would go away with medicine, others empty handed, all looking ill, however. When my turn came, I put on a sick look and stuck out my arm, complaining of some imaginary illness. As the hakim searched for my pulse, he fired off a barrage of questions: Where are you from? I gave him the name of some city or another. Who referred you to me? I wasn't ready for that question, so I paused and then gave the name of one of my friends. His forehead creased slightly as though he were trying to place the name, but he said nothing. Then he let go of my wrist and asked, "How soon could you come back again?" I told him I was here these days and could come back whenever he liked. The hakim gave me a week's medicine and told me to return in three days for him to check my pulse. The medicine was dirt cheap. When I got home I put it away. The truth is, I was quite impressed by the man's personality. He spoke gently and with a natural poise. I had pictured a completely different sort of person, but found nothing in his manner that betrayed his deliberate attempt to attract people to himself.

Three days went by and I returned to the hakim. After a good deal of thought I had already decided to come right down to business. I quietly sat down in a corner at the rear of a group of people. When the people in front of me got up, instead of stepping forward I would slip behind some others. My strategy paid off. By about two o'clock in the afternoon I was the only one left. The hakim didn't even give me a chance to open my mouth.

"What's the matter, son?" he smiled. "Why are you playing hide-and-seek?"

I grinned sheepishly. Even before I said a thing my secret was out.

"How did you find out?" I asked.

"I'm no novice at checking pulse, been doing so for fifty years," the hakim explained. "There's nothing wrong with yours. I just went along and gave you some medicine. I knew you'd come back again." He stared me in the eye and said, "Now what's going on?"

I started out timidly and took some time to come to the point. "I am just a common landholder," I told him. "Chaudhri Zafar Sahib had worked as a magistrate for some time in our town. I met him in connection with some case and later became friends with him. Chaudhri Sahib was very fond of me and I frequently called on him at home. My family and I were taken by the grace and courtesy of

Begum Sahiba (Kausar) even more than that of Chaudhri Sahib. When I read about the unfortunate incident in the newspaper, I was extremely shocked. I know that you are on intimate terms with Begum Sahiba's family. I have come now hoping that you might put me in contact with the deceased's mother so that I could offer her my sympathies in person. And yes, if there is any way I can help in this matter, I am ready, even to the extent of testifying in court. We are beholden to Begum Sahiba for her many favors. The first day I came to you I was a bit unnerved seeing so many people around."

The hakim asked me why I hadn't gone directly to Qusur. I explained that first of all I wasn't acquainted with Begum Sahiba's family and then again I had come to know that her mother wasn't keeping well. So I thought it better to speak with him and maybe through him go to Qusur.

The hakim brooded over the matter for some time, giving me a suspicious look every now and then. An experienced man though he was he couldn't see through my ruse. He was taken in by my sincerity. Finally, he said, "I'm going to Qusur on Monday. You may come with me."

I thanked him and started to leave. Just then he added, "The medicine you took? Bring it back with you. It can help someone else. These herbal drugs are hard to come by these days."

My meeting with Kausar's mother is by far the strangest incident in my twenty-year diary. The entry reads:

February 3: A chilly day. We took the 10:30 bus to Qusur. I had brought one of my books along to impress the hakim and impressed he was. I got a few more things out of him during the bus ride. Kausar's uncle, a certain Nawab Sher Muhammad Khan, was the head of the house. For some years now he had given up the trappings of his nawabi and started up a dry goods business which along with managing his lands he was running quite successfully. The manor house stood over more than an acre and the compound was enclosed by a six-foot-high, double-brick wall which a thick layer of moss had turned to a dark olive hue. In older times it was probably the estate of a rich moneylender. In the corner of the compound stood a crumbling temple building. A poor family who perhaps took care of the cattle and ran errands lived in it. There were a few peepal and banyan trees to which two water buffalos and a goat were tied, and piles of dung dotted the compound area. A bunch of half-naked urchins played nearby in the sun.

A servant deferentially greeted the hakim on the veranda and shortly thereafter escorted him inside. He returned a short while later and asked if I wished to sit in the sun or inside. I said inside. I was taken into a large living room. The furniture inside the room was massive but comfortable, the color somewhat subdued and soft, and the atmosphere quiet leisurely.

Half an hour went by. Tea was served. A handsome young lad passed through the room and greeted me, slightly bowing. Although I was not directly involved in the case, my heart was still thumping loudly. I was barely able to drink half a cup of tea. Children's voices could be heard from farther inside the house. Must be Zafar's children, I thought. Servants were scurrying about. Time dragged on interminably...

At this point the entire tone of my diary changes. The lifeless style marked by choppy sentences and staccato rhythms leaps into a controlled, coherent and flowing narrative as if my fitful heart had finally calmed down.

I had expected that when invited inside I would have to speak to Kausar's mother from behind a curtain. This was the only thought that gave me any comfort. I felt as if I would reach my objective and yet remain anonymous, my true identity in no danger of being revealed, thus escaping the dangers that normally attend the fulfillment of a difficult undertaking. I would be part of the action, and somehow also detached from it.

When I followed the servant through the mansion's central courtyard and went through the door at the end of the hall, I didn't have time even to glance at the room's decor. On a large white bed lay a white-haired old woman propped up against a big pillow. Even the wrinkled skin of her face was a radiant white. She had a delicate but withered features. Only her large almond-colored eyes seemed fully alert and alive. The thing that totally overwhelmed my senses was the predominant color of white: white bed, the pile of numerous small, white pillows, the lady's white blouse, white scarf, white face, white hair, the delicate white bones of her hands, white table cloth, white vase filled with white flowers. I greeted her with the formal bow of respect.

"Please sit down," came the unexpectedly vibrant, ringing voice.

I sat down in a chair placed at the foot of the bed. Only then did I notice a child of about four sitting on the bed. The woman's hand was resting on the child's back, and after briefly looking at me, she was now looking at the child, smiling, as if asking both the child and myself, "You know each other, don't you?"

All at once my mind went totally blank. The room expanded into a huge hall and the hakim sitting nearby shrunk into a miniscule speck in the distance. Finally my instinct for timely excuses came to my rescue.

"Intisar wouldn't remember me," I said. "By the time I got around to go and congratulate them on her birth, Zafar had already been transferred to another place."

Kausar's mother didn't say anything. She just let her hand stay at the child's back and went on looking at him. Then she patted his head and put her hand with the other in her lap.

"Shah-ji tells me you're a writer."

"He's too kind," I said with modesty. "I'm just a common landholder. Farming gives me some free time to write a little now and then."

"My son was a poet," she stated. Her voice betrayed no sorrow; in fact she said that with the same respect, pride and joy one feels when talking about a revered ancestor.

"What was his pen-name?" I asked, innocently.

She turned her face to look at the small flowers in the vase. Then she spoke in a very feeble voice, as if talking to herself, "No pen-name."

"Excuse me?"

"You don't really want to know his name," she said in a mildly accusatory tone. "In fact, all you're asking is if his work was ever published, who published it and when. Isn't that it?"

"Yes," I said, genuinely embarrassed.

"He never published a thing," she said, again softly. "But he was a poet all the same."

"I hear he's living abroad these days."

"Kausar told you that?"

"Yes."

"Then you know she hadn't yet been born when he left. But Kausar knew every little thing about him," she said. "Both of my children were somewhat extraordinary."

I thought that it was a good time to offer formal condolences. And I did. But she just sat there, lost, as if she hadn't heard a word I said. All at once I felt that I must have said something wrong. There wasn't the remotest trace of mourning, or even of regret in that room. Her face was expressionless—no sorrow, no happiness either, only age.

For a long time she sat motionless—a graven image staring at her hands. The child slid off the bed and darted from the room. Another round of tea arrived. There were only two cups. The young woman who brought the tea poured for us, the hakim and me, a cup each. I choked down a gulp. All at once the room went dark. Startled, I looked outside. The room's atmosphere had so bewildered me that the shadow of a small cloud passing overhead was sufficient to terrify me. I was overwhelmed by the urge to drop everything and get out of there. And get out of there pretty damn quick. I slowly set my cup back down on the table.

Her hands quivered a little and she looked up at me. "Shah-ji tells me you knew my daughter well," she said.

"Yes."

"Then you know about the incident?"

I cleared my throat and said, "As much as was reported in the newspapers."

"So what do you think about my daughter?"

I stared at her in silence. I couldn't think of anything to say.

"You said you knew my daughter well," she repeated. "Now what do you think about her?"

"I...I was shocked...after hearing about it," I stammered.

"You know very well what I was asking. If you don't want to say it, then I will. Everyone thinks she was immoral."

"I never said that." I mustered up some courage. "I don't jump to conclusions before I know all the facts."

"If you're really telling the truth, then you're very naive. You don't even know about yourself."

"What do you mean by that?"

"You've already made up your mind. Nothing more will change it."

"While I lack the courage to contradict you, I must say that that is not my opinion."

Even though Kausar's mother blinked her eyes a few times, her gaze remained fixed on me.

"Maybe you're right," she said. "You're still only one man, not the whole world."

Without taking her eyes off me she again became perfectly motionless as though her spirit had escaped her body for a short while.

"The truth cannot remain hidden forever," I said. "Someday it's bound to come out."

"I alone know the truth."

"Then why not tell the world?"

"Would that restore my daughter's honor?" she asked, still drilling me with her gaze. "When a man kills his wife after accusing her of being unfaithful, unfaithful she remains in the eyes of the world. Surely you've seen a lot of such instances. Don't you know? When a man kills a woman, it's all her fault. When she kills him, it's still her fault. Courts only decide the crime. The infidelity of a woman is never disputed." Her voice faltered and stopped.

I stared at her in silence. When she spoke again, it was as though she was not speaking to me but only reproving herself. "Of course men automatically accept a woman's infidelity. What's worse, even those of her own sex do. How cruel! She's left on her own."

The woman who lay before me in a heap of bones was telling me in her gentle but crisp voice about something I had never thought of before. Her words overwhelmed my heart, my mind, my senses. What was the truth? What actually did happen? Once again she drifted off into silence, looking intently at her hands in her lap.

"Of course the laws of nature are immutable," I said. "But man has created his own laws to live in society and has set down punishment for each infraction of those laws. If you don't tell the truth about the incident, how on earth can justice be done?"

"Truth has nothing to do with justice," she said. "What do you want me to say anyway? To testify against Zafar? But what is his crime?"

My mouth dropped open, and I looked from her to the hakim and back again completely dumbfounded. Finally I said, "Excuse me, I don't follow you."

"Zafar is innocent," she said with slow deliberation.

Just then the hakim got up from his chair. It was obvious from his expression that he didn't want to prolong this exchange. He grabbed his walking stick dangling from the back of his chair and asked to be excused. "I think you must rest now," he said. "We've bothered you enough."

I, too, got up from my chair. Kausar's mother, who was meanwhile looking again at the bouquet of flowers in the vase, suddenly turned around to look at me and then to the hakim, to whom she motioned to stop.

"Please sit down," she said. "I want to talk with this young man." She gestured to me. "Sit down. I want to tell you the truth behind the incident. Of my family, only my brother is left now and he won't even listen to me. But my son would if he were here today. You're a writer, perhaps you'll understand. You remind me of my son."

There was something in the way she looked and spoke that made the hakim and I sit down again. Again and again she nervously clasped and unclasped her hands. Finally she began:

"About eight months ago my daughter came to me and said, 'Mother, I don't care anymore.' That's all she would say." The old lady lifted her eyes to mine and continued. "I didn't pay much attention to what she said. I thought, 'When have women ever...' Well, you're a man, so I don't expect you to understand this. But the truth is a woman never loses the pain she feels the day she's married and has to leave her home. Most women don't even know the source of this pain and what it is they have lost. But life goes on. I decided that some such thing was bothering my daughter and it would work itself out in time. How was I to know it would come to this? She who was a part of my body, I couldn't see what was going on inside her.

"She would come and visit me every few months or so. But after she said that she would come every few weeks. She'd leave the children with me and go roam the fields the whole day. One evening she returned and I was shocked by her appearance. In the space of a few months she had completely changed. Her face was no longer vibrant with life. I had her sit down next to me and asked, 'What's wrong, child? Are you feeling well?'

"'Mother,' she said, 'this is the first time in months that you've really looked at me. You tell me.'

"I was stunned. She was telling the truth. I had been so preoccupied with her children that I had stopped paying any attention to her. I said, 'Child, why ask a poor old woman like me? Tell me, what have you done to yourself?'

"'I've told you already,' she said, 'I just don't care any more.'

"'That alone couldn't do all this to you. I really don't think so. Tell me, are you eating alright?'

"For the first time in her life my daughter lost her patience with me, 'Mother,' she said, 'why aren't you listening to me? Why don't you pay attention to me? I said that I just don't care.'

"I was silent. Then and there I realized that the matter wasn't all that simple. There was something behind all this. So, that evening, after everyone had gone to sleep, I again broached the question with her. 'Child, speak plainly. Zafar is treating you alright, isn't he?'

"She said, 'Mother, I have no complaints about Zafar. He's an extremely good man.'

"Well, after all, they had been married for some time now and we all know the problems that can or do occur. 'Zafar hasn't stopped loving you, has he?' I asked.

"'He's as devoted as ever to me and the children,' she answered.

"I said, 'Child, I'm not talking about devotion. I'm asking if your husband loves you as much as he did before.'

"'He does,' she said. 'More than ever. Why are you asking me all this? I said that I don't have any complaints about Zafar.'

"'Then perhaps he's tight with the money?' I asked.

"'No, I handle the money and Zafar keeps none for himself.'

"'This is beyond me,' I said. 'Now what is really troubling you?'

"Kausar just stared at me incredulously. Then she spoke up, 'Mother, I just feel fed up with it all.'

"I shut up, ardently hoping that, God willing, she'd settle down of her own. Shah-ji knows all about it. He gave her some medicine and also prayed for her. But Kausar's heart was not about to ease any.

"She kept coming back. She never shed any tears in my presence but I know she was crying inside. A few times Zafar came and took her back. My sister-in-law said that menstrual irregularity sometimes induces such a condition and that a doctor should see her. Everybody had an opinion. I wore myself out questioning Kausar. It wasn't some irregularity of her period or deficiency of milk, still she kept saying, 'I don't care anymore. Why do you keep harping at me? If I could tell you I would.'

"One day I said, 'Daughter, not just husbands but God has given wives the right as well. I'm your mother. You mustn't keep things from me. Now tell me, are you in love with someone else?'

"Kausar simply sat there gawking at me. Finally she said, 'No, mother. It's not that. Don't even mention it again. I don't want to hear anything said against Zafar.'

"I was completely exasperated. She was not prepared to listen to anything. Everything seemed alright. God had provided her with everything. What could be wrong? She said, 'Sure, God has provided me with everything. But is that all there is to it?'

"'What more can there be?' I said.

"'I don't know,' she replied.

"'Child, you must perform your prayers.'

"'I do,' she said. 'Regularly. I even say all the special prayers you taught me, but that doesn't seem to do me any good. My heart is still restless. I don't know what's happened to me...'"

The old lady opened her two delicately boned old hands resting in her lap and droned on in a monotone, her face now a bit flushed. As I listened to her I was struck time and time again with the feeling that Kausar was alive, not dead, and this was her voice. Only when the old lady paused to take a breath did I again become aware of my surroundings. Outside, the clouds had covered the sky and the darkness was creeping into the room. She continued:

"Shah-ji, you should remember. You taught her a few special

prayers. When she was here I had her sit in my room and do them. She was fast losing her appetite. After a while she dropped those prayers altogether. If I was around she would perform her ritual prayers or else let them lapse, too. She was wasting away. She stopped nursing her six-month-old baby, saying, 'I don't want anyone to touch me.' Some said that she had gone crazy. Now I know crazy. Back in our old neighborhood in Delhi there was a whole family of crazies. They didn't know their feet from their heads. My girl wasn't crazy in the head. She was perfectly lucid and kept asking people, 'Tell me, oh please tell me what's wrong...' She would feel ashamed when she saw Zafar and quietly go back with him. I'd be cut to the quick. What had my daughter done? She wasn't unfaithful, deceitful or a common thief, so why must she feel so ashamed? If Zafar weren't so thick headed, if he had been a little more patient and didn't let suspicion get the better of him, it just might have worked out. Kausar would have come around. Zafar knew his way around but he didn't know this sort of thing. Isn't it just like a man?

"Kausar came one day and said to me, 'Mother, I'm not going back.'

"'Daughter,' I said, 'have you lost your mind? Heaven forbid!'

"'Would you throw me out of your house?' she asked.

"'Of course, never,' I said. 'But a woman's place is in her husband's house, child.'

"'And this is your husband's house?' she said.

"'Fate, daughter, fate...' I replied.

"'Not at all,' she said. 'It's rather our life. There is no fixed place.'

"Her words made my head spin. She wasn't crazy. Her mind was filled with questions that had never occurred to anyone. I said, 'Child, to this day I still don't know what's bothering you.'

"'That's what I keep asking myself,' she replied.

"That was the last day. She went out and didn't return until very late. In the evening Zafar showed up. It was getting on toward night and there was still no sign of Kausar. Her uncle, cousin, all the servants and even the farmhands were out looking for her. Zafar began to question me: 'Where did she go? When? Why?' I told him straight out that I didn't know, adding a little later, 'Son, listen to me. Although Kausar was once a part of me, I still don't know what's going on in her head. Tell me, what's bothering her?'

"He replied, 'Exactly what I want to know.'

"A little before seven in the evening Kausar showed up. Seeing

Zafar, she lowered her eyes out of shame. I knew then that she'd go back with him in the morning. I said, 'Young lady, where did you wander off to? Where have you been?'
"'I went to Lahore,' she replied.
"'To your house?'
"'No.'
"'Then where did you go?'
"'I just wandered around.'
"'Wandered around—where?'
"'In the park.'
"She looked out of sorts. From that moment I had the premonition that something terrible was about to happen. But I hadn't imagined that that was the last time I was to see my daughter's face, to hear her voice. Though in my heart she isn't dead, nor will she ever be. She is always there with her glazed eyes and her voice ringing in my ears.

"None of us said anything then but that night, after the children had gone to bed, Kausar came and sat next to me on my bed. Zafar was right behind her and sat in the very chair you're sitting in now. He looked as if his patience was finally running out. He said, 'Mother, ask her if there's anything she doesn't have.' So I said, 'Kausar, speak up. Your husband's asking you a question. It's your duty to reply.'

"She sat there with her head bowed and said softly, 'I don't lack a thing.'

"Zafar then asked her, 'What do you want?'
"'Yes, answer him, child,' I said. 'What don't you have? Status? Wealth? Education? Just what? I'm not saying that things always go right, but there's a reason for everything. Some woman's husband turns out bad, a wife beater, a drunk. Some men can have no children. Some are poor, some sick. Some get embroiled in lawsuits. Some are sinners, some take up with other women. When something like this occurs, there's always a reason behind it. But you have two darling children. Your husband loves you. He has status and doesn't run around. He's entirely devoted to you and doesn't deprive you of anything. So what do you want?'

"Kausar looked up at me and said, 'Mother, I don't know. What can I say?'

"Zafar remained suspicious and said, 'What do you mean you don't know? What haven't I provided you with? I have given you a house, servants, money—haven't I? I'm a man of status. I've my own property and a good reputation. What more do you want?'

"With her head still hung low Kausar answered, 'Nothing.'

"'Look at me when I'm talking to you,' said Zafar. 'You're never straight with me. For a whole year it's been, "Nothing, nothing," "Alright, alright," and "I don't know, I don't know."'

"Kausar lifted her head to look at him, but it was as if she were looking at him through a fog.

"Zafar said, 'I'm your husband. I want you to be happy. For the first four years of our marriage you were happy with me. What's happened now? Have I changed? Speak up! Am I still the same man?'

"'Yes,' she replied.

"'Aren't I healthy?'

"'Yes.'

"'I haven't lost my looks, have I?'

"'No.'

"'Do I love the children? Do I think of your happiness? Do I work hard? Have I made a name for myself?'

"'Yes, yes.'

"'Do I go straight to work and come straight home?' Zafar asked. 'Come on, do I go anywhere besides the house?'

"'No.'

"'I have breakfast at home, go to the office and come straight home, read the newspapers, do some work, eat and go straight to bed. That's my daily routine—right?'

"'That's right.'

"Zafar went on: 'I don't go to the club. I don't gamble. I don't carouse. I stick around the house. I give all the money to you. Isn't that right? Speak up!'

"'That's right.'

"'Then what's the problem? What do you want? Tell me and I'll be happy to get it for you. You want jewels?'

"Kausar shook her head and said, 'No.'

"'You want clothes?'

"She again shook her head and said, 'No.'

"'You want some furniture?'

"Kausar was no longer answering by voice but only shaking her head. She sat there looking in Zafar's direction, but it seemed more like she had stopped seeing. I put my hand on her shoulder and said, 'Child, say something.'

"She turned her head to look at me, as if coming back to life. Her frozen look unlocked, her face assumed color. I gained some hope. I lifted my hand to stroke her head when all at once she pressed her hands down hard over her ears, as if her head was about to burst from some unbearable noise, and tumbled into my lap, face down, like a lifeless object. I was caught completely by surprise and panicked. 'What's the matter, child?' I asked. 'Tell me, what's the matter?'

"She lifted her head to look at me with dulled eyes. She stared at me for the longest time before saying, 'Mother, I do know one thing. There's more to life than all those things. I don't know what it is but my heart tells me...'

"She screamed and burst into tears; managing between great, wracking sobs to get out, 'I don't know, but my heart tells me there must be! I just don't know! What can I do?'

"She clung to me. Her misery made me oblivious to everything. With these hands I supported her. Beneath her clothing she was just skin and bones. I was absolutely conviced then that my daughter was telling me the truth. She wasn't lying. People may think whatever they will."

When her voice ceased, a heavy silence fell over the room. She lifted her gaunt face first to the hakim and then to me. "Now whom will I tell?" she said. "Who would believe my daughter? Zafar was looking at her as though he couldn't believe his eyes or his ears. Anyway, she left with him early in the morning with her eyes downcast, silent as ever. That was the last day I heard her voice, and saw her bright face. Zafar was a man, became a killer, and will probably hang. But my daughter isn't dead; she still lives in my heart. Whom can I tell? And what? What would my testimony amount to?"

She kept looking at me for an answer. Then suddenly she sat straight up, off the pillow, gestured with her hand and said, "I have one statement to make. If anyone wants to hear it, then listen!" Her eyes narrowed, her face became flushed. When she opened her mouth such a yell came out that I involuntarily leapt to my feet. "If anyone wants to hear it, then listen!" she roared. "Guilty my daughter may have been, unfaithful she was not!"

Her voice hadn't quite died out when the bundle of bones fell back on the bed. She flopped over onto her side and turned her face away.

I wrote the above entry in my diary after I returned to Ayaz's house. I remember nothing of the return journey. Perhaps the hakim tried to get me talking but I probably mumbled disinterested replies. My head was buzzing. Nasim was at home. I exchanged a few brief words with her and went straight off to my room, bolting the door behind me. I picked up a pen and sat down with my diary. There was no need to pause, recall or go over anything; it felt as though every single word the old lady had uttered was etched in deep relief on the walls of my mind, shining bright for all to see.

When I stopped writing I was completely exhausted. I lay down on the bed and closed my eyes. The face of Kausar's mother floated before me—drained, creased with age—and I heard her slow, flat voice: "My daughter was telling the truth. She wasn't lying. What more can I say?" All at once I perceived that the face had changed: the wrinkles had disappeared and it had become the beaming face of a young woman. I had never seen that face before, nevertheless it looked strangely familiar. She was saying in a child's terror-stricken voice, "Mother, I don't know what it is, but one thing I'm sure of..." Startled, I opened my eyes and shut them again. The face was still there. When I opened my eyes a second time, someone was violently knocking on the door. I realized that I had been asleep for many hours.

I got up and opened the door. It was Ayaz. I noticed it was evening. We sat in front of the fireplace and drank some tea. My mind was finally settling down.

"You look as if you're just back from a long journey," Ayaz laughed. "So you've seen Kausar's mother?"

"Yes."

"Find anything out?"

I went into my room and returned with the diary. "It's all in here."

Ayaz took the diary from me but didn't open it as he was busy talking with Nasim. I gathered from their conversation that some people were coming over for dinner that evening. He said a few things about it and then went into his room with the diary. Nasim, too, got up after a bit and went into the kitchen. I sat there and played with their children. The fire began to die down, so I shoved a few more logs on. The logs smoked a bit and then burst into flames. The sky had been overcast the entire day and it had finally started to rain. Ayaz stayed in his room for some time. As often happens before the arrival of guests, the house was filled with an air of hushed expectancy, save for the sound of Nasim moving around and talking in the dining and kitchen area. The children were somewhere near her, quietly occupied with themselves. Ayaz still hadn't come out of his room.

There, sitting alone by the fire, a strange thought crossed my mind: I'll never write again. That troubled me. To shake it off, I began to think about the guests. I had never taken a real interest in the get-togethers at Ayaz's, but after such a full day I looked forward expectantly, even impatiently, to the guests' arrival. I was totally frazzled by the day's events.

After about an hour Ayaz emerged from his room. He quietly handed me the diary and went over to stand in front of the fireplace with his arms folded and legs slightly spread out. He stood there staring into the flames for a long time. At one point Nasim entered the room and asked, "Aren't you going to change?"

"In a minute," Ayaz answered. He still didn't say anything to me, just gave me a deep, penetrating look a couple of times as if he wanted to say something but couldn't. Then he suddenly turned around and went off to change. I watched him leave the room. The way he walked with shoulders slouched, his entire frame sagging, his head drooping, gave me the impression of a man who had lost something invaluable, or as though some thought had reached its peak and burned out.

It was an excellent party. I have been present at many elegant parties and sumptuous receptions at Ayaz's house, but none more enjoyable than this one. Its flavor is still fresh in my mind, untouched by the ravages of time. I feel as though that evening my mind was like a freshly squeezed honeycomb with its myriad cells empty, open and ready to fill themselves with the fresh syrup of the world.

There were five guests at the dinner table. I knew them all. There were two lawyers, Khaliq and Mubashshir. The former was Ayaz's age and had gone to school with him, the latter was a young barrister. The third guest was Faiyaz, editor of an English daily. At one time Ayaz had fought a case for him and later Faiyaz prevailed upon Ayaz to write some articles which he published in his newspaper. At the time Ayaz was writing a column for a different newspaper. The other two guests were Azhar and his wife, who were, of course, family. They were the first to arrive. I got up and opened the door for them. They chatted with me a minute or two and then went inside where Azhar's wife Kulsum went into Nasim's room and started chatting with her, while Azhar spent a few minutes roaming around the dining room, kitchen and back porch talking with children and servants, then himself went into the room where his sister and brother-in-law were getting ready for the party.

A little later Khaliq and Faiyaz arrived together. The three of us stood before the fire warming our hands and asking after each other's health. In entered Ayaz and Azhar. Greetings over, Khaliq brought up something that had to do with the courts and which they had probably been discussing earlier in the day as well. Faiyaz turned to me and asked about one of my stories which he thought had political overtones and which had recently appeared in a popular spicy magazine. I was somewhat surprised that he went in for that sort of magazine. I never thought much of Faiyaz even though he edited a large English daily. Still, I am a firm believer in the saying that if a man attains a certain status, he more or less develops the abilities that go along with it. Faiyaz had a domineering look about him. He was in his fifties, his hair was long and grey, he wore thick, black-rimmed glasses and always dressed in a white kurta-pajama suit with a white cotton waistcoat. In winter he would throw a white sherwani-coat over all. His speech was very refined and authoritative, and he gave the impression of a man who knew what he was talking about. In my experience I have always been disappointed in the real competence of people like him. Faiyaz, therefore, in spite of his earnestness and position, always came off as somewhat of an impostor to me.

Still talking, we had sat down. That night I wasn't at all in the mood to talk about my creative writing. Faiyaz, being well-mannered, stopped asking me about my writing the moment he noticed my reluctance and began to express his opinion of it instead. Ayaz's group was conversing in especially loud tones. Nasim and the children's voices came in from the other room. A short while later, Faiyaz suddenly leapt to his feet. I turned around and saw Nasim and Kulsum enter the room.

"Oh, don't get up," Nasim addressed everyone as she motioned for us to remain seated. "Well, hello! We haven't seen you around in quite a while," she said across the room to Faiyaz as she took a chair next to Azhar. "Where have you been keeping yourself?"

"Where have I been keeping myself?" Faiyaz exclaimed. "I've been sitting in my office swatting flies and waiting for your dinner invitation."

"Well," Nasim said with mild sarcasm. "One hears, though, that you've been keeping very busy these days."

"Who gives a hoot about me, anyway?" Faiyaz said as he quickly arose and took a chair next to Nasim. I ended up sitting by myself. After a while I got up and went over to the window, drew the curtains and looked outside. It was raining hard. The room behind me was humming with people's voices but there remained a dead stillness in my heart. I shut the curtains and returned to the party.

The seven of us were sitting with our chairs pulled into a semicircle. Faiyaz was still talking to Nasim. Kulsum was sitting to my right. Though we had been acquainted for quite some time, we never really had the chance to get to know each other better. She was sitting quietly. I said a few words to her by way of formality. During a pause in the conversation, Nasim asked Ayaz, "Come to think of it, Mr. Mubashshir hasn't shown up yet."

"You're right," said Ayaz as he looked at his watch.

"Well, you do know Mubashshir is a very busy man," Khaliq said earnestly. "I offered to give him a ride but he refused. Actually, he had to go to some union meeting at the Law College."

"Well, we'll wait another five minutes," Ayaz said slowly. Nasim nodded in agreement.

"The weather is nasty," Faiyaz said. "I doubt if he can make it."

"He's a very reliable man," Khaliq interjected. "He'll let us know."

A few minutes later the phone rang and Ayaz got up to answer it. Everyone expected it to be Mubashshir and Ayaz returned to say that it was one of Azhar's assistants who wanted to give Azhar an important message about a motion coming before the court the next morning. Ayaz then delivered Azhar the message.

"You should have given me the phone!" Azhar said.

"Oh, come on," Ayaz said. "You've gathered around you a whole bunch of dummies. And this clown, I know him inside out. He's just trying to mess up the party—that's all."

Khaliq said mischievously, "Azhar! Watch out for your brother-in-law. He's set on torpedoing your practice."

"Khaliq," said Nasim, "if you're here to make trouble, then watch out..."

"Or you won't get any food," Faiyaz butted in. Khaliq broke out laughing.

Just then the doorbell rang. Ayaz opened the door and, what do you know, it was Mubashshir, his face and hair drenched. He took off his wet glasses and stomped on the doormat to shake the water off his shoes. His face, always wearing a look of mild surprise, looked positively astonished now, as if he was having difficulty figuring out what had happened to him. His condition looked so pathetic that everyone laughed in sympathy. Ayaz helped him take off his raincoat, hung it behind the door and ushered him over to the fireplace.

"All this just between the gate and here!" Mubashshir said in an astonished voice.

"How did you get here?" Ayaz asked.

"Some kids had a beat-up van. They dropped me off."

"What's going on at the college these days?" Azhar asked.

As Mubashshir warmed his hands before the fire, he talked about what had happened at the college union. Meanwhile he had dried his glasses with his handkerchief and put them back on his piercing dark eyes. It seemed he had completely forgotten his accidental soaking and was now fully caught up in the new situation at the college. Nasim brought a towel for him and then left the room. As he talked he rubbed his hair dry with it, then fished a small comb out of his pocket and began to comb back his hair without the aid of a mirror. His skull was wide and rather good-looking. As I watched him casually comb his hair, it occurred to me that this guy would never have to worry about going bald. His muscular body seemed to have been poured into his suit. He was into athletics at the university and one of those people who have success and popularity written all over their faces. Even Kulsum, who normally wore a very bland expression, was taking noticeably keen interest in what Mubashshir was saying.

A little later Nasim returned, looked around at us and announced, "Dinner is ready."

Nasim had always said that delicious food must also look delicious. One look at the table and I was again convinced how right she was: diced onions, browned to perfection, sprinkled over the pilav; slices of hard-boiled eggs tastefully arranged on the shami kabobs. Cucumbers, tomato and peeled orange slices garnishing the salad dishes; slivers of white almonds and other dried fruit appearing on the dishes of rice pudding like studded pearls.

Khaliq and Azhar, each rubbing his hands together gleefully, praised the food but even more Nasim. Faiyaz leaned over the table, inhaled the rich aroma, and holding his breath spread his arms and looked to the sky with eyes closed as though making apparent that he was in heaven. Only Mubashshir remained beside me looking with both wonder and seriousness at the food as though unable to decide whether to begin eating it or do something else.

"Please be seated," Nasim finally said. "Start eating. You've talked enough already."

We pulled our chairs up to the table and started passing the food. "Here you go." "Please." "Don't you want any?" "Please start." "*Bhai*, you don't need anymore, pass it over here." "Why are you starving me to death?" "*Wah,* the aroma of the food is driving me crazy!" "Then why do we have to give you any? Your sense of smell has already done it for us!" "Ha ha ha!" "Ha ha!" Amidst the small talk the dinner started. A delicious aroma arose from the steaming dishes of rice.

After a few minutes the conversation died down, replaced by the clinking of dishes and spoons, frequently punctuated by exclamations of *"Wah! Wah!"* "Simply wonderful!" "Lord be praised!" Mubashshir was sitting next to me. He had piled his plate full and was enthusiastically shoveling down his food. Watching him, it seemed that taste meant nothing to him and he was only eating to appease his hunger. A shy person by nature, Mubashshir felt totally out of place in a formal situation. We sat quietly eating. Halfway through his plate, Mubashshir turned to me and said, "You've read the new ordinance, haven't you?" When I professed my ignorance, he related to me what far-reaching effects it could have on civil rights.

By now we were taking second helpings and the conversation was beginning to pick up again. At the other end of the table Khaliq and Faiyaz were speculating about Ayaz's future. Faiyaz was pressing Ayaz to accept the government position which had been offered to him a second time that year. Even though this was a close, informal circle, a topic like this was not freely discussed. It would seem the sumptuous meal and the convivial atmosphere had prompted Faiyaz to volunteer his feelings about the matter. I had an uneasy feeling when I heard him bring up the topic.

Mubashshir, leaning over his plate, went on methodically picking up the remaining grains of rice with two fingers and popping them into his mouth. His face began to flush. All at once he quit picking at his food, grabbed a spoon to serve himself but instead he waved it in the air and said, "Why?"

Everyone heard the question but it took Faiyaz, who was still rambling on, a few seconds to wind down. A complete silence fell over the table.

"Why?" Mubashshir repeated.

"I don't get you," Faiyaz said.

"On what basis are you advising Ayaz Sahib to take a government job?"

"Whoever said I was advising him?" Faiyaz answered. "I was merely expressing my opinion."

"That's precisely what I meant," Mubashshir said. "Your opinion is based on what?"

Faiyaz's expression changed. He collected himself and after a moment of thought answered, "In my opinion capable people like Ayaz should take over and run the country's affairs."

"So you think people not in the government aren't? What about the lawyers, doctors, school teachers and street vendors? You think they have nothing to do with it?"

"My dear fellow, that is *not* my opinion. You know very well what I was talking about," Faiyaz answered with characteristic politeness. "The job of formulating government policy is *the* most important job and everyone who is capable must step forward and accept the responsibility."

"And just what is the policy of *this* government?" Mubashshir retorted. "Do you have any idea what it's doing?"

"All the more reason for people like Ayaz to get involved so that when the government tries to pull something underhanded, somebody's there to check up on it."

"You're not making any sense," Mubashshir said. "Are the ones doing the checking up on the inside or on the outside?"

"If any capable people were in the government, it wouldn't be doing anything underhanded in the first place," Faiyaz said. His face was flushed. He was beginning to feel he was losing the argument.

"The government has a whole slew of them already," said Mubashshir sarcastically. "What you really mean is that Ayaz should join the club."

"What?"

"Faiyaz Sahib, I have read your editorial supporting the new ordinance. You made it perfectly clear that in your opinion there is no dearth of bright people in the government and they are already doing a commendable job. Now then, you don't need Ayaz—do you?"

Such discussions were a commonplace at Ayaz's but they generally remained impartial and impersonal, no more than a mere pastime in this family full of lawyers. However, Mubashshir's words were a direct attack on Faiyaz's integrity and caused everyone around the table to become tense. Faiyaz had run out of answers. Ayaz, who'd normally support Mubashshir in such circumstances, had now leaned back in his chair and was quietly sitting there fiddling with a spoon. I noticed a strange glint in his eyes, as if he wanted to end the argument but at the same time was also revelling in its unpleasantness. At any rate, he made no move to diffuse it. Mubashshir, spoon in hand, stared at everyone in turn.

Just then, like a godsend, in came the sound of a child crying somewhere in the house, breaking suddenly the tension of the past few minutes. Everyone jumped to activity. Nasim instantly leapt up and scurried off. Kulsum picked up the rice pudding, laughed and said, "Well now, don't let all this talk make you forget the desert!"

Khaliq quickly jumped to his feet, took the pudding bowl from Kulsum's hands, then holding it and still standing he said as though making a speech: "Ladies and gentlemen. What brings us here this evening is the desert. As soon as we have eaten it, we'll be on our way."

Just as he was sitting down, it probably occurred to him that his comment was inappropriate as it could be construed as yet another jibe at Faiyaz, so he quickly added another joke, an equally bad one, aimed at himself, and followed it with a laugh. Ayaz and Azhar joined in. Then Azhar brought up something else.

Nasim hauled in the bawling child who suddenly became the center of attention. The child's nanny followed but she stopped at the threshold of the dining room. The child was probably frightened in his sleep. Azhar clowned around in front of him to quieten him down. Then everyone in turn tried to attract the child's attention, even Faiyaz, who quickly stood up, put his thumbs to his temples, wiggled his fingers and began to crow like a rooster. The child was flabbergasted by all this activity and quieted down for a few moments before he started crying again. In a few minutes the former gaiety and calm had returned to the room.

Ayaz's youngest son was quite attached to me. After he had finally stopped crying, his mother tried to get him to go back to bed but the excitement of all the people around had fully awakened him. I got up and stretched my arms out to him. The child toddled over to me. I sat down and lifted him onto my lap and began to pick the nuts off my rice pudding and feed it to him. Apples and oranges were being served now. After a slight hesitation Faiyaz and Mubashshir opened up. Faiyaz even made light of what had happened before and Mubashshir responded with good cheer. Everyone was still at the table when Azhar announced he was ready to leave. A wave of customary disappointment swept over the group.

"One of the family can get away with eating and running off," Khaliq quipped. "If we had the gall to do it, then it'd be 'You take this for a hotel or something?'"

Azhar began to laugh. Nasim shook a finger at Khaliq and said, "You turn everything into a joke, don't you?"

Khaliq joined both hands in front of his chest and bowed his head with affected humility. After a few minutes Azhar and Kulsum rose, which caused everyone to follow suit, quickly wiping their hands and cleaning their teeth with toothpicks. When I tried to get up, the child screwed up his face and snatched up the knife and fork he had been playing with. I sat down again. As they were leaving, Azhar and Kulsum kissed the child goodbye. I said goodbye to them from my chair. Everyone left the dining room. I was left with the child sitting in my lap. The sounds of "Good night" being said came from the outer room. Azhar and Kulsum were leaving. Then the front door shut and the sound of a car starting was heard. The rest came back inside and sat down in front of the fireplace. Nasim went into the kitchen to fix some coffee. I entertained the child by making different configurations on the tablecloth with the knife and fork. Story-telling was the basis of our relationship. Now, in the midst of his play, he suddenly remembered one of the stories I had told him some time ago and began pestering me to tell it once again. But I started telling him a different one—a short one. The sound of laughter filtered in from the other room. When Nasim walked through with the coffee, she said, "Come along. This child will keep you sitting here all night."

I got up and followed her into the other room. The fire was burning low so Ayaz brought in a few dry logs for it. Minutes later they flared up. The boy was still clinging to me. I was holding him with one hand and drinking my coffee with the other. Khaliq, Mubashshir and Ayaz were talking about a lawyer they knew who had gone crooked and was fast getting a bad reputation in the courts. I finished my coffee and as I was setting the cup down on the table noticed that Nasim had picked up my diary from the table and was absentmindedly flipping through it while talking with Faiyaz. After a while the child began to doze off. Nasim noticed this and got up.

"Sorry, I've got to go," she said as she picked up the child from my lap.

Faiyaz, Khaliq and Mubashshir started getting up but Nasim quickly asked them to sit down, adding, "Ayaz doesn't go to bed before midnight and I'm getting sleepy. So good night, all of you."

"Thank you very much for the excellent dinner," Faiyaz said.

"When do we come again, Nasim?" Khaliq asked. "Just say the day and we'll start..."

"Fasting?" Faiyaz cut in.

"Come over whenever you like, Khaliq. You know you're always welcome here," Nasim said. "And now, good-bye."

"Good-bye," Mubashshir hastily said.

"Good-bye."

Nasim's departure was followed by a lull in the conversation. Then Khaliq and Ayaz picked up where they had left off. Mubashshir dropped out of the conversation and was now sitting quietly by himself staring with fascination into the leaping flames. Faiyaz, looking carefree, filled his pipe and lit up. The pipe smoke mixed with Khaliq's cigarette smoke filled the room. I got up, went over to the window, opened a shutter and looked outside. A cold, moist gust of wind slapped my face. I took several deep breaths of the fresh air. The room hummed with the soft, satiated voices of Khaliq, Ayaz and Faiyaz. The rain came intermittently. The light shimmered off the wet grass, the trees in the garden, the traffic on the road and the distant houses.

"Is it still raining?" Ayaz asked.

"Yes," I answered.

The wind was nippy, I shivered slightly. I shut the window and went back. Ayaz, Khaliq and Faiyaz were now talking about the general conditions in the country but the nature of their conversation remained limited to personal affairs: who'd become what, who was doing what and who was involved in what. The topic was interesting and I soon found myself taking part in it. Mubashshir was still sitting in a daze. After a while he said one or two things but mostly remained sitting in quiet contentment. The evening's food and circle of friends had a soothing effect on me. Our faces reflected deep satisfaction and happiness and our conversation was soft and aimless. In this happy atmosphere we barely noticed the passage of an hour. Finally Khaliq ran his fingers through his henna-dyed hair and said to Faiyaz, "Well, you intend to spend the whole night here?"

Faiyaz, Mubashshir and Khaliq all got up. I followed suit, and so did Ayaz finally. Khaliq put on his overcoat, Mubashshir his raincoat and fastened it up.

"Well," Khaliq said as he put his hand out to Ayaz, "good-bye."

Ayaz shook his hand and then we all shook hands. Ayaz opened the door. It was raining again and there was still a strong wind blowing. Ayaz shivered from the chill. Khaliq's car was parked near the veranda. He opened the door and quickly slipped in. Faiyaz sat in front with him and Mubashshir took the back seat.

The doors slammed shut and the car started. Everyone in the car as well as Ayaz and I on the veranda waved good-bye. Splashing mud and water, the car left through the gate. Ayaz was looking out at the road. The rain was beginning to stop but the gusting wind carried the remaining fine drizzle halfway into the veranda. Ayaz stuck his hands into his pockets and leaned against the wall. I began to feel chilly.

"Come on," I said. "Do you want to get soaked?"

Ayaz remained as he was. The taillights of the car disappeared as it went around the corner but Ayaz's eyes remained transfixed on the darkness left behind. He had spent a few hours in the company of close friends. Now it was about midnight and everyone had gone home. In the swooping stillness of late evening I felt for a moment as though I was looking at a stranger. Ayaz had loosened his tie and the knot was dangling on his chest. His hair was greying and his face was a confluence of youth and age. I felt I wasn't standing on Ayaz's veranda but somewhere else, in some alien place. The world seemed insubstantial.

"Let's go in," he finally said. "Never mind closing the gate."

We went back into the room which felt a lot cosier than the chilly outside. Ayaz shut the door and looked at his watch.

"It's getting on toward midnight," he yawned. "Nasim?" he called out of habit, then said to himself, "Must have gone to bed." Then he said to me, "Well, it's time for you to do your reading and writing. I'm going to bed. See you tomorrow."

I suddenly realized I was thirsty so I went out to the kitchen. As I filled my glass I glanced out the window and caught the silhouette of someone's head. I turned off the faucet and peered harder. Someone was sitting in a chair. That part of the back veranda was screened off on two sides and used as a sun porch during the day. I set my glass down on the counter and tiptoed to the rear door which had been left ajar. I stuck my head out and looked around. For a few moments I couldn't see a thing. When my eyes finally became accustomed to the darkness I took a step outside. I was standing in the dark and could see clearly. It was Nasim. She was sitting straight up in a chair with a shawl thrown around her shoulders and her arms crossed in front of her. My diary was in her lap.

"Nasim," I called out softly.

She glanced up at me and then quickly turned her face away, but not before I noticed that she was crying. I instinctively reached out for the light switch but stopped short and began to look around uncertainly. The clouds were thinning out, allowing the moonlight to filter through the trees. It was February weather at its worst. I was just about to call her again but held back. She remained sitting, rigid, in the chair, motionless and without sound, as if in a world of her own. I left her there and went back inside.

I returned to the living room and sat down in a chair before the fireplace in which the fire had gone cold. I waited for Ayaz. He'd come looking for Nasim fairly soon, I figured. She'd come out from the kitchen and he'd ask her, "Where were you?" "I've been here all the time," she would say as she'd smile slowly. "I just went out for some fresh air." Then she'd follow him into the bedroom.

Twenty years have passed since then. A lot has happened. Ayaz managed to get Zafar's death penalty commuted to life imprisonment. Some time later he accepted a government position. After two years of being the Advocate General, he resigned and resumed his practice. Shortly thereafter he joined an up-and-coming political party. He ran on his party's ticket and won by an overwhelming majority in a constituency of Lahore. When his party formed the government he became the Minister of Law. For a while he was also the Deputy Minister of Commerce. What a time! We were all riding high. Then all at once the world turned upside down. Nowadays he is serving time for certain improprieties. Whether he committed them or not is quite another story. As a man's power grows, so does his ability to excuse away any wrongdoings. But Ayaz appears satisfied with his life. He utilized his abilities to the fullest extent. What more could a man want?

Once a month I go to Lahore to visit Ayaz. He's gotten B-class in jail. Yesterday when I visited him I found him slightly ill. "It's just a little indigestion, nothing more," he said. "The idiots have changed the cook again."

I asked him who the present cook was and he answered, "Some slob. He's doing time for killing his wife. He doesn't know the first thing about cooking, that's for sure. I sent in a complaint today. I don't want to cause Nasim any trouble." Then, as if suddenly remembering the old incident, he said, "Do you remember the time we were defending a guy who had killed his wife?"

"I remember."

For some time he stared out the small window of his cell as though trying to recall it all. Then he laughed and said, "You did some real detective work in that case."

I laughed along. It all seemed to pass before my eyes again.

Most of the time now Ayaz talks with me about the past, as

though he's making up for the time when he couldn't afford to and I'd end up returning after visiting with Nasim while he worked. Every once in a while he would say, "You have a talent. Why waste it? Write a story about your country. Don't you see," he'd become excited, "this country has killed and buried history."

At such moments my heart goes out to him. He is one of those people who only brush against greatness. Twenty years ago who could have known a whole generation would go through this. Where are all those people now?

Mubashshir had joined the political party with Ayaz and worked his way up the position of Provincial Minister. The man was clever. Seeing the wind blow the other way he resigned just in time and returned to private practice. These days he's a top attorney and collects large fees from the government, prosecuting members of his own former party.

Faiyaz became very influential for the first four or five years and acquired a good deal of property. Then he began a press and retired from journalism. He and Khaliq remained friends to the very end. Every evening without fail they would meet in a fashionable restaurant where they would sit late into the night. One evening in that very restaurant Khaliq was eating when he dropped face first on to the table, dead.

Only Nasim managed to emerge from this ordeal unscathed. She's the same old Nasim. She remained steadfastly by Ayaz's side through the good times as well as the bad. Her parents have passed away. Her two boys are studying in the U.S. and Germany. She goes to visit Ayaz once a week. Mostly I run into her at the prison and then usually go back to the house with her. There's only one servant left in the house to take care of all the work for her. The mansion is deserted. Azhar and his wife drop by to see her every so often. (They still carry a grudge against Ayaz and Nasim dating from the time when Ayaz was in power.) The rest of the time she's alone in the house. She reads the letters from her sons and spends days writing them replies. In her room are piles of old newspapers and magazines with pictures of Ayaz and her in them which she picks up now and then to browse through just to kill time. Most of the time, though, she sits in her room looking out the window to where the crabgrass is sprouting in the garden. Her room remains dark late into the night. Her features have aged prematurely but she is still careful about the way she dresses. This is one habit she's kept up. Right from the beginning she's had exquisite taste. When I see her, she's always dressed elegantly. But I have eyes and I can see. Beneath this finery she's skin and bones. Many times I wonder what she's done to deserve this. She's lived her life in honor and dignity. I feel pained.

As for my life, thank God it's going along. But I haven't written a story in twenty years, although I've been religiously keeping my diary in which I put down everything that happens to me.

That's all—

The Journey Back

From our relations with women we learn about ourselves.

We eighteen men lived in that house. It had been slated for demolition for quite some time already, but they hadn't gotten around to it. This story is from the time when I first left my country and came here. I stuck around in London for a week, but couldn't find work. The agent who got us over here shoved an address or two at us and disappeared. These addresses were supposed to give us some place to go. In the process of looking one up, I wound up in Birmingham. I ran into some luck there; I got work within just a few days. So I stayed on. That was how Birmingham became my city and that house my home for the next two years.

Then, as luck would have it, a strange incident came about in that house. It blasted us like a bomb and scattered us all over the place. We had all entered the country illegally, and were working clandestinely. On the day the incident occurred, we took to our heels and split. The four or five men who happened to be in the house at the time got the chance to grab their things; the rest who were out just took off. We ran to wherever our feet took us. I ended up in Scotland, and lived in Glasgow for several years.

It has been years since that day, but in all this time I have yet to run into a single one of my former housemates. I often wonder about how things come to pass. Life seems to hurl us into such strange situations, leaving us alone to grope around in the dark for the answers. Saqib is the only person from that time whom I see once or twice a year. But then, Saqib is something else again. First, he lives in a fixed place; second, he was inextricably involved in the incident which destroyed our house and home.

Now life has become quite easy. After scraping to get by for several years, I have obtained citizenship of this country. I had to spend three months in jail during those last days because one of my own countrymen turned me in. But luckily, the immigration law changed just then. Prior to that, my lawyer was fighting the case. He told the authorities that I had been living and working here for over five years and paying all my taxes. Moreover, I was never implicated in any crime, big or small. My affair with Margaret McTagart, whom I had become involved with in Glasgow, also came up during the discussion. I was living in her house. I also had a son by her. But we never went as far as getting married. The question just didn't arise. How could it? I already had a wife and kids back home. So I tried to keep the whole thing from being brought up, but my lawyer said that this sort of thing was not considered bad here at all—in fact, it would strengthen my case. And that's just what it did.

Anyway, the immigration law changed in the middle of all this, and I was suddenly as free as anyone else to live in this country. The winters in Scotland had frozen my bones. As soon as I got out of prison I came here, near London. The weather is good here. I landed a job at the post office—a solid government job. I have to do a lot of overtime though, about as much as regular time. I bought my own house and got my wife and kids over.

As for Margaret...there isn't anything between us anymore. I just send support money for Majid regularly—the son I named after my uncle. He is doing fine, growing up comfortably with Margaret's other two children. I say what difference does it make whether he lives here or there; in the end he is still my son. One day when he grows up, he'll come to me himself.

My kids are with me now. They speak English like the British. I could not ask for much more. But there's one thing: you can't even find a moment to breathe. Now that I'm in the hospital, I have some free time at last. I lie quietly all day long, thinking about old times. This is the first time in my life that I've been in a hospital. Where I come from, they don't believe in putting people in hospital. You stayed home until you got well—and that was that! I've always been as fit as can be and, thank God, I've never been sick in all my life. It was a minor accident that brought me here this time, not some disease or anything like that. If it were up to me, I would simply get up and go to work, but the doctor gives the orders around here. I'm stuck in bed and they've been running tests for the last few days. So I'm taking it easy.

The hospital is really something else—so grand, it looks like a palace. The floors are shiny and the beds sparkling white. Most of the doctors and nurses are either from our part of the world or from Black Africa. Their uniforms are sparkling white, too. The food is great, and everything in the bathroom is immaculate—as if this were some high class hotel. Yet strangely enough, I feel increasingly more homesick than ever. That's the only thing which bothers me. I feel restless. I can't seem to get those early memories out of my mind—things from my country, things from this country—it's as if my entire life is passing before my eyes.

Maybe I can't get my mind off that whole Birmingham period because of something unusual that happened recently. A few days before I was admitted to the hospital, I had gone to visit Saqib. There they told me that Saqib was being sent back. The news made me quite sad. I have not stopped thinking about the old times ever since. The events stream into my mind one by one, as if they were all linked together on a chain. That house in Birmingham, where I spent my first two years in this country, pops into my mind like a picture. I haven't been back there since I left. People say that the city has pulled down all the old housing and the whole area is being rebuilt. But the house stands intact in my mind, as if I was there just yesterday.

We eighteen men lived in that house. The landlord was an old Jew. In the postwar years he had bought up several old houses for a pittance and rented them out, while he moved to a classy section of town himself. (Our neighborhood too was once among the cleaner and more affluent areas of the city.) The place was full of working class men who lived with their families, cooped up in one or two rented rooms. Their women, Raza Ali told me, swept the sidewalks in the evening.

Raza Ali had come to this country just after World War Two. The real flux of people from other countries didn't really begin until after the fifties. Most of them were either people from our part of the world or Black Africans. Within less than a decade, this predominantly white city was swarming with colored people. Realizing that there was money to be made, these immigrants practically worked like dogs and were soon able to buy their own houses.

I was told all this by Raza Ali. He was a native of Surat, India, where he started working on ships when he was 12 years old. He could speak several languages: Surti, Bengali, Madrasi, Panjabi—all of them. Once, when his ship came to this country, he got off and stayed. And if I am not mistaken, he was probably the oldest Indian living in all of Birmingham.

Raza Ali said that the area had already begun its decline with the rented housing. Then when the whites saw us coming, they took off. The value of the houses dropped dramatically. Our people bought them up in easy installments. Most of the white tenants had left on their own; the fumes of cooking chillies eventually drove the rest of them out. Their places were filled by newcomers from our country. As the number of our people grew, stores selling our type of groceries began to open up. Gradually we could get anything: whole wheat flour, dals, red peppers, spices, halal meat, non-halal meat, sweets made from ghee, mustard greens, bitter gourds, green chillies—you name it. Restaurants serving our kind of food opened too. Now the white people flock to them; they eat hot, spicy curry and wash it down with gallons of water. But before, merely walking through the area made their eyes water.

People living on bigger streets obtained licenses from the city to convert their porches into small cafés. Back then, these cafés used to be the focus of the expatriates' lives. Nowadays the situation is quite different. We have really settled in this country. We have jobs, wives and kids, and a social life. Mosques and temples have cropped up and we have our own committees to sit on. There is money in our pockets, TVs in our living rooms, cars in our driveways, and we even celebrate our children's birthdays. In short, things are very good now. But back then, none of that existed. The cafés were the only places where we could meet, spend time and find out about employment. People from the same region generally huddled around the tables in groups. The customs and bureaucratic procedures of the country were explained to the newcomers. Records were played all day long. The cafés were probably the first places from where the melodious sounds of our qawwalis and ghazals were heard in this country.

I met Raza Ali in one of these cafés many years later. By then he was already a decrepit old man. He would go from one café to the next all day long. He didn't socialize with any particular group; he mixed with all of them—Bengalis, Panjabis, and so on. People bought him tea throughout the day, because he knew all there was to know about the workings of different offices in this country, and was always ready to offer advice on anything. Raza Ali was really a fine man. He had lived a truly strange life. He began working on ships at the age of twelve, and returned to his village once or twice a year. He was married on one such visit; he was sixteen then. When I met him, his own daughter was already a married woman. He showed me his small collection of pictures, which he kept carefully tucked away in an envelope. Most of the pictures were of him as a young man standing arm in arm with his shipmates at different ports, or on board. The rest were of his daughter—as a child , a young girl, and a married woman—and of her children, whom Raza Ali had never met.

Raza Ali told me that although he had only gone to see his wife ten or fifteen times in his life and never spent more than a month at a time with her, he had been sending her money regularly for forty years. "No matter where I went," he would say, "I sent money off promptly on the 30th of the month, I never missed a single one." He had been living in the same dingy room throughout his thirty years in this country. In all that time, he had only been home once for two weeks, when his daughter got married. Once when I asked him why he never brought his wife over here, he said that she was happy where she was. That was it. I heard that he had lived with a white woman for a while in the beginning, but then he left her and went back to living alone in a room. He spent year after year working in small factories. In the evenings, he sat in cafés and pubs, talking away in undertones to his fellow countrymen, as if he were muttering strange incantations.

That was how his life passed, day after day. Looking at him, it seemed as if he would go on for a hundred years. But in the end, his health deteriorated. He died within a year of our last meeting. Some fellow Surtis got together and buried him with help from the Social Welfare Department. The Welfare people burned his old clothes, made a bundle of his papers and pictures and sent if off to his village.

Raza Ali never got anywhere. Things were relatively easy job-wise back when he first came. He really could have made it with a little effort, but he was already set in his ways. He kept drifting from place to place like a ship. That time was very rough on our people. (It was bad enough when we came along later, but those were the days of real exile. Now things are a lot better, but we knew hardship in our time also.) Legal restrictions were placed on immigration. The Jews made a fuss; the government gave in and closed the borders. As a result, a trade of smuggling foreigners into the country started up. I can't think of anyone from my time who came here any other way. I myself had to sell my wife's jewelry to come up with five thousand, just to get an agent to arrange for a passport—and a fake one at that! And how we were hussled on to the trucks and wagons and what we went through in order to get here is yet another story. We were hit with more debts upon our arrival: working papers had to be made—there went another fifty pounds; it took a hundred more to pay off some fellow countryman to wrangle a deal with his foreman to fix you up with a job in the factory. It took two years just to work off these debts. And on top of all was this nagging fear of being apprehended by the law, which would send everything down the drain. The only consolation we had was knowing that we were all in the same boat. Anyway, once we figured some things out about this country, we began to move around with a little more freedom. Earlier on though, we all sat locked up inside that house like eighteen prisoners. I think I got to know that house more intimately during that time than any prisoner would ever come to know his cell.

We spent all that time which ordinary people spend shopping, seeing people, or in all sorts of recreational activities inside that house. The Jews are a very clever people. They never sold any of their houses to us, they only replaced the tenants. Now we rented from them instead of the white people. They never laid down a cent for the upkeep of the houses, but they jacked up the rent to twice the going rate. It was the same way with our house. It dated back to the time of Queen Victoria, and seemed to have been slowly deteriorating ever since. Decay had worked itself deep into the walls; they were covered with mold and giant yawning patches where chunks of plaster had fallen off. White dust floated down from the ceiling in a continuous drift, as if it were snowing indoors. Breathing in this white lime dust turned out to be a health hazard. Several people developed hacking coughs, and everyone came down with head colds, flu, and chest ailments. Poor Ghulam Muhammad got pneumonia. He laid around moaning for days on end. He was damned lucky he survived. Our health improved some as we gradually ventured out to see a doctor. For the first six months though, no one dared to have a health card made, fearing that the doctor would turn us in. But this country has good doctors. They treat the ill, they don't clean out their pockets or prescribe the wrong kind of medicine, as our doctors do back home. But even after we got the cards, no one ever called the doctor to the house, despite the fact that we had a phone and the health card said that we had the right to housecalls.

Rights?—ha! What sort of rights did we have in those days? All of our scrambling around only amounted to one thing: make a living—somehow. If you ask me, I'd say we came to plant a seedling here and, we planted it. Putting down roots in foreign soil is no picnic, you know. It takes a lot out of you. Well that's just the way life goes. A lot of things are different now, no doubt about that. But the times are still rough; just ask some newcomer and you'll see. No time is ever easy. Still, so much has changed for the better. New housing codes have been put into effect. Adequate ventilation is required by law. The houses tend to be small, no quarrel over that, but there are windows in every wall—they are quite large, and let in a lot of sunlight.

But that house of ours was as dark as a dungeon. There was a lot of land to go around during the Victorian period, so the houses were built rather large. The windows were a different story, however: always very narrow, like those in cathedrals. Those houses were like dark, dank caves with numerous rooms, both large and small. Ours had ten rooms. Well, actually, only nine. The tenth was a tiny pigeonhole tucked away under the roof—the attic. The house boasted of an underground room too—something these English people call a "cellah". And what an incredible cellar it was—there was never less than a foot of water covering the floor!

Six Mirpuris occupied the three rooms on the first floor, which also had a kitchen and a bathroom. The four rooms on the second floor were taken up by half a dozen men from some village near Hafizabad and two Bengalis. The third floor had only two rooms, both pretty small. Ghulam Muhammad and I shared one, and Husain Shah had the other all to himself. And then there was Saqib, who lived in his attic pigeonhole. Saqib used the wooden ladder outside our door to get into the attic. He would climb the ladder, push the square wooden board out of the ceiling, and with his hands planted just inside, heave himself up there. He sat down, hanging his legs through the hole. Then, still sitting there, he would bend down, take off his boots, and pull up his legs. There wasn't any room to stand or turn around, there was barely even enough space for the mattress on the floor. Saqib manoeuvred himself over the mattress in a sitting position and laid down. A bare light bulb dangled from an electric wire wrapped around a nail. Saqib kept his things in small wooden shelves built into the wall. His few pieces of clothing were always neatly folded and tucked away under his pillow. On one side, where the roof sloped down, there was a skylight with panes of frosted glass.

Sometimes Saqib got so tired, between working a full day and making the effort to climb to the attic, that he wouldn't even have the strength to reach down and untie his boots. On such occasions, he would sit with his feet hanging down through the hole for minutes on end. Other times, he turned on the light and took out one of his magazines. We read movie magazines from time to time, but Saqib never gave those so much as a glance; he only read Urdu literary journals. Once he picked one up he read it for hours, completely forgetting about his boots. That would create a strange scene: two immobile legs draped over the edge of the attic opening, as if they belonged to a corpse. And that made Ghulam Muhammad quite nervous. Unable to bear it any longer, he would stick his head out the door time and time again and yell, "Hey Saqiba! your feet are going to swell up and burst. Take off your boots."

Saqib was happy living in his attic. He only had to pay fifty shillings rent. When our rent doubled the next year, his only went up fifteen shillings.

The Jews no longer bothered to repair the houses. They knew the whole area was going under; sooner or later the government would pay them some compensation and pull it all down. So why throw away the money? Gradually, all the big houses were condemned and slated for demolition. But carrying out this sort of thing obviously takes time. The landlords' policy was simple: if they were still intact, milk them for money. The trade of smuggling people into the country had picked up steam around that time, and that turned out to be a real bonanza for those landlords. Illegal aliens like us would pay anything for a safe hole to hide in. The landlords packed in as many of us as they could and then demanded incredible amounts of rent. Anyone who squawked about it got quietly reported to the immigration people and then arrested at work. Although it is embarrassing, I must admit that many of these landlords were our own people. Yet who could really blame them? They were expatriates like us, living in exile. They only did what they did to get their feet on the ground. But the Jews—what was their excuse? They had everything.

As time wore on the character of the neighborhood changed altogether. It didn't take the prostitutes very long to pour in once they heard there was a great demand for them. That was more good news for the landlords. The prostitutes ran an illegal business, so they were ready to pay any price for a place to live quietly. They didn't have to stray very far for work—there was business for them right down the alley. When I moved in, there were basically two kinds of people in the area—prostitutes and illegal aliens. The rest were café and pub owners. Occasionally, a few students would rent out a room here and there. We all coexisted peacefully. The landlords were raking in the profits from everywhere. Our rent went from three to six pounds within a year—but it didn't pay to open our mouths, we just laid it out. There weren't any other expenses —just a little for bread and butter and some for bus fare. The rest was either sent home or saved up.

Our lives were confined to the four walls of that house for a whole year. It had three floors and an attic, but the tenants were divided into two groups. The split was created by the kitchen situation. The first two floors used the kitchen downstairs. It had regular cabinets, a table and chairs. Our kitchen—if it could be called a kitchen—was on the third floor at the top of the stairs. The landlord had simply installed a small gas stove in the hallway and put a tiny table next to it. There was a water tap and basin by a wall. Ghulam Muhammad, Husain Shah, Saqib and I cooked and ate there. Well, I should say that Saqib never actually cooked. He couldn't even boil water. He bought a week's worth of groceries every Saturday and handed them over to Husain Shah, who cooked them for him. In exchange, Saqib wrote all his letters—Husain Shah was completely illiterate—did all his shopping, and sometimes even washed his clothes. But Husain Shah got more than his fair share. To be more specific, he exaggerated the estimated amount of groceries Saqib needed, and then proceeded to eat up half of what Saqib bought behind his back.

Husain Shah was a Pathan who came from a village in Cambellpore. He was short and stout, built like a rock. He had a thick mustache and his two front teeth were broken—which made him look a bit amusing. Yet Husain Shah had an unaffected air of authority about him. He had never been rough with anyone, but he always seemed ready to get up and beat you up. That was why everyone always did exactly what he said—no questions asked. With Saqib, he was especially gentle and loving; he even offered to take him in for free several times, but Saqib was quite happy in the attic.

Ghulam Muhammad was my roommate. He was from Gujrat, Pakistan. He used to be a sergeant in the army. He came six months before I did. By the time I arrived, his life had been pretty much set. I discovered that fact on the first day I set foot in the room. So many years have passed since then, but the scene is still vivid in my mind: It was evening. In this country, it gets dark at around four o'clock during the winter—like an eternal night. And to top that off, I was brought to a house which was as dark as a tunnel in the first place. Ghulam Muhammad lived alone in the room at the time. When I first walked in, I couldn't see a damned thing. I felt around for the light switch and tried it, but nothing happened; the room was just as dark as it had been. Fumbling around, I located a mattress on the floor and sank down on it. It was dark coming up the stairs too. The man who took me to the house left me half way up the stairs. When I got to the top I could not see in the dark, so I cracked my shin against the jutting edge of the gas stove, and it still hurts.

I will remember that day for as long as I live. I sat in the dark huddled against the wall for two or three hours. There was a light on in Husain Shah's room, but his door was closed. Later he turned off the light, opened the door and went off to work. Then the only light left in the room was the miniscule amount filtering in through the window facing the street. When my eyes fully adjusted to the dark, I saw that there was a light bulb hanging in the room. It may have been burnt out. I flipped the switch two or three times, but nothing happened. The mattress I was sitting on was lumpy; the sheets and blankets had been more or less heaped onto it. Some things were lying on a wooden table—probably cooking pans—but it was too dark to really tell. Aside from that, there was nothing else in the room.

I was shaking from hunger. A little later I heard footsteps outside on the staircase. Someone came up, dropped a mattress and some blankets outside the door and went down again. I wrapped myself up in one of the blankets and plopped back down on the mattress. Oh, if anyone ever asks me how it feels to be a man in exile, I am sure my mind would flash straight back to that time. I had been scrambling around for God knows how long until then. I didn't have a permanent place to stay. Then that night I had finally found a room. What a relief! But what sort of relief was that? There I was, starving, with my body practically going into convulsions.

It's pretty strange that in the years that followed I never had the opportunity to think about it, but now that I'm in the hospital and have some free time, the memory of that night has suddenly thrust itself upon me with all its horrors. The entire period just sits there, suspended before my eyes. It makes me wonder if we ever really leave the past behind or whether we carry it around forever inside us.

My stomach was empty—I remember that well enough. I had spent the whole day running around, so I couldn't get anything to eat or drink. Nobody said a word to me when I got to that house, let alone offer me something to eat. I was pointed to a dark room and that was the end of it. Gradually the tenants in the house went off to work, while the others returned and went straight to sleep. Fatigue finally got the best of me and I dozed off. Ghulam Muhammad came in at half-past eight—his footsteps woke me up. Seeing me rouse myself, he just stared at me for some time but didn't utter a word. Then he almost walked right over me to get to the table. He was buried in a heavy overcoat and had a railway engineer's cap on his head with flaps coming down over his ears. His pants were tucked inside army boots. I could see well enough because my eyes were fully adjusted to the dark. But Ghulam Muhammad had just walked in the door and was moving around with ease, as if the darkness didn't hamper his vision at all. He whipped out some bread from one pocket of the overcoat, a can of prepared beans from the other and then dropped them both on the table. After opening the can with a pocket knife, he dumped the contents into a frying pan and carried it to the stove. He lit the stove and placed the pan on a burner—all in the pitch darkness. When the beans started to hiss, he brought the pan back into the room. Sitting down on the mattress, he began to shovel the beans down with bread and butter. As he ate, he slopped the butter on the bread like a mason slaps mortar onto bricks. He suddenly stopped his hand in midair and spoke, "Your first day here?"

"Yes," I answered.

"Did you get something to eat?"

I was famished, but I said, "Oh yes—please continue."

Ghulam Muhammad wiped that frying pan clean with the bread in two minutes flat. Shoving the pan aside on the floor, he sprang to his feet. First he took off his hat, then his coat; he hung them on a nail driven into the back of the door. Then he was down on the mattress again, unlacing his boots. I hopped off his mattress. He gestured toward the door with his elbow, still undoing his boots, and said, "Go get your mattress." That was the last thing he said that night.

I hauled the mattress inside and shoved it against the wall on the other side of the room, laying the blankets on top. Meanwhile, Ghulam Muhammad had removed his boots and set them together near the foot of his mattress. Then it was time for his pants—taking them off, he laid them out over his boots. He was wearing longjohns which were stuffed into thick socks. (He never took the socks off or, for that matter, his sweater.) After unbuttoning his collar, he slipped under the covers and went to sleep. Within a couple of minutes he was snoring away. I was still standing up near my mattress, too numb to move. My hunger had subsided some, but the fear in my heart raged on—nothing could dampen it. For some strange reason, I just couldn't get myself to lie down and go to sleep. That first night proved to be quite an ordeal.

Ghulam Muhammad sat bolt upright when his alarm went off the next morning. He threw the blankets aside and scooted down to the end of the bed, still sitting. His pants were already laid out; he just pulled them over his legs. When his feet popped out of the legs, he shoved them into his boots and tucked the pants into them. Then he stood up, zipped up his pants, buttoned his collar, threw on the overcoat and stuck the cap on his head. Ghulam Muhammad stopped to take a look at himself in the mirror hanging on the back of the door: he smoothed down his mustache with his hand, lifted his cap off and placed it back on his head neatly. Apparently, the man didn't need lights; his eyes seemed to work just fine without them. Then he opened the door and walked out. The hands of the clock were still glowing; he was up and out in exactly two minutes. I was absolutely flabbergasted by the man's flurry of activity. For as long as I lived with him, that was the way he was. As I said, his life was pretty much fixed: he was out the door by 7:30 in the morning and trooped back at precisely 8:30 in the evening. He worked seven days a week. He used the bathroom and ate breakfast at the factory. He paid three pounds rent and got by on another three for the rest of his expenses. He told me that within a year's time he had saved enough to buy several acres of land back in his village.

The man never ceased to amaze me: he worked the whole day in the factory and spent the entire night in the dark house. It was only later that I came to know that it was not so amazing after all. That was how everyone else in the house generally lived, and what I myself ended up doing after a while: leaving for work before it got light and returning well after dark. In a way it was for the best. Our safety lay in our anonymity. Anyway, when I got work, I took money out of my first week's salary to buy two lightbulbs. I put one in my room and the other in the hallway above the staircase. And that's how we eventually stopped living in pitch darkness at night.

Saqib arrived three months after I did and set himself up in the attic. Saqib—well he was different, from all of us. I made it through high school but he had gone to college, for a couple of years anyway. He was also terribly young and delicate. There was only his mother back home. No wife, no kids. He wrote his mother every week, and sent back money once a month. That's why he only worked eight hours a day. When the foreman bugged him, he did some overtime, otherwise he sat around reading in his attic or down in our room. He was from the city. The rest of us came from villages. He was also educated. That's why when anyone needed to write a letter in English, he took care of it for us. A Bengali did it for the people downstairs. A few weeks after I moved in, I cooked for Ghulam Muhammad once or twice, and eventually he also ate cooked food. That was how the four of us on the top floor ended up as a clan of some sort.

We didn't have much to do with the people living downstairs. We said "Hello!" when we ran into each other, but that was about it. We had a toilet to ourselves upstairs. Anyhow, who had time to go to the bathroom at home? Most of us used the facilities at work, except of course Husain Shah. He spent enough time in the bathroom for all three of us put together. He worked the night shift. When he came home early in the morning, he offered his prayers. He used to say the night shift was invented just for him, because it allowed him to stay home during the day and offer his obligatory prayers. We did go downstairs to bathe every Sunday, but that was only a weekly affair. And in the winter we bathed on every other Sunday.

The Mirpuris on the first floor kept to themselves too. It was pretty much the same for the Hafizabadis on the second floor, but they had to contend with the Bengalis who were stuck living on the same floor. Those two were always jabbering away continuously in Bengali. But actually, the Hafizabadis had a good deal on their hands—they got the best out of the Bengalis. One was master at cooking, and made food for the whole floor. The other knew Urdu and English besides his native Bengali. He took care of everyone's correspondence and did the weekly grocery shopping as well. Shopping was the biggest hassle. It involved going out on the street and to the stores during the day, then dragging back armloads of groceries—all the time taking the risk of being seen by everyone. That was dangerous work back in those days. But it was different in the factories; we roamed around quite freely, even though we came across all sorts of people there. Our white masters got a lot of work out of us; in return, they provided us with protection. We knew they would never let go of us: after all, we put in twelve hours a day and did all the menial labor and the dirtiest work. The country was booming in those days. The factories were roaring with business and there were never enough workers to go around. The white workers had already managed to get fat raises and were not about to do heavy or messy work. So we got assigned to it—you know the sort of job I'm talking about, cleaning up, loading and unloading, working outside in the snow and so on. On top of it, we never took time off or missed a day of work, and we were always ready to fill in for any white worker who failed to show up. Most importantly, we never asked for a pay raise.

The management knew all about our illegal status in the country and that we were working for them on fake permits. But as I said, they stood to gain a lot from us; so they looked the other way. Some of them even pocketed our insurance money instead of giving it to the government. Rumor had it that our names didn't even appear on the factory payroll—in other words, we didn't exist. But our anonymity turned out to be a blessing in disguise. It may sound odd but we felt relatively well protected in that house of fraud. In fact, we felt more secure there than we did at home.

But the weekly shopping—that was something entirely different. Going out on streets teeming with all sorts of strangers was a hazardous undertaking. Illegal aliens usually got picked up in stores shopping for food. So whenever any of us had to go shopping, he made sure to wrap himself carefully in a heavy overcoat, with his face half buried under a bulky hat; and we only went out at closing time, when most people had already headed back home. Everyone always tried to weasel out of the ordeal, foisting the responsibility onto someone else. The first two floors had their Bengalis. The Bengalis weren't all that naive, but what could they do, being outnumbered six to one by the Hafizabadis and Mirpuris. So one of them ended up cooking for the Hafizabadis, while the other did the shopping for both floors. In return, they were left alone. On our floor, Husain Shah and I took turns to go out for groceries at first, but then Saqib came along. He didn't mind going out at all. He was only too glad to do that. Oh he was young—what would he know of the fear that plagued us?

Well, that was what we did outside the house: go to work and buy groceries. We spent the rest of our time indoors, getting ready for work and cooking meals, or catching up on sleep. Where was the time to idle away chatting? Once in a while when I didn't have to work overtime I came straight home and cooked enough food to last me two to three days. Then Saqib and I would sit down and talk or play cards. The only time we saw our other housemates was on Sundays. Since five of us worked weekends also, there were only thirteen of us at home Sundays. It was like a country fair all day long—people bustling all over the house borrowing this or that, paying off debts, doing their laundry, getting letters out, cramming a whole week's chores into one day.

We all came together for two activities on Sundays. The first was going to the movies. The Sikh residents rented out a theatre in the neighborhood and showed our desi films. Altogether there were two films and four shows. Later they bought the place and ran films seven days a week. Our entire community turned up there. People rushed through whatever they were doing—even the sick came crawling out of their beds at the prospect. A few hundred people would show up. Seeing a film isn't such a big thing now. We are free to go see whatever movie we want—English, German, American —movies that take your breath away and make your head spin by their sheer wonder. Back then though, the movie used to be the highlight of the week. And we waited for it all week long. After lunch we changed into fresh clothes and gathered in one of the Mirpuri rooms downstairs. The show began at four o'clock, and we had fixed three o'clock as the time of our grand departure. Already at a quarter to three, we would begin shouting at the dawdlers to move it. There was no question at all about going there in twos and fours—we always went en masse. There was safety in numbers.

At precisely three o'clock, the thirteen of us filed out in our well-pressed, clean clothes and shining boots and marched off to the movies. There would be droves of people everywhere heading toward the theatre at that time, making it impossible for the police or any other white man to figure out who among us was a legal alien and who illegal. All they knew was that today was our movie day and they could expect a large crowd. And they would not touch a crowd with a ten-foot pole. Oh these British—they are a cunning lot! They go about their business in a quiet sort of way. Anyway, whether legal or illegal, we all stuck together on Sundays. And though the bobbies had difficulty telling the legal ones from the illegal, we ourselves had none. One glance and we knew who was who. The illegals moved on the street in a peculiar sort of manner. Even now, when I see a band of them on a sidewalk, I can tell. They have a certain way of hanging close together, acting totally absorbed in the conversation, and every once in a while dropping their heads to sneak a glance around, as if they were peeping around the edge of a wall; they'll never look you square in the face. But old habits die hard. Even now when we are free of the legal hassles, have our own property and good jobs, we cannot rid ourselves entirely of our old ways. Every time we run into some respectable person from back home, we find ourselves covering up, afraid that he might sense our low class origin. It's not easy to shed the tell-tale signs of poverty. Whether it's poverty of body or soul, I say it's a curse, a crime—no one should have to bear it.

I went back home during vacation last year and brought a car along. We are allowed to bring cars in with us. The people of my own community treated me with respect, but those government big shots and their ilk—there was nothing but contempt and low regard for us in their eyes. For all their education, they don't know a damned thing about life. They think it's a matter of being rich or poor—well it isn't; it's a matter of honor. In a new country, the only thing immigrants lack is respect. They are willing to work, and they also make money, a lot of it sometimes; but what comes the hardest is respect. Even if you have to scrape to make ends meet back in your country, lineage confers a measure of respect upon you at least. In exile, you have no identity; your sole possession is your life. Those people who have never set foot outside their country—well what do they know? They have no right to slight us. We used up a whole lifetime to plant a seedling here, to build the foundation of honor for a whole group of people.

But anyhow, I am talking of the time when the only dignity and freedom we had was a film show once a week. A few hundred of us paraded right through white territory down to that movie theatre. And we wore whatever we damn well pleased: a coat and pants, pajama, shalwar-kurta—anything. You could hear the Urdu and Panjabi film songs blasting from loudspeakers standing blocks away. There was nothing to fear. We all laughed and talked with each other, trading news from back home, yacking about who was coming over, who was going back, who got arrested, who was biding time in Germany, what agent was squandering whose life, who was giving good black market rates for currency exchange, which factory had openings for work, and so on and so forth....

Some of the white passersby would stop and stare at our crowd. A couple of bobbies always hung around to keep things in order, but they stood quietly to one side. Sometimes when a really popular film came along, a near riot broke out over buying tickets; that got the bobbies into action. They'd wave their arms and shout to restore the peace, but they never used their clubs.

A completely different scene awaited you in the theatre hall: you were greeted by a volley of popular film songs by Lata Mangaishkar, Muhammad Rafi, Nur Jahan, and others. And when the film started, it put you into a familiar world: your own movie stars, your own language, dances, songs, jokes, the same story line, the same scenes—you felt as if you had never left your country.

Ah the films!—they're pretty strange things anyhow. There were many times when I would be so absorbed in the story that I wouldn't know where I was until the lights came on, and even then it took a few seconds to really reorient myself. It was an odd feeling. Lots of people cried at the tear-jerkers—the crescendo of sniffles told you so. But me—I never cried. No matter how involved I got in a picture, I never forgot that it was only a story. I did learn something interesting by going there though: one grows tender hearted when far from home. We thought about our homes, wives and children constantly—the very same things we never much concerned ourselves with before. Going over those memories was like cutting our hearts out. Oh you could marry someone and raise a family here, but where would you get the satisfaction of speaking your native language? Our manner of speech and our gait, our style of clothes, long sunny days, the sounds and smells of home, the gentle touch—these things just don't exist here. I tell you, I've seen big, solid men with skill and plenty of money break down and cry their hearts out at these movies, as if they were suddenly told they were stricken with some incurable disease. When the theatre lights went up at the end of the film, you could see everyone's face radiating with satisfaction, which, however, didn't last long. It was already dimmed by the time they had reached the exit. On the way back we talked about the movie and repeated its jokes. And so a weekly event would pass by.

The second major event took place after we had returned home. The hour between eight and nine in the evening was reserved for the prostitutes' visit. A horde of them lived right on our street. We hired them for Sundays—there was a fixed agreement for the time and rate. I heard that before I came people went to them on their own and paid individually. Then everyone got together and decided that it was a waste of money. Husain Shah came up with the alternative which everyone liked: the prostitutes were to be hired for a fixed time and rate. And they were to come to our house. Husain Shah really knew how to handle our Jewish landlord. Anyway, everyone put their money into a kitty. The whole thing was given to whichever prostitute happened to come. Then all of us went in to see her one by one. New tenants moving into the house were told about the system; the decision to join or not was left to them. As far as I know, Saqib was the only one who turned the offer down, and his refusal made us happy. He was just a kid, and we loved him like a son.

Husain Shah was in charge of running the system. Three prostitutes worked for us. One of them came each Sunday. The woman who came three weeks before was supposed to show up for the fourth Sunday. If one showed up twice in a row because the other was busy or something, she was paid less. The agreement was final. Husain Shah stuck to it and made no exceptions. The prostitutes had contracted themselves out to other places in the same way.

Every Sunday, at eight o'clock sharp, one of the prostitutes would appear at our house, all spruced up. We would all be sitting inside waiting. She would trot in calling, "Come on boys, feeding time!" and go up to the second floor. There was a Hafizabadi room up there set aside for this particular event. All of us would crowd outside, talking softly amongst ourselves. But as the action picked up, the laughing and joking got louder and louder.

Husain Shah was always number one in the line. Everyone knew he would go first—it was a given. All else aside, he was a namazi. He was followed by four other namazis—three Mirpuris and Sherbaz, a Hafizabadi. These namazis were compulsive about their ritual bathing, almost to the point of absurdity. They'd insert their coins in the hot water meter ahead of time so they could wash themselves as soon as they were fininshed with the prostitute. This and their obsessive devoutness gave them a status of respect. The rest of us got our chance only after these saints had finished up and already headed downstairs to bathe.

A barage of dirty jokes was hurled at each person as he emerged from the room. The line outside the door ran all the way downstairs, and anyone coming out of that room had to bear the brunt of our squeals of laughter and nasty comments. But the ordeal never discouraged any of us waiting in line; we simply tried to move our place up a notch by hook or by crook, which resulted in a lot of pushing and shoving. But even this jostling around had an order to it—people stood and squabbled within their own group.

The Hafizabadis got to go next because we used their room. Whoever came after them depended on seniority in the house: the longer one had lived there, the higher his place in the line. Obviously, the rule didn't apply to the Bengalis. They came last of all, even though they had been living in the house long enough to belong somewhere in the middle. They always got kicked to the tail end. The prostitutes didn't take long to catch on to the fact that the Bengalis had the lowest standing in the house; they joined the bandwagon of abuse. They began to raise hell as soon as the Bengalis stepped into the room. Yelps of "Animal! Animal!" came booming out of the room. The Bengalis didn't get much time with them—the prostitutes dispensed with them as fast as they could. Then came the drama: the woman would stomp out of the room in a huff, hollering, "Where's Husain Shah?" If he was taking a bath, she trooped downstairs and banged on the bathroom door, shouting, "I don't ever want to see that animal's face again! Even ten pounds wouldn't be enough for that job—do you hear?"

Humiliated beyond limit, the Bengalis would try to utter something in their defense, before heading straight off to their rooms. It was the same show every Sunday, and became part of the weekly entertainment. We teased the Bengalis about this once in a while, but somewhere deep down we were jealous of them: we wondered what it was they possessed that we didn't. We used to egg them on to find out what it was. In the end the Bengalis got their revenge on us—and what a revenge! But when things were just moving along, we never missed an opportunity to take advantage of them or amuse ourselves at their expense.

Our Sundays lasted half the night. Just after nine o'clock, people began lining up for the bathroom. It took about an hour and a half for everyone to bathe. The namazis rushed off to their rooms to offer their prayers as soon as they were through bathing. As Sunday is the day of worship in this country, they dutifully took themselves to the task. One could hear their repenting voices and ardent prayers reverberating through their doors for hours. The rest of us split up into small groups and headed into different rooms to play cards. That was when the agents showed up to collect their weekly payments from those of us still laboring under their debts. Often times this prompted a lot of verbal abuse being hurled back and forth, but those agents never left without their money. Once they were gone, we went back to our card games, talking to each other softly—about the news back home, the price of land, how the crops were doing, inflation, and so on. Those who were overcome by sleep would get up and go off to bed, leaving the rest immersed in a strange melancholy. A hushed silence swept over the house and our voices began to trail off, as if something vital was slipping out from inside us. And so our Sunday fare fizzled out. Once again we would wait through our mundane weekly routine for the next one to come around. Nobody knew where the time went.

That was how things went for us. But then about a year later, something changed the entire character of our house. Returning from work one night, I knew something was up the minute I stepped into the house. Upstairs, I heard a woman's voice coming from Husain Shah's room. Saqib clambered down from his attic and into my room, telling me that Husain Shah had brought a white woman home. We hushed up, putting our ears against the wall. A little later, in walked Ghulam Muhammad and the lights went on. Almost as a reflex action, both Saqib and I brought our fingers to our lips to keep him quiet and we motioned for him to turn the light back off. Ghulam Muhammad, the one set in his ways, was rattled. The situation had caught him off guard. He started glancing around the room with a puzzled look on his face. Then he caught on, shut off the light and plopped down beside us. When we whispered the news to him, his eyes popped out. He asked, "Is she a hooker?" and, without waiting for an answer, stuck his ear to the wall. The three of us sat there listening to the voices behind the wall for a long time.

Now it is true Husain Shah was illiterate, but he managed to get around in English well enough. He was doing most of the talking, but every now and then we heard the woman say a few words too. Every time her soft voice filtered through the wall, we involuntarily strained to listen more intently. We couldn't catch a thing she said, but even so, our hearts began to pound every time she opened her mouth. Ghulam Muhammad was so overwhelmed he completely forgot his set ways. The thought of eating never crossed our minds. How could it? Eating meant cooking, and cooking meant turning on the light and making all sorts of noises. There was no contemplating anything like that in our dazed immobility. We feared that the slightest sound or movement on our part might hush up the woman and send her scrambling away from the house. And Ghulam Muhammad—well, he kept asking over and over, "Is she a hooker?"

But how would we know what she was? Sometimes we nodded yes, sometimes we shook no. Then, a little while later, Ghulam Muhammad asked, "Is she going to stay here?"

We felt as if he had voiced the same question which had been pervading our thoughts from the very start. It seemed obvious that she would, but we were afraid to believe it. After all, no woman had ever spent the night in this house. We'd seen plenty of our men carrying on with white women, but we knew they were all prostitutes. That any woman—prostitute or not—would come here and actually set up house was beyond our wildest imagination. As time passed, we became obsessed with the question. We were concentrating so hard on listening that we almost forgot to breathe. Every now and then, snippets of the conversation drifted into the room.

We didn't give a damn about what they were saying, or even about what was happening on the other side of the wall. We only wanted to know one thing: was this woman going to stay here? The entire routine of our household depended on the answer. It sounds pretty foolish when you think back on it now, but it was almost as if something was cluing us in on what was to come.

We sat with our limbs stiff and our ears glued to the wall for a couple of hours. It was well past the time for Husain Shah to go to work. Our stomachs were grumbling from hunger, but nobody stirred from his place. Suddenly, the voices stopped. After several minutes of silence, Saqib tiptoed over to the door. When he came back he said there was no light under Husain Shah's door. We were absolutely flabbergasted. I mean—my God—they had turned off the light and gone to sleep! We had never seen Husain Shah miss a day of work, either.

Gradually the tension in our bodies began to subside, and we got up. Ghulam Muhammad turned on the light. I padded out of the room quietly to fix dinner. But we couldn't keep our ears and eyes off the man's door, as if whatever had happened behind it had somehow changed everything for us. It was the same with the lower floors. Nobody had gone to sleep yet. Everyone was walking about on tiptoe. Every now and then one of them would stand on the stairs listening for a few minutes, and then retreat back down. Whispers echoed everywhere. And although quiet hovered over the house, it buzzed like a beehive from all the activity.

When we sat down on our mattresses to eat, we found out that Saqib didn't get his dinner. He told us that Husain Shah had cooked something, but walked away with the food into his room. Saqib simply stayed up in the attic. We asked him to come down and we shared our food with him. That was also the first night that Husain Shah didn't go through his gargling ritual, do his ablutions, or offer his prayers. Ghulam Muhammad asked Saqib over the meal, "Why don't you join our group for your meals?" Saqib nodded. From that day on he started eating with us, and we were freed from the hazards of shopping. He bought groceries for all three of us, and Ghulam Muhammad started eating half of the boy's share. So it seemed to work out well for everyone.

The next day Husain Shah went to the doctor and got a sick notice for three days. He sent it to his foreman with one of the Hafizabadis. Nobody had the guts to approach Husain Shah about what was going on. This continued for three days. He only came out of his room to use the toilet or cook. After he was through cooking, he'd carry the food into his room and shut the door behind him. It seemed that he had completely forgotten about Saqib.

Nobody saw the woman for three days either. On the fourth day —a Saturday—she finally emerged and paced around our floor for a few minutes. When I came back from work, I saw her standing near the stove talking to Saqib. She was a thin, young woman, with blonde hair and blue eyes. She was draped in a long, loose robe that hung down to her feet. She was wearing thick socks and slippers. The minute she saw me, she shuffled off to Husain Shah's room like an invalid. Saqib shot up to the attic. A couple of minutes later he leaped back down and burst into my room.

"So what was she saying?" I asked.

Saqib blanched and lost his tongue. Then he managed, "Nothing."

"What do you mean nothing?" I persisted. "She was talking."

Saqib tried to catch his breath for a bit, and then said, "Her name is Mary."

"Well what was she saying?"

"She was talking."

"What was she talking *about?*"

"She said hello to me first, and called me herself," Saqib explained.

"OK, so she spoke to you first," I conceded. "But what the devil was she saying?"

"She asked me what kind of work I did, what time I went to work and what time I got home—that's all."

"Why?"

"How would I know? Just to talk, I guess."

"What do you mean, just to talk?" I asked. "What else was she saying?"

"Nothing."

"That's a lie—she was talking to you for a long time."

Saqib tensed up, thinking. After a pause he said, "She has an upset stomach."

I looked straight at him, which made him even more nervous. He looked so comical that I burst out laughing. Saqib calmed down a bit, laughing with me.

"Our food has made her ill," he said. "She said she likes our curry and chapatis very much, but the chillies upset her stomach."

We both plopped down on the mattress with our eyes still wandering outside. Her stomach was upset all right—she went to the toilet two or three times while we sat there. We filled Ghulam Muhammad in on everything when he got home. He dropped down beside us, turning toward the door. When the woman passed by again, Ghulam Muhammad lunged forward in order to see her go into the toilet and shut the door. Then he turned to us and said, "She's a hooker all right."

Saqib stuck up for her then and there, but Ghulam Muhammad was adamant; he could not be persuaded to change his mind about the woman. Meanwhile Husain Shah returned from shopping. This time he had bought some cooking pots too. That evening, the woman cooked English food. We only got up to cook our own meal after she had gone back to the room with the frying pan. We were standing by the stove cooking when she came out to do the dishes.

She said hello and we returned the greeting. She quietly washed the dishes under the tap and, on her way back to the room, smiled at us pleasantly. We were struck dumb, unable to move or even utter a word. It was the smell of the food burning that jolted me back to life. I leaped for the stove and poured some water on the curry. But we were still completely dazed. All at once it seemed that our thoughts had fallen out of our heads.

Oh, how the slightest gesture can touch you to the core! Prostitute or whatever, what difference did it make? After all, she cooked food and washed dishes right in front of us—why, she even smiled at us like a fellow human being. Wasn't that enough? How just one word, or even a simple smile, can transform everything! We were suddenly in touch with ourselves. For the first time ever, this country no longer seemed so distant and inaccessible. We ate our meal in silence, turned off the light and went to sleep with a new warmth in our hearts.

Indeed we had our first real encounter with this country on that evening. The next day—a Sunday—Mary's stomach got much worse. She feebly made her way down the stairs and called the doctor. Silence swept over the whole house: everyone dropped whatever they were doing and listened to her talk to the doctor over the phone. That was the first time anyone had used that phone to call the doctor. In spite of it being Sunday, with the house full, it was dead silent everywhere. Everyone suddenly seemed to disappear into their rooms where they sat waiting for the doctor to arrive, tense with apprehension. A while later the Bengalis stirred and started cleaning. Within a short time they had the kitchen, bathroom and stairs sparkling clean. Dead silence gripped the house once again. Everyone's eyes were glued to the door.

An hour went by. Then the doctor showed up. He rang the bell, but no one budged. Just then Husain Shah suddenly decided that he needed to use the toilet. He bolted into the bathroom and locked himself inside. The three of us inched away from the door, out of view of anyone passing through the hallway. When the bell rang again, one of the residents downstairs forced one of the Bengalis out to answer the door. A Mirpuri told us later how the Bengali slunk behind the door as he opened it. The doctor walked in and stood there looking bewildered, peering around. The Bengali slithered out from behind the door. The doctor asked for Mary, and the Bengali chap motioned him upstairs. The doctor came up to our floor, where Mary was standing outside her door. He examined her, wrote out a prescription and shot out of the house in five minutes flat! He never bothered to give the house a second glance.

A few incipient noises rose timidly, and the house suddenly sprang to life, as if waking up from a dead sleep. That was when our Sunday really began. The stairs reverberated with the sound of people scurrying up and down, and pots and pans clanged in the kitchen filled with the mouth-watering aroma of cooking spices. The whole house buzzed with the noise of the Mirpuris, Hafizabadis and Bengalis as they chattered away in their strange tongues. Husain Shah, out of the bathroom now, went out to fill the prescription. As usual, we ate lunch, spit-polished our shoes, and went off to the movies. But Husain Shah didn't come along; he stayed home with Mary. God, were we happy that day. There was a bold spring to our step and our eyes sparkled with a rush of confidence. It suddenly seemed we were no longer the degenerates everybody could walk all over. On the way back from the movie, we discussed the story and joked around with each other. Then, half way to the house, we stopped talking abruptly, as if remembering something. A strange hush spread over us as the house drew nearer. When we finally got home, we slipped in through the door and quietly retreated into one of the Mirpuri rooms. The waiting began... Although no one ever said anything, we all knew exactly what was going through everyone else's heads, and what it was we were waiting for.

A little while later Ghulam Muhammad shot upstairs and walked around our room for a bit, checking the situation out. He came back and reported, "They're in the room," sitting down in his place once again.

Time ticked on. A couple of us tried to make conversation but couldn't say more than a few words before dropping back into silence. Time was just flitting away and there was still no solution to the present dilemma. Saqib got up and left the room—no doubt to go up to the attic and pore over one of his literary magazines. No one paid attention to him; he was never part of this anyhow.

We knew very well that Mary was a, well that sort of woman. Even so, her presence had made a difference. After all, didn't she live in the house, cook food and use the toilet? She even behaved as if she were Husain Shah's woman. Under these circumstances, it seemed grossly improper to have a prostitute come to the premises. As a result, the desire which possessed us like clockwork every Sunday was suddenly gone. We found ourselves face to face with a tremendous problem.

At last, Husain Shah came downstairs and appeared on the scene; it seemed that there would be a solution after all. This was the first time that he associated with us since Mary's arrival. He just sat silently with us for a few minutes, twirling the end of his mustache with his fingers, staring into space. A Hafizabadi opened his mouth, which sort of startled all of us.

"Shah-ji, how is bibi feeling now?" the Hafizabadi asked.

A few seconds of complete silence followed. Husain Shah just gaped at the fellow. Then suddenly, everyone started to mumble, asking after Mary's health.

Husain Shah nodded, answering, "She's better now." Then he sprang to his feet and began scanning the room with his eyes. "Well," he began, "you can do it here," he gestured with his hand. "But keep it down."

Then he was gone. Everyone started talking at once. The silent vigil was over. It seemed as if a crushing weight had been lifted off our shoulders.

One of the Bengalis was talked into running to the door when the bell rang. He was to tell the woman to keep quiet and to direct her straight into a Mirpuri room on the first floor. It was decided that we wouldn't queue up outside the door—everyone would wait in the room right where they sat now. Then we would go in one by one.

Although we were still snickering and smirking after hashing through the plan, there was something essential missing. The whole thing felt so insipid. And we knew it—Ghulam Muhammad and I more than anyone else. It was different for the two of us. The moment our eyes met through the uproar in the room, we became aware of our amazingly similar feelings. And we stood up together.

"You can count us out," said Ghulam Muhammad to one of the Mirpuris. He gaped back at us, dumbfounded. We left the room.

That night, neither of us bothered to bathe. We sat quietly in our room for a couple of hours. Not one sound trailed upstairs from the action below. After a while we got up to cook dinner. We were washing the dishes when Mary walked out of her room to warm up some milk. She smiled at us and said hello. We smiled and greeted her back. Then, gathering some courage, Saqib asked her after her health. She told us she was feeling better. When we had finished and returned to our room, she was still standing by the stove heating the milk.

After quite some time, the sound of people bathing or eating supper downstairs meandered up into our room. Obviously they were done. We went down to kill time. Nobody said anything about the evening's event. Instead we discussed matters closer to the heart. The arrival of the agents was followed by the usual altercations over payment, and they left with their money. The conversation droned on. The card games started up and we talked about things back home. But we made sure to keep our voices down, as we used to do in our homes before our elders. There was a calm in our voices and not a trace of worry as we talked about our parents, and our wives and kids.

That Sunday night was a turning point in our lives. We scarcely knew it then, it's only in retrospect that it seems so. We were transformed. We felt like we had really begun to settle here. Of course that didn't mean we were forsaking our own country. People who leave their homes to strike roots in a foreign land and go through the hardships involved never stray very far from their homeland emotionally. They don't leave their country behind until they die. Yes, they adapt to new ways of course, but they never give up the old ones, for as long as they live. So let's just say we were picking up a new habit: to get right into the centre and go for it, rather than crouch around timidly in the shadows as we had all along done.

That an unrestrained existence, a life free of fear could be such a blessing didn't dawn on us until we bumped into Mary on the stairs next Saturday. She was carrying a shopping bag. When she saw us, she asked, "Aren't you going shopping?" We didn't know what to say, but then we answered yes.

"Alright," she went on, "let's go together."

Saqib and I grabbed our bags and scurried off behind her. We were in the market within a few minutes. Until then, shopping to us meant stepping into a shop timidly, hurriedly whisking whatever we needed into the basket, doling out the money, throwing the stuff into our bags, and getting the hell out of there. But with Mary around it was different that day. Inside the first shop, she picked up a few things, checked their prices and put them back down. She began grumbling that the shop was too damned expensive and left. We followed her out. The shopkeeper gaped at us, but didn't say a word. In the next store Mary did buy a few things, but put the others back on the shelf after seeing the price. Outside, when she looked at our empty bags, she asked, "Didn't you buy your groceries?"

Saqib pointed to a big store and told her we would buy them there. But she said, "That store is very expensive—everything's cheaper in this one. So why don't you get what you need here?"

We went back into the shop. Mary picked out some inexpensive items for us after looking at our lists, and put them into the basket.

When we came out of the shop we had finished half our shopping. Mary had a fight with the shop woman in the third store. She took one look at the prices and told the woman that the same items sold cheaper at the other store. That woman turned out to be a real bitch. She started to say, you get what you pay for—low prices, low quality, but Mary cut her short saying that the products were identical and put out by the same company. The woman snapped that in that case, Mary was welcome to leave and shop there instead. Mary started for the door, grumbling away.

The woman began to sputter, "We don't need your sort here."

Mary caught it half-way out the door, turned around and shot back, "We are all the same here. If you are such a princess, well, you'd better go sit home, or take your shop elsewhere." And with that, she marched out.

We were scared out of our wits, all the same we felt confident—even happy. It was a strange feeling.

The shopkeeper in the fourth store was an old man who knew Mary. She completed her purchases there. We followed right along with her, buying the rest of our stuff. This was absolutely the first time that we actually picked up an item, checked its price, put it down and chose a different one. In other words, this was the first time we really went shopping.

When she was paying for the stuff, Mary stood there talking with the man about this and that, and introduced us to him as her "friends."

The shopkeeper said, "Welcome, Gentlemen!"

By the time we got out of the shop it had already begun drizzling. It's always drizzling in this country. We waited for it to stop in the doorway of the shop, and then we set out for home. Mary walked along slowly on the way back, looking at the displays in the show windows. We had never spent our shopping time like this. But we went along quietly with whatever Mary did. The market was bustling with shoppers. In the meantime, I spotted a bobby. He was on patrol, coming from ahead. I glanced at Saqib; he had seen him too. Our first impulse was to dash across the market to the other side, but how could we go and leave Mary?

Mary was standing near a window looking at some women's clothing. We turned to hide our faces from the bobby, just standing there. Then Mary started off. Now there was no getting away from the man—we had to come face to face with him. When he got closer, he turned out to be another friend of Mary's. Mary stopped, calling him over. She talked to him for a few minutes while we stood there against our will, glancing about furtively. Then Mary said something to him in jest, walking off. These British—always cracking their little jokes. They don't mean anything! The bobby smiled and answered her. Moving off, he called out: "Some fine gentlemen your friends are—they don't even carry your bags for you!"

Mary looked at us, laughing, and walked away. A little further on Saqib insisted on taking Mary's bags. We slowly walked along talking and reached home. Opening the door and stepping in the house, we really felt it—yes, we really *live* here, and this is *our* house.

Mary blended in completely within a couple of weeks. We cooked and went shopping together. Sometimes she would come into our room and stand there talking with us for a while. She got on quite well with Saqib. Saqib would come home from work and spend most of his time talking with Mary. Sometimes she'd send him out on an errand. Ghulam Muhammad and I never went into Mary's room, but Saqib did. He told us that she had invited him in. Sometimes he'd be sitting in the room when Husain Shah came home from work. He didn't mind Saqib visiting Mary.

Husain Shah worked it out with his foreman to get the day shift. Now he was at work during the day and home at night. A couple of weeks after this he started offering his prayers once again. The only difference was that he'd make up for the missed ones after his night prayer. So the whole thing took him a couple of hours. Mary was astonished by all this. Sometimes she'd mention it in a joking tone to Saqib, but she respected Husain Shah a great deal and never said anything to him. Mary—well she had a story of her own. As I heard it from her, Husain Shah and Saqib, it went something like this:

She came from Newcastle, a city in the northern part of this country. Her parents lived in a village just outside the city. Her father was an old drunk. He'd have a go at the bottle and then rail at his wife and daughter. One day he came home from the tavern and got annoyed. He really started letting his wife have it when the woman grabbed a knife from the kitchen and plunged it into his belly. He lay there writhing on the floor until he died. Mary's mother was arrested.

Mary must have been about ten or eleven then. She had a brother too—about a year older than her. The Social Welfare Department started to look after them. Mary's mother went on trial and got fifteen years hard labor. Mary became a permanent ward of the state, and was raised in one of its institutions. Her brother lived in a different one, but they saw each other quite often.

Mary grew up there, went to school and so on. As soon as she turned seventeen, she sprang loose—they couldn't keep her there legally after that age. She stayed on in Newcastle for a couple of years. She lived in a small room and worked odd jobs. Then she got mixed up with the hippies. They are a strange lot. They wander about like a bunch of vagrants. When they run out of money they take a trip to the Social Welfare Department and squeeze out whatever they can. Once in a great while, one of them will get a few days' work, and split the money with the rest. Otherwise they lived off handouts and begging, indulging in opium, hash and whatever. Mary travelled all over the country with one of their groups.

Meanwhile the news caught up with Mary that her mother had been released from jail on good conduct after doing only half her sentence and that she had returned home. Right then, Mary abandoned her hippie group and went back to her hometown. Her brother had disappeared without a trace. She lived with her mother in public housing for six months. During this time her mother had started drinking. The old lady would hit the bottle, call her daughter every dirty name in the book, and beat her senseless, as if she had just replaced Mary's father. Mary finally got fed up and left.

For the next two years, Mary lived in Manchester where she found work in an Irishman's shop. Soon she became his mistress, and he put her up in a rented room. One and a half years passed by without incident. But the guy had a wife and kids, and the wife found out about Mary one day. She was a big, fat Irish woman. She thundered her way into Mary's room and attacked her, beating her black and blue. On her way out the door she threatened to come after Mary with a knife if she ever saw her in the city again.

Naturally Mary fled, terrified. She didn't stop until she got to Birmingham. Here she stayed with an old acquaintance for a couple of weeks. One day she ran into Jamaica George. There are lots of Black Jamaicans here; many of them make their money by pushing drugs or running prostitution rings. Jamaica George was something of a tycoon in that business; his turf was another neighborhood like ours. He was the terror of the whole area, but to Mary he was exceptionally kind and treated her as his woman. In those days Mary was never without a car, and she ran the house. She lived with him for three years.

Ah, but that kind of money-making carries its own hazards. To Mary's misfortune, Jamaica George's enemies finished him off one day. It was a recent murder—we'd heard about it too. Jamaica George had a younger brother who took over the business. But he lacked his brother's guts and brains—he just didn't have what it took to run this sort of thing. And so the business fell apart. Soon he started badgering Mary—told her to get out and go turn a few tricks if she wanted to keep living there. Mary refused flat out. When things really got rough and she thought she couldn't take it anymore, she left. Mary told us herself that there was no way in hell she'd ever sell her body even if her life depended on it. A few days later, she stumbled upon Husain Shah in a café and came home with him.

By this account, Mary must have been nearly twenty-seven years old, but she didn't look any more than nineteen or twenty. If you stop to think about it, she had a pretty hard life; yet oddly enough, it didn't seem to have left its scars on her. Her face radiated the innocence of a young girl, fresh out of school. The sight of her continually beaming face never ceased to confound us: how could anyone remain so cheerful after all the hardship she had been through? Once we praised her for her fortitude and she quickly retorted, "Oh you men—what do you know? The slightest difficulty and off you go over the edge. We know, yes we have really seen life."

Mary didn't have any vices. She didn't drink or use opium. She only smoked—indeed, chain smoked—cigarettes. But smoking cigarettes—you could hardly count that as anything in this land of vices. Mary treated Husain Shah with utmost respect and never left him to look after anything. As soon as she got over her upset stomach, she learned how to cook our type of food. She'd ask Husain Shah or me something every day. She was a real whiz—within a few days she was making delicious curries for Husain Shah. She'd put less spices in the food if she were going to eat some herself, but most of the time she cooked two separate dishes—English for herself and desi for Husain Shah. She was not one to run away from hard work: the whole evening she would stand there cooking with us, talking away. Even Ghulam Muhammad, who by nature didn't speak much and was otherwise unyielding in his set ways, would talk with Mary. New life seemed to have burst into flower on our floor.

By and by Mary started visiting the ground floor as well. Earlier on, all she did was say hello on her way up or down, but now she would stop over and talk a bit. Occasionally, she'd also go down to borrow some spices and seasonings. She used the tap upstairs to wash Husain Shah's and her own clothes in the beginning, but now she used the bathroom downstairs. Then, as time wore on, she struck up a casual friendship with the Hafizabadis on the second floor. Well it was bound to happen; Mary was the friendly sort after all. When she got bored during the day she'd go visit them. She would hear the guys who worked nights puttering around after they got their sleep and she would talk with them. No one from the lower floors had ever come upstairs during the first year, but now it often happened that one Hafizabadi or the other found his way to our floor in the evening. He'd sit on the stairs if we happened to be cooking, otherwise he'd come into our room and start chatting. Thanks to Mary, we had become friends with the Hafizabadis.

Once a week, the Hafizabadis sent some curry upstairs with somebody. "Don't worry, Mary," he would say, supported by the chorus of the rest of them standing on the landing, "there aren't many chillies in it." Thanking them, Mary would take the food. She always looked charming—as if the grace of accepting things came naturally to her.

Whenever Husain Shah rolled out his prayer mat, she took her cigarettes and came by our room. After standing in the doorway talking for a while, she'd urge us to go downstairs with her. Downstairs, she'd go into one of the Hafizabadi rooms and plop down on a mattress with the rest, pass her cigarettes around and talk lightheartedly. When her cigarettes ran out, she smoked ours.

Mary took a great interest in our country. She'd say that she had seen its people but not the place. She wore us out with her questions. She asked about our lifestyle, our customs and traditions, the weather, education and upbringing, what the houses looked like, about our women and children, songs, films—she wanted to know about everything! One time she even went to see our Sunday movie. Husain Shah had stopped coming ever since she arrived, but one Sunday she dragged him along. She told us she liked the film very much.

Mary enjoyed talking with us about our families. She learned the names of everyone's wife by heart. Her memory was phenomenal —she never mixed up the names. Whenever she ran into us she'd ask, "Any letter from home?" Sometimes she'd ask us to read the letter aloud—in our own language. She didn't understand a word of Urdu, but she'd sit there listening attentively all the same. Then we gave her a translation in our broken English—that made her happy.

Often at night, some Hafizabadi would come bounding up the stairs saying, "Look, Mary! A letter from my wife!" Mary's face would light up as she replied, "Really? A letter from Sakina? Well what does she write? And how is she?" She asked about each and every one of our family.

Mary showed great interest in our religion, too. She used to ask us things we didn't know the answers to ourselves. Sherbaz the Hafizabadi, a devout man who offered his prayers regularly, took it upon himself to educate her about the precepts of our religion. A trip downstairs would bring the dutiful Sherbaz to her side to get on with her religious instruction. Soon she became very well acquainted with our religion and thought very highly of it. She said that although she was not given to being religious herself, she thought religion was a "good thing." And that Sherbaz—he bet his bloody life that one day sooner or later, Mary was destined to become a Muslim. She had a flicker of faith in her, he said.

She hung out downstairs until she heard Husain Shah shuffling around in the room upstairs. She'd spring up and say, "He's done praying—I must go now." Sometimes we went up with her, other times we stayed on downstairs blabbing away with the Hafizabadis. One Sunday we heard that all the Hafizabadis had decided to call it quits with the prostitutes. Only the two Bengalis from their floor still hung on. The Hafizabadis used to call them a pair of jackrabbits—said they couldn't sit still until they had their fling with a woman. Embarrassed, the Bengalis would say, "Alright, alright—one of these days we will stop. What more do you want?"

It wasn't until a couple of months after Mary arrived that her stomach began to show. She had been pregnant for quite a few months, it seemed, which was why she always wore loose-fitting clothes. Not really knowing what to think, we quietly discussed her condition among ourselves for a couple of days. We didn't notice anything different about her behavior. She was still the same cheerful girl who chatted lightheartedly with everyone, washing away whatever uncomfortable feelings we might have had about the pregnancy. How could we find fault with her? She was already unlucky enough as it was. Yet it didn't seem to affect her warm and giving nature. She cared for everyone and never gave anyone the slightest cause to feel bad or offended. And then Sherbaz began saying that any child was God's blessing and we wouldn't hold it against her.

Mary began growing weaker every day. Her face became sallow and she heaved herself up and down the stairs, huffing and puffing. But her failing strength never stopped her from cooking for Husain Shah. We all began to look after her. When she went to the hospital for her weekly checkup, one of the Hafizabadis working on the night shift always went along since Husain Shah was away during the day.

It was about this time that a fight broke out on the first floor one night. It all started when Akram's agent suddenly began squeezing him for more money. Akram had quietly paid it out the week before, but he blew up this time around. We already knew the guy was being a real bastard. Angry voices began booming upstairs as the argument got vicious. We all came out of our rooms and huddled together on the stairs listening. The agent was threatening Akram with arrest; Akram was protesting back that the only reason the guy was giving him a run for his life was because he was helpless. Mary asked us who the loudmouth was, so we told her it was an agent. As she knew nothing about our deal with the agents, she asked, "Agent? What agent?" And we quickly filled her in. She asked us to go downstairs with her, that she'd deal with the agent. We told her nothing was to be gained by sticking our nose into someone else's quarrels. "Why not?" she shot back. "Nobody comes into *this* house and starts messing around with one of us."

Well, she waddled her way downstairs. At first she just sat down on the bottom step to catch her breath. And that agent—he really spilled his guts the moment he caught sight of a white woman. You should have seen the way Mary got up and gave it to him. She started off in a low enough tone but soon she was thundering:

"I say who the bloody hell do you think you are? What's your name? What do you want here? Only good, honest, hard-working laborers live here. What are you yelling about? What—you think someone is trying to rob you? Oh, I know your sort all too well. Nobody here is doing you any harm. Arrested—you think you could get someone arrested? Go ahead and give it a try. I know all the police around here, and I'll have you thrown in jail before you know it! In this country no one is illegal. You are the only criminals. Yes you, who go about fleecing the poor!" She opened the door as she talked on, pointing outside. "Get out of here—now! If I ever see your face in this house again you'll be on your way to jail. We've got laws in this country—remember?"

That agent didn't waste another moment standing there, he flew straight out the door. Mary, who had quite worn herself out in the meantime, slumped down on the stairs. Husain Shah sat next to her, supporting her. The Mirpuris stood around her, petrified. When Mary recovered her strength, she began telling them, "It's alright—there's nothing to be afraid of. You have to fend for yourself. They can't do anything to you."

Mary may not have known very much about our rather precarious situation in this country, but she still stuck her neck out for us in whatever way she could. Word got out about the incident and the agents realized that they couldn't push us around anymore. Now they came quietly, took whatever amount they were given, and went away just as quietly. And Akram's agent—he was so bloody unnerved he didn't show up for two weeks in a row! And when he did start coming again, he hung outside on the doorstep, sending in word that he was there, and quietly waited for the money. Then he beat a hasty retreat.

Now the Mirpuris also began coming up to our floor, and gradually Mary got to know them as well as she knew the Hafizabadis and us. Whenever Mary came back from a shopping trip alone, she'd sit downstairs with them for a while to catch her breath. The Mirpuris served her tea and carried her groceries upstairs for her. Akram worked the night shift, so he started escorting Mary back and forth to the hospital in a taxi. The house was declared off limits to the prostitutes, following Sherbaz's impassioned plea that this sort of business was out of place in a house about to be blessed with a child. It was only the two Bengalis and a degenerate Mirpuri who still wouldn't give it up, but they went and disgraced themselves somewhere else.

On the day Mary went into labor, she called the hospital, and an ambulance was sent to pick her up. When she came back on the fourth day, Sherbaz had arranged for a special ceremony: a cover-to-cover recitation of the Holy Quran. Everyone in the house except Husain Shah gathered in Sherbaz's room that evening, reciting as much of the Quran as they could remember. Sherbaz had also bought a basket of our desi sweetmeats for the occasion from one of our shops. We had come in fresh, clean clothes and were sitting on cushions in a semicircle. Sherbaz finished off a long passage from the Quran with a prayer. Smiling, Mary watched the whole thing. Then when everyone spread their hands, palms turned toward their faces, for the benedictory prayer, Mary followed right along with us. Just before the sweets were passed around, each of us placed a pound note for the child into Mary's hand. Mary thanked us as she accepted the money. Then we tasted the sweets and carried on happily. That was the first day that a baby's cry ever rang through the house; it was like a boisterous joy reverberating about its room and hallways.

Husain Shah made himself scarce for a couple of days, but then he began carting the kid around the house too. Everyone suggested that Mary name the child Michael George, and she did. But sometimes she'd tell us that one of these days she meant to go and have his name entered in the records as Michael George Husain Shah. The baby's looks were a bit unusual. His white complexion was complemented by the kinky hair and pudgy lips of a Jamaican. But he was a lovely child, with the cheerful temperament of his mother. He never bawled on for hours like other babies. Within a few months he became so popular that Mary couldn't keep track of his whereabouts: he'd be bouncing around in the arms of one housemate or another.

The house had taken on an unusual gaiety: Mirpuris would be on the second floor, Hafizabadis on the first, and the three of us—well, we were all over the place too. We were coming out of our shells now. We shared food back and forth, gave advice and generally tried to help each other out. Suddenly, it started to feel like home there in exile. When I thought back on that day I had arrived—what a comparison! it was so bloody dark you couldn't even see the stairs. Now lights shined in all the rooms and even on the landings well into the night. It's said that there's a blessing in sticking together. How true! We saw it with our own eyes.

This gaiety, this wonderful household accord showed signs of strain when Husain Shah began talking about his nephew back home. He mentioned him casually once or twice, saying that he'd received a letter from him. We didn't think much of it—we all had relatives back home. Well apparently, the matter didn't stop there; that was just the beginning of it. A few days later we heard Mary shouting in Husain Shah's room. We were surprised: we had never heard her raise her voice before, so we cocked our ears. A little while later she emerged from the room looking quite distraught. She didn't so much as look at us or say a word. She headed straight downstairs and out the door, the child in her arms. Since the time she had started living here she had stepped out of the house only to run errands, but never like this at night, when there did not seem to be any good reason to go out. Returning a couple of hours later, she went straight into her room. From that night onward, Mary wasn't the same woman. We saw a strange change creep over her day by day.

Mary's innate exuberance began to fade. The smiles and courteous words all but disappeared from her lips. And although things appeared to go on as before, Mary herself had definitely changed, so much, in fact, that if you saw her a month ago and again now, you'd have difficulty recognizing her. Her skin furrowed and bunched up like someone exposed to prolonged cold. Often times now, she would cook dinner and retreat to her room before any of us got home from work. We didn't see her much—only when she came out to wash the dishes or go to the bathroom. On such occasions, she'd just say hello or, at most, exchange a few, brief words. She went out shopping alone and was otherwise completely caught up in caring for the child, talking to him incessantly.

Husain Shah seemed to have dropped out of sight too. He'd come back from work and shoot into his room. The rest of us still got together just as before, but now only on the first two floors; no one came up to our floor anymore. We speculated about Husain Shah and Mary, but none of us knew what was really brewing. Even our own conversations had become less and less frequent now. Our voices no longer rang through the house; a palpable tension seemed to weigh down on its every beam, threatening to break them all. We broke up early on in the evening and retired to our rooms. Saqib went back to reading his literary journals. Ghulam Muhammad totally stopped socializing within a couple of weeks and returned to his set life.

Then one day when Mary was still busy cooking, Saqib returned unexpectedly early. Instead of making straight for his attic, he stopped and finally decided to talk to her about what was going on. Mary gave him the whole story: "Husain Shah is asking me to marry his nephew. Says that the boy is poor and can't afford to come up with the money for an agent. If I agree to marry him, he would be able to enter the country legally—I mean look at this, can you believe it?"

Saqib repeated it to us that night. Then we trotted downstairs to tell the rest. People were amazed. Who had ever heard of such a thing! Everyone sided with Mary on the matter. And Sherbaz —well, it was his considered opinion that this business of blood-related men sharing the same woman violated the precepts established both by God and His Prophet.

Everyone shuddered with a "God forbid!" Right then and there it was decided that something must be done to stop Husain Shah from such a rash act. But what should be done? We agreed that first we should hear what Husain Shah had to say about the whole thing. Two or three days passed by as we waited for the opportunity to talk with him. In the meantime, all the buzzing and hushed-up air of secrecy clued Husain Shah in on what was going on. He ended up coming to us himself, sitting down with us in a Hafizabadi's room. And he had a different story to tell.

Husain Shah explained that although it was true that he wanted Mary to marry his nephew, the marriage was only to be on paper.

"Who in the world is talking about a real marriage," he said. "What —you don't really think I've completely gone off my rocker to send my own woman off to marry someone else? I explained all of this to Mary: I'm only asking her to go through the motions... Just to meet the legal requirements. All we have to do is comply with this point of their law so the boy can come here. That's it! The boy won't be any more involved than that. Things will continue just as they are now. But Mary—her brains are scrambled. She can't understand any of this."

A few people chimed in with a yes. We had heard of a similar case. A woman was paid to go through this type of "paper marriage" and that was how one of our people was granted resident status here.

"So put a stranger up to it or get your own woman to do it— what's the difference?" Husain Shah went on. "It's only a marriage on paper, right?"

Several people went along with Husain Shah while the rest of us just gaped at him.

Husain Shah started up again: "We've all been through a lot of hardship here—haven't we? Even now we live in hiding. Agents, police, government, foremen—everybody lords it over us here. Now one of our own people finally has the chance to enter the country legally, so why not take advantage of it? I was just a boy when my father died. My brother took me in and raised me. He just passed away. Now there's only his son. The boy is very poor. It will be hard enough for him to scrape up the money for his passage here, let alone enough to pay off an agent.

"What does Mary stand to lose? All she has to do is put her signature on a piece of paper. This is her country; who can dispute what she does? The boy can come here openly and legally. He knows something about electrical work. He'll earn good money. It'll help him, but it'll help us too. And besides, I do have some rights over Mary—don't I? I picked her up off the street and brought her into my own house. I treat her with respect. Can't I ask for this much? I spend my own hard-earned money on her: food, clothing—everything. I give her all the comforts in the world. I've helped her in every way. I've got no secrets from you. I've even accepted her illegitimate son as my own—what more can she ask for? If it was one of our own women, she'd have given her life for me! This one can't even scrawl her name on a piece of paper!

"Wouldn't you say our primary obligation is to help our own relatives? That's the reason why we are putting up with all this hardship. Let's face it, our lives are dependent on our relatives, and ultimately, it's they who come running to help us—not these thankless white people. Look how much I've sacrificed for her. She was being crushed by the blows of fate—I took her in and made her into a queen! I take care of her every need—what, she can't even help me out a little...for once? You are my brothers. We all have the same needs, the same obligations. You decide: if you were in my place, what would you do?"

Husain Shah's explanation took a load off our minds; everything was clear. We agreed with him. And Sherbaz said that Husain Shah was absolutely right—looking after our relatives was a moral duty —why, even a religious obligation!

If you look at it, we were indeed dependent on our relatives, just as they were on us. Husain Shah wasn't out of line. He'd bent over backwards for Mary. She did not have anything at all to lose by signing that piece of paper, did she? and Husain Shah had so much to gain.

Anyway we didn't say anything to Mary, but we told Saqib that if he happened to chat with her, he should get her to understand the whole thing: Husain Shah didn't mean any harm by what he said. Something like this could really help one of us out. Mary would get a lot out of it too—Husain Shah would be beholden to her forever.

Saqib agreed to do it. Mary was friendly with all of us, true, but we knew that she cared a great deal more for Saqib.

A few days later Saqib told us that he'd spoken to Mary.

"Well what did she say?" I asked.

"Nothing," Saqib replied. "She just gawked at me as if she couldn't believe what she was hearing. Then she went straight off to her room without saying a word."

It was right about then that Husain Shah received some official-looking manila envelopes from the government. He just took them into his room. Mary's behaviour didn't improve any—in fact, it took a turn for the worse. She'd completely stopped talking, as if she'd been struck dumb. When she ventured out of her room, her eyes stayed fixed on the baby in her arms. She never even gave us a sidelong glance, let alone mutter a hello.

Then she started neglecting her household chores as well. She would just throw anything together at mealtimes, cooking food in any old way, and heat up milk for the baby two or three times a day. The dirty dishes piled up under the tap. Husain Shah would usually end up doing them. She previously did the laundry everyday downstairs in the bathroom, or at least every other day. Now she stood at the tap upstairs and washed the baby's clothes, leaving the rest in a dirty heap. She'd do the wash once a week if she felt like it; otherwise, Husain Shah had to haul the whole pile to the launderette.

Mary had given up her loose maternity clothes and gone back to wearing dresses after the birth of Michael George, but she'd become so neglectful of her appearance that she'd wear the same dress for a whole week straight. She never had been one for makeup, but always took special care of her hair. She shampooed it with warm water everyday and kept it neatly combed. Now she let it get oily—who knows how many days lapsed before she washed it—and it hung down in stringy curls, like a bunch of bedsprings. It seemed as if she were slowly withdrawing from the world and into herself. The former lustre was gone from her eyes; they had greyed over as if she were losing her sight.

When he was free, Husain Shah would sometimes sit around with us, dropping a comment: "Stubborn as a mule! Doesn't understand a bloody thing!" And then he'd mutter, "Women have their heads screwed on backwards!"

We couldn't understand what was wrong with Mary. The matter was settled. And when you come right down to it, there was not much to it anyway. Why, then, was she making such a big fuss over it? Well we knew she was asking for it and was going to get it one of these days...and she did.

A big scene was in progress one day when I returned from work. Mary was screaming and shouting. (Boy, when she was angry, it seemed as if she were speaking some other language!) We couldn't understand a word. Husain Shah's half-raised voice butted in every now and then with a "Shut up! Shut up!" And that was it.

As people returned from work, they stood listening to Mary's yelling in their rooms or on the stairs. In the middle of all the commotion we heard a series of blows, the kind you hear when someone is beating the dirt out of the rug. Suddenly, Mary stopped yelling. We stood there straining to listen, but there was dead silence. Just then we heard the sound of someone falling to the floor, followed by the sound of Mary crying. We'd heard our own women rant and rave, but we'd never heard anything quite like Mary's wails. Her choking sobs sounded as if she were grasping in her throat for her life, but it was slipping away anyhow.

We stood there listening for quite some time. The sobs subsided and died out. The lights in Husain Shah's room went out a few minutes later. We stirred from our places and began fixing dinner.

The usual mealtime clanging of pots and pans permeated the house. We'd already finished eating, entertaining the thought of going downstairs to set up a card game when Husain Shah's lights suddenly came on. He came out to warm up some milk for the baby. He took the warm milk into his room and the lights went back off again a little while later. Not another sound came out from that room for the rest of the night.

Mary wasn't to be seen for the next three days. When she finally did come out, she looked pale and terribly weak. Back when she had first moved into the house, she had these dark circles under her eyes, but a few weeks of rest and a proper diet had restored her health. The color returned to her cheeks and the dark circles went away. Now they had reappeared once again.

Her health returned surprisingly quickly this time. It seemed as if she had come to an inner decision during those three days. Life is full of lessons: we have to help each other out; it's all a matter of give and take. It's just that women's minds work differently. But it seemed that Mary was finally beginning to grasp the meaning of Husain Shah's words.

Within about a week Mary was back to her former self: gracious, kind, cheerful. She began gaining back her strength. Once again she started mixing with us, and we started doing our household chores together. The color came back to her face and it regained its sharpness. But those dark circles—they didn't go away this time. Mary's temperament got better and so did the atmosphere in the house; it seemed as if she were living just the way she wanted. Still, those dark circles never left her for as long as she lived with us. It was the only noticeable physical change in her and it told us that although her behavior had returned to what it was before, deep down something had also irrevocably changed. We knew something was different, but we couldn't put our finger on it. Anyway we grew accustomed to it with time. But looking back now, I think the thing we were vaguely aware of, was that Mary had made up her mind.

And so she had: it was obvious from her manner when she emerged from her room three days later. Her polite formalities had given way to an outright boldness. She had always treated Husain Shah with the utmost respect, but now she openly bossed him around in front of everyone: "Husain, do this! Do that!" "Husain, don't do that!" " Oh Husain, how many times have I told you—don't do it that way, do it like this!"

Her once deferential manner toward us (she never failed to add a "please" or a "thank you" to whatever she said) had also changed.

Now just about everything we did or said provoked some sort of criticism. When I think about it now, it seems as if she may have been reverting to her true nature. Yet at the time, her conduct didn't bother us, let alone appear unpleasant or offensive. Ah—if only we had known what was coming, we would have tried to avert it then and there.

Mary began acting as though she ran the house. Soon she had put its affairs back in order. If she spotted the slightest mess on the landings or in the kitchen on her way in and out, she'd snort in disgust and set the residents of that floor to work. When she found anyone sitting idle, she'd say, "Hey, get off your duff and give me a hand. Come along—stop lazing about."

This didn't bother Husain Shah either—he almost seemed to enjoy doing his assigned chores. The atmosphere of the house had completely turned around. Now Mary talked with everyone about Husain Shah's nephew Irshad without any hesitation or reserve, as though it were something all very ordinary. She'd already completed the legal papers and submitted them to the Home Office.

A couple of policemen—one uniformed, the other in plainclothes—came and knocked at our door one day. They asked for Mary and marched straight upstairs. As soon as she heard them, Mary quickly deposited her baby with us and dashed back to her room before they got upstairs. She had fixed up her room nicely. Against one wall was the bed, and a table and two chairs stood against the other. Canned food was stacked up on a table in the corner. Near the bed, a mirror hung above a small makeup table with a lamp on it. The windows in Mary's room were the only ones in the house which boasted of curtains.

The police were in there with her for quite a while. Mary served them tea as she talked with them. They finished their investigation and got up to go. She saw them out. Later she told us that it had all gone splendidly, that she expected no snags. Husain Shah was overjoyed. A couple of weeks later the paperwork was finally completed and sent off to Irshad. Then the wait for his arrival began.

Irshad was entering the country strictly above the board, so he didn't have to hustle his way underground through Europe on buses and trucks like the rest of us had to; he was coming by plane. Husain Shah and Mary took a bus down to London to pick him up on the day he arrived and returned with him the same evening. Mary seemed to be acting a bit too friendly with Irshad—talking and joking with him as frankly as she would with any of us. Irshad, however, was too overwhelmed to react or answer her. Besides, he still didn't feel quite at home speaking English.

Mary had asked us to cook dinner for them the day before; Ghulam Muhammad and I went to great lengths preparing a nice meal. When they got back they picked up the food and took it into Husain Shah's room. They talked softly among themselves for a while after they ate, with the door shut. Ghulam Muhammad went to sleep at his regular time but Saqib and I stayed up. Earlier, Mary had instructed us to put Irshad's mattress into our room. We had to remove the table which Ghulam Muhammad used for his pots and pans to squeeze in the third mattress, even then it barely fit: the door wouldn't open all the way. But it all worked out in the end.

Their talking must have stopped some time around midnight. The door opened and Irshad padded into our room. There was no walking space on the floor; Irshad trod over my mattress to get to his own. Soon he had snuggled up in the blanket. He seemed very happy with the desi food we had cooked for him. "Everything's great here!" he chortled. "Just like back home." I reassured him in every way I could. He was exhausted and fell fast asleep.

Irshad must have been in his mid-twenties. He was a handsome young man, tall and well built. The ends of his thick, black mustache pointed downward, and he wore his hair cropped short. He was the kind of young man one takes instant liking to. And although the inconvenience of cramming the extra mattress into our room had vexed us somewhat, the feeling vanished almost from the instant we met him.

Since Mary had already set the wedding date with the marriage bureau, the "paper marriage" took place a few days after Irshad's arrival on a Saturday afternoon. Husain Shah and Saqib accompanied them to the office. Being illegal aliens, they were understandably nervous about walking into such a place, but Mary dragged them along anyhow. They acted as witnesses. Husain Shah pulled out an expensive gold ring from his pocket; he'd bought it just for the wedding. It was given to Mary during the ceremony.

Mary was wearing a white, silk dress bought especially for the occasion. She had done up her hair and put on some make-up. It was the first time we had seen her all decked out like this. As she was leaving the house for the marriage bureau, we all stood there gaping at her. She looked beautiful. She left the baby in our care.

The four of them returned home from the marriage bureau in a taxicab. Mary was holding a bouquet of flowers. I was standing downstairs then. A Mirpuri was holding Mary's baby. She was smiling, chatting away with Husain Shah, Irshad and Saqib. Just as she walked in the door, her gaze fell on me. Without bothering to look anywhere else, she thrust the bouquet straight into my hands. As I was trying to hold it, she leaned forward and stole a kiss on my cheek. Everyone burst out laughing. So did she. Then she said, "I'm the one who got married. But it's you who is blushing! Why— you've turned a bright red!" And my cheeks became redder still.

Well that gave everyone the chance to laugh. Mary took the baby in her arms kissing it on the head and cheeks, and climbed upstairs. Husain Shah and Irshad followed her up. We felt like having a celebration of some sort; after all, occasions such as this didn't come around every day. We went up to the second floor to consult with Sherbaz, but he hastily pushed the door shut as he rebuked us bitterly, "Have you lost your senses? Celebration—for what? Get on with your work."

We sat there talking for a little while and then got up and busied ourselves with the chores. Mary had also changed her clothes for an ordinary dress to get going on the housework. The ring stayed on her finger for a few days, but she eventually removed that too and put it away somewhere.

Sherbaz was right of course. Nothing had changed in the house; things went on just as before. Irshad continued sleeping in our room, Husain Shah and Mary in theirs. Irshad's paperwork had all been taken care of and sent off to the respective offices. He strode right out in broad daylight and had his employment and medical cards made up as if it were nothing special at all. Then he began standing in line at the employment exchange. Why, Irshad had all the rights of any white!

Jobs were easy to come by in those days. Irshad took a test of some sort in a factory. Since he had some electrical knowhow, he easily passed the test. He was off to work the very next day. And poof! Money in his pocket within the same week. Irshad didn't have to work in the shadows, always ready to hide. He worked days and brought home a good salary every Friday. Occasionally, when the foreman asked, he'd put in some overtime; otherwise he had the whole weekend off.

All of us felt a certain pride about Irshad's status too. He commanded the same sort of respect in the house as Husain Shah and Sherbaz, but he never allowed it to go to his head; he was as deferential as ever. And he respected Husain Shah and Mary immensely. He never intruded in on their privacy. And even though he ate with us, he dutifully gave a part of his salary to Husain Shah every Friday. We thought he was paying off the debt for his fare, little by little. Later on, though, we found out that he had paid the plane fare himself. He was only giving him the money out of the sense of obligation a nephew ought to feel toward his uncle. Husain Shah fed us a different line about it. He said it was a good excuse to save money, and that in time Irshad would get it all back. God alone knows. Well, it was between nephew and uncle. Besides, Husain Shah had really been very kind to Irshad. He could do him no harm. Things were going just fine.

Oh, if only everything had kept on as it was and nothing had come in the way of anyone's happiness! But that was not to be. The stars had a different plan. It's said that life in exile is like moving through an obstacle course with tricks at every turn. How true! Things changed slowly as time wore on.

Irshad enjoyed freedom. He could go anywhere and talk openly with whomever he pleased. Maybe if he had been a virtual prisoner like us, he would have stayed on the right track: going to work, coming back home, and earning his money. Being a prisoner is a curse all right, but in exile it's actually a blessing: it forces you to concentrate on what really matters, not on trifles.

Oh, the games of fate... Thinking about it now, it seems that this freedom itself ruined him in the end. He naturally began to look around more and more as he got his feet planted firmly on the ground. The first thing he did was make friends with people outside the house. Next he let his hair grow long. Finally, he started going to the pubs. (In this country a bar is called a "pub.") Well there's one thing I'll say for Irshad: he never got hooked on alcohol, but he did on freedom.

He only went to the pub once a week, on Fridays. He'd pick up his paycheck and head straight to the pub from work. He knocked on Husain Shah's door when he returned home, very late. Husain Shah would often be asleep. Grumbling, he'd get up and open the door. Irshad would talk with him pleasantly and hand over the weekly sum. Once or twice Husain Shah tried to stop him from going to the pub. Irshad heard him out in silence. Later, Husain Shah asked Sherbaz to talk to the boy and straighten him out. Sherbaz came to our room and gave him a talk on the evils of drinking, presenting the Islamic view of the matter. The graphic description of the suffering awaiting drinkers in the next world scared Irshad off, and he solemnly vowed to mend his ways. But when Friday rolled around six days later, he was back in the pub.

Husain Shah finally blew up one day. Irshad walked in one Friday at about ten in the evening and promptly knocked on Husain Shah's door. He opened it and cursed Irshad angrily, "Get out of here you drunken sod!" He ranted on, "Don't you ever show your face to me after one of your drinking bouts. I don't need your money!"

Irshad was grinning sheepishly in the doorway when Mary called out from inside the room, "Relax. He goes to the pub once a week—so what? Get off his back!"

Mary siding with Irshad stumped Husain Shah—he couldn't come up with an answer. He just kicked the door shut and went back in.

Next morning, he quietly accepted the money from Irshad.

Irshad changed his payment schedule from that day on: he'd give him the money on Saturday mornings instead of Friday nights.

Friday nights Irshad came straight to our room and threw himself down on his mattress. He'd jabber away with Saqib and me late into the night. He was young and strong, and didn't get drunk easily. But he did drink enough to open up. As he grew bolder, he even talked about Husain Shah with us. His initial joking manner gave way to a more serious tone. He often spoke bitterly about him: "He sleeps on a bed. Leaves us here to rot on the floor."

Like a disciple, Saqib was clinging to Irshad more and more. And soon enough, just what we had long dreaded came to pass. Saqib didn't return home at his usual time one Friday evening, but walked in with Irshad around ten or eleven. He was in bad shape. He lunged for the tap and threw up. He had been vomiting the whole way home. He was under that tap puking his guts out for a full hour. Then the dry heaves started and it seemed like he was choking to death. Irshad, Husain Shah, Mary and I hung close to help him. Ghulam Muhammad stuck around for a little while too, then he went off to bed.

Husain Shah and I were pacing around, trying to think of some way to stop the violent spasms, but there was nothing we could do. Who can cure someone sick on alcohol? With both hands Mary rubbed his back, smirking as if this wasn't anything serious. "Don't worry," she said. "It's always like this the first time. He'll be fine soon enough."

Yet, when Saqib's throat clamped shut and his eyes bulged out for seconds on end, Mary looked worried. Then as soon as he started breathing normally again and groaned, "Oh God help me! I'll never go near the place again!" Mary's lips cracked back into a smile. She'd flash mischievous looks at Irshad, comforting Saqib at the same time, as if this were all some sort of game.

Husain Shah was exploding into fits of anger. "You cursed

thing!" he lashed out at Irshad. "You're dragging this boy down along with you and you don't even give a damn! If I'd known you'd wreak such havoc I would never have let you *think* about setting foot in this country!"

Mary tried calming him down several times. She was right: Saqib's fits slowly petered out. When we were helping Saqib up to his attic that night, we heard him repenting for his little escapade, promising never to drink again through his drunken haze.

But how long does a drunk's repentance last? Ghulam Muhammad, Husain Shah, Sherbaz and I all worked on putting some sense into Saqib all week long. However, when next Friday came along, he was right back at the pub with Irshad; they got in late that night. Saqib and Irshad became a pair from that day on. Irshad was a legal resident; he didn't have to worry about anything. But Saqib was an illegal alien, and we worried about him constantly. Some Friday nights when the two of them came swaggering home arm in arm, singing away at the top of their lungs and attracting a lot of attention on the streets, we'd be half-dead with worry. But as time rolled on we began to pay less attention to it. We called them barroom chums.

Now Irshad had really started to try out his wings. Earlier on, he had so much respect for Husain Shah that he never ventured near his and Mary's room uninvited. But now he was in and out of that room all the time, visiting with Mary. I really don't think Irshad was at fault. Mary's encouragement had spurred him on. What can a man do when a woman is bent on getting her way? It became all too clear one evening, when Mary was nowhere to be found. It was a Friday. Husain Shah returned from work and began asking us where Mary might be. But no one had a clue. The baby was on the second floor with the Hafizabadis. Husain Shah went down and got the child. An hour or so went by. Husain Shah never took his eyes off the door. Still no sign of Mary. He wandered around the house with the baby, talking. Then he went back upstairs to his room. Mary had cooked and left his dinner for him. But he didn't touch it. All he did was sit in his room. He'd come out every now and then, pace around at the top of the stairs, lean over the bannister, go to the bathroom and then back to his room. It was the first time any of us had seen him in such an anxious state; he looked terribly distraught. Finally tired out, he performed ablutions and offered his prayer; he finished it in half the usual time. Then he shut himself up in his room and just sat there quietly.

Mary came trooping home with Irshad and Saqib some time after ten o'clock that night. We had already suspected as much; we knew we had been right all along when we saw them together. As soon as Husain Shah heard them, he shot out of the room and stood at the top of the stairs, his face flushed with anger. I felt sure that something awful was about to happen. I was alone, awake in my room. When I saw Husain Shah come out, I quickly turned my light off, so whatever it was would happen out *there*.

Mary, Irshad and Saqib were coming up the stairs. Saqib and Irshad were quiet, but Mary talked on in a cheery voice as if she didn't have a care in the world. "Hello," she said pleasantly, reaching the top. Husain Shah's eyes grew wide in utter disbelief that she could be actually standing before him, chatting away so cheerfully. "You're still up?" she said as she came and stood right next to him. My door was half open; I was sitting in the dark watching everything. The red left Husain Shah's face as he regained his composure. Mary bounced up and kissed him on the cheek. Then she put her arm around his back and led him into their room.

Well, under my breath I thanked God that the crisis was averted; my fears had been groundless. I laid down on my mattress. Saqib scrambled up the ladder to his attic. Irshad walked into our room, stepped over me to reach his mattress, and wrapped himself up in his blanket. I waited for the snoring to start. He never failed to snore whenever he returned from the pub. We had to live with Ghulam Muhammad's snoring everyday. Irshad did his share of grumbling about that, but every Friday I had to put up with their snoring duet.

Mary warmed up Husain Shah's food and took it into the room. He ate it in silence. After he finished they closed the door, but the light stayed on. And then for the first time Husain Shah spoke. His voice was halting, subdued; one could barely make out what he was saying, but his voice was audible all the same. He droned on like that for quite some time, as if he were gently reproving her. Mary remained utterly silent for some time, but when she finally did speak, her voice was loud, angry, sharp. God knows what she said, but whatever it was, it shut both of them up The light went off and they went to sleep. And there I was, trying to fall asleep amidst Irshad and Ghulam Muhammad's snoring duet. Lying there I thought, we just made it past another potential crisis. Things would be alright for now. The thought gave me a sense of relief, and I quickly fell asleep.

I have to laugh when I look back on that now. What place does "relief" have in this world? But that's the way things were in those days. If our life made it from one step to the next without hardship, it would give us a sense of relief. And every night was another hurdle to get over, with its own hazards. If we made it through the night, we made it past one more hurdle. I tell you, no one should have to live through a time like that. But that's life, isn't it? Well, at least we were able to live in relative comfort and peace for a while during the time I'm speaking of now.

The next morning, a Saturday, Husain Shah took the money from Irshad in silence. Mary and Irshad drew closer with the passage of time. Saqib was part of their group, but Mary's true interest was directed toward Irshad. His name was always on her lips. One day we heard that Irshad got himself put on the night shift. Now he was at work during the night and spent all day with Mary. When Husain Shah saw this happening, he got himself transferred to the night shift too, but that took some doing. Scarcely a week had gone by when Irshad switched back to the day shift. The two of them were scrambling for the shifts. Husain Shah wrangled his way back onto the day shift.

Things probably worked out for Husain Shah because he got on well with his foreman... He'd given him a bottle of whisky on Christmas and bought him a basket of fruits and quantities of our desi sweetmeats on both 'Ids. Back home we'd heard that white people didn't go in for this sort of thing, but almost as soon as we set foot in this country, we discovered that this wasn't the case— just about anything goes here. But in all fairness I must say one thing: these people appreciate skill. Yes they do. Husain Shah couldn't possibly compete with the skill Irshad had in his hands. The condition of the country has gone from bad to worse now, but in those days skilled workers had no dearth of job opportunities. They were valued everywhere, and people paid attention to them.

When Irshad changed his shift around for the third time, Husain Shah was stuck with the day shift. The five or six weeks which passed by in the meantime gave Irshad the opportunity to get closer to Mary. Often times Irshad would be home when Husain Shah went off to work. He spent long hours in Mary's room, chatting with her or doing her favors. When the shift thing was no longer the issue, they got what they wanted. Now they even started closing the door.

Husain Shah worked the whole day and slept home at night. Irshad was home during the day and gone at night. Irshad's schedule was pretty much fixed now. Husain Shah would be long gone by the time Irshad got home early in the morning. Mary got up and cooked Irshad a meal as soon as he walked in through the door. Irshad played with the baby. When he was done eating, they'd talk, waiting for the baby to fall asleep. When the child, fed and tired from play, fell back asleep, Irshad and Mary shut the door to the room and went to bed.

Come afternoon, they got up. The door swung open and the day's work began. Saqib joined them at around five o'clock when he returned. If he didn't go in on his own, Mary was sure to call him. Irshad packed himself some food for the night and went off to work a little after six. Right after he left, Mary started cooking Husain Shah's dinner. Husain Shah came home some time after eight. Time rolled on without incident; our days were spent in peace and quiet.

The next few weeks brought along a couple more changes: Husain Shah quit doing overtime. Now he left for work at seven and returned just after five. Irshad left Mary's room promptly at five o'clock and came into ours. But Mary's attitude remained unchanged. Once Husain Shah had returned, she'd invite Irshad and Saqib into the room. They both stayed there until it was time for Irshad to go to work, or else they were just in and out the whole time. Husain Shah had stopped talking to his nephew because of the friction between them. The only contact they had was on Saturdays, when Irshad slipped him a fixed amount of money. Now the couple of hours they got to spend together every day eased the strain on their relationship, but they still couldn't talk as easily as before.

Then one day we saw Husain Shah going out with the three of them. It was Saturday. Mary, Saqib and Irshad started going to the pub on Saturdays because Irshad had to work Friday nights. Husain Shah usually stayed home and took care of the child. Mary came into our room that day and left the child with us, saying, "Husain Shah is coming along with us."

We didn't believe it until we actually saw him going out the door with them. From that day on, the four of them began going to the pub together every week. Because they stayed out quite late at the pub, Husain Shah would miss his prayers on Saturdays and be obliged to make up for them. That was the only thing which changed in his routine. He offered his prayers regularly on the other six days of the week, and carried out the rest of his household responsibilities also. His life had an innate order to it. A flourishing tree comes to mind when I think about him now; that same sort of order exists in those trees. Husain Shah's presence was what kept the whole house together. But there was a whole host of forces working against him. And we could vaguely sense it.

One day Husain Shah returned from work early. This had never happened before. Doing overtime, well that was a daily thing with him. If he wasn't scheduled for it, he'd take the place of someone who'd failed to show up. But coming home early—it was out of the question. Later we came to know that he wasn't feeling well that day. He took the afternoon off because he had developed a severe headache. Mary's door was shut when he came in. Finding it locked, he headed into our room, which was empty at the time. He laid down on my mattress to get some rest.

Ali Muhammad, one of the Hafizabadis, told us about all of this. He was home at the time because he worked the night shift. Husain Shah got up about an hour later. Mary's door was still shut. He quietly slipped out of the house. I myself witnessed the rest of what happened. Home from work, I was standing in my doorway when Husain Shah slowly lumbered up the stairs. As he passed by me, I caught a whiff of alcohol. The pubs weren't open yet; he must have bought the booze at a store and gulped it down.

Mary's door was open now. Irshad and Saqib were sitting in there with her. Husain Shah stopped in the doorway. The three of them glanced his way and Mary interrupted her conversation only long enough to say "Hello" to him. Husain Shah made no reply; he remained planted in the doorway.

The conversation inside the room suddenly stopped as they all turned toward Husain Shah. Saqib and Irshad were sitting in the chairs and Mary was stretched out on the bed, leaning on her elbow. I don't know what they saw on Husain Shah's face, for he had his back turned toward me, but whatever it was, they stirred out of their places one by one, with their eyes fixed on him. First Mary slowly rose to her feet from the bed. Then Saqib got up from his chair.

Husain Shah's eyes bore down on Irshad. Suddenly, he was standing right in front of him. Extending one arm, he picked Irshad up by his hair. With the other hand, he whacked him across his face. Then he swung back, smacking Irshad so hard with the back of his hand that his face jerked up toward the ceiling. He put the front of his hand to work again, slapping Irshad just above the eyes. A squeak of "Uncle!" was the only thing that escaped from Irshad's mouth between the blows.

Scrambling out of the room, Saqib stood staring from the doorway. Husain Shah clenched his fist and rammed it into Irshad's jaw. The force of the blow knocked his head out of Husain Shah's grip, and Irshad fell against the wall with a thud. Mary leapt in front of Husain Shah shrieking, "Husain Shah! come to your senses! What are you doing!" Husain Shah shoved her out of the way so violently that she tumbled and landed on the bed. "He's your brother's son!" Mary screeched from the bed. "You're going to kill him! You'll kill him!"

Like a statue, Husain Shah stood firm in the middle of the room, legs stretched apart, arms hanging down. His chest was the only thing that betrayed any sign of movement. He stared at Irshad through the narrow slits of his eyelids, as if he were squinting in the dark. The lights hadn't yet been turned on, but the daylight was ebbing away. The dim outlines of Husain Shah's muscular body seemed to spread from wall to wall, filling up the entire room. Irshad was a burly youth with his body well groomed, sleek and supple from his life of leisure, seemingly able to glide through the air as he ascended the stairs. But right then he was down on his knees in front of Husain Shah like a delicate child. Fifty years of manual labor had forged muscles of steel in Husain Shah's limbs. Emotion surged out of his aged bones like an electrical current.

Irshad was a mess. A broken front tooth sat in the palm of one hand. His lips were split open. Blood trickled over his chin and fell onto his shirt. His eyes were frozen in terror. When Husain Shah took a step toward him, his face instantly took on the expression of a hounded animal meeting its death. "Uncle!" he sputtered from his slumped position on the floor, "I'll turn you in! You are staying here illegally. I'll turn everyone in!"

Irshad's words had no effect on Husain Shah at all; it was as if he hadn't even heard him. He bent down and yanked Irshad off the floor as if he were a bale of cotton. Mary screamed. Husain Shah lifted Irshad up over his head and hurled him out of the door like a ball. He landed at our feet with a big thud. The whole house shook from the impact. Inside the room, Husain Shah stood directly in front of Mary, arms out at his sides, panting away. We thought he was going to go for her next. But he didn't move an inch. Gradually his breathing became normal; it was as if his anger had dissolved like foam. He turned around and kicked the door shut.

The whole house was silent, except for the gentle sobbing of the baby who had been awakened by the commotion a short while ago. Minutes passed by like that. We were all gathered on the stairs outside the room. Saqib and I lifted Irshad off the floor. He rinsed his mouth out a couple of times and washed his face at the tap before he went into our room and sat down on his mattress. Everyone filed in, one by one flopping down on the mattresses. No one said a word.

A little while later Irshad got up, took off his shirt and threw it in a corner. He slipped on a fresh one and went off to work. No one else stirred from his place. Gradually we began talking of other things; no one mentioned the evening's incident. But every now and then we'd look at each other remembering it and shake our heads in regret. There was only one thought in our minds: this fight spelled trouble for all of us. Irshad was the only legal immigrant in the house. If he decided to carry out his threat, it would be the end of it for all of us.

Strangely enough, all our hopes were now riding on Mary. We considered her to be the root cause of the whole thing, but we knew that if anyone could straighten out this mess, it was she and she alone. And before the night was out, we were proven right.

An hour later Husain Shah's door opened. Mary came out and started cooking Husain Shah's meal. She was standing at the stove when Husain Shah came out to go to the bathroom. Sherbaz got up, glancing at us, and went and stood at the door. When Husain Shah came out of the bathroom, Sherbaz put a hand on his shoulder and led him into our room. Husain Shah sat off to one side.

"Whatever has happened has happened," Sherbaz began to explain. "Forget about this. Irshad is still a child. He's your own blood. You're an intelligent man. There is so much to be gained by sticking together. After all, would there be anyone around today to say our Prophet's name if the Muslims hadn't stuck together? The only way we'll get anywhere at all is if we stick together."

Husain Shah sat with his head down and quietly heard Sherbaz out. He didn't say anything, but the look of embarrassment on his face reassured us. And then when Mary called out sharply. "Husain Shah, come and eat," from the other room and he got up and left the room, we felt completely relaxed.

Mary came out to wash the dishes a little while later when we were cooking our dinner. Ghulam Muhammad had returned from work meanwhile. We related the evening's incident to him, but we also told him that there was nothing to worry about. Husain Shah was sitting in his room with the baby on his lap. Mary was talking cheerfully with Saqib as she was doing the dishes. That night when we turned off the lights to go to bed, we could hardly believe that a storm had crashed through the house just three hours ago.

Whatever misgivings we had were washed away in the next few

weeks. Irshad had acted honorably toward his uncle and hadn't turned him in. Saqib told us that he had begged forgiveness from his uncle, and Husain Shah had forgiven him. So the matter had ended peaceably. Husain Shah only missed one visit to the pub. That was on the Saturday following the incident, when Mary, Irshad and Saqib went without him. By the end of the following week, things had returned to normal. Husain Shah worked days, Irshad nights, and nothing got in anyone's way. And so, once again, the four of them started going to the pub together. Irshad never skipped a payment to Husain Shah. In fact, Saqib told us that he had increased the amount by a few pounds to win his uncle back. Well, God alone knows the truth, but Husain Shah did seem outwardly content.

Everything would have kept going just fine if Mary had remained within her limits. Now she had full control over everything and wanted for nothing. But, it's as the elders say, a woman will always revert to her base nature. Now it's true that Saqib and Mary had got on well from the start, but things never went any further. Once Husain Shah and Irshad had patched up their differences and everything was moving along on an even keel, Mary suddenly began showing interest in Saqib.

Saqib was a young, naive boy. Everyone in the house treated him like their own child. No one thought anything of his relationship with Mary at first. But when they started shutting the door to the room, it made us wonder. Saqib came home at five o'clock. If Irshad happened to be out or busy in the house somewhere, Mary grabbed the chance to call Saqib into the room, closing the door after him. This went on for quite some time before Husain Shah and Irshad found out about it. How long could it have gone on behind their backs when they all lived under the same roof? Irshad got wind of it first, and then Husain Shah found out too. Husain Shah didn't say anything but Irshad confronted Mary with it. But what did she care? She told him to shut up.

Saqib's behavior started to change. Earlier on, he told us everything Mary said. Not any more. He started keeping secrets from us. He still ate with us, but socialized less and less. It seemed as if the closer he got to Mary, the further he drifted away from us. Saqib's English was much better than ours, and he was deservedly proud of it. The ease with which he spoke it had brought them close together in a way. Saqib dropped reading his Urdu literary journals and picked up English magazines instead. He was always talking on and on with her, or else reading portions of the magazines out loud to her. Even with us, he'd break into English in mid-conversation —things went as far as that.

And Mary—well she had become outright shameless. She no longer cared whether Irshad was just outside the room or if Husain Shah was home; she'd call Saqib into her room and shut the door whenever she pleased. And they'd stay in there for as long as they wanted. Neither Irshad nor Husain Shah attempted to get her to open the door. In fact, they'd deliberately go busy themselves elsewhere in the house until the door opened, when they'd walk in there as if nothing had happened.

On the surface it looked as though things were working out the way we had hoped they would. Everyone was happy in his place, and the house was running smoothly. But things were not what they seemed. It was strange how we had been swept by a mounting feeling of anxiety now, when things seemed to be going so smoothly, compared to our calm during their frequent brawls and fights earlier on. But smoothly—ha! How so? Well that's what life is all about. When two threads get tangled up, you can still undo the knot; but when they begin to fray, the whole piece of fabric threatens to unravel. After that it's only a matter of time until the whole thing simply falls apart. To spare ourselves anxiety, we pretended not to notice what was going on. But everything was falling to pieces right before our eyes. More and more we were feeling as if we were standing on a riverbank which would cave in any day soon.

A radical change was coming over Saqib. Mary's room and his attic were the only places you could find him then. He'd only join us for meals, and even then he'd only say a few words and leave. He began skipping shifts at work. Sometimes he called in sick, or just failed to show up, and other times he left right in the middle of his shift. I can say this much for Mary—she did reprimand Saqib for missing work. "Saqib," she'd say, "hard work and hard work alone keeps this country going. Nobody will care for you if you don't work."

But it was getting more and more difficult for Saqib to stay away from Mary. Lying on his mattress up in the attic with his face near the trap door, his eyes were always riveted on Mary's door. And when he wasn't in his room, he followed her around like a shadow, his gaze trained on her, as if he were half-crazed.

The four of them had even stopped going to the pub together. Rancor loomed in Irshad's heart. So he picked a fight with Saqib on the way back from the pub one day and really let him have it. Mary and Husain Shah stepped in and yanked them apart, but Saqib had already taken quite a beating; blood dripped from his nose and mouth. That was the last time Saqib went along with them to the pub.

A few days later Husain Shah and Irshad got into an argument over money. Because he had started buying expensive clothes for himself and Mary, Irshad was left with less money to spare. Husain Shah didn't say anything for a couple of weeks, but blew up at him when he got less than the set amount again the third week. At least that's what Saqib told us. And he'd got it straight from Husain Shah and Mary. Irshad's version was different, however. According to him Husain Shah had bought up a lot of land back home in the village for himself and his son, though he had told Irshad that any land he bought with Irshad's money would be specifically for him. Well, Irshad said that if his uncle was taking money as compensation for arranging his paper marriage with Mary, then whatever he'd already given him was quite enough. He had no intention of handing over another penny. After all, he had legal rights. Well, whatever it was, Husain Shah and Irshad had a falling out over it.

The three of them started going to the pub with Mary separately. Nobody had a fixed day; when Mary felt like going out, she'd just take one of them along. That was how she ended up going to the pub three times a week, and they once each. Soon Mary started to cook for Saqib as well. The only time we ever saw Saqib at all was at mealtimes, and now even that ended. Mary had taken it upon herself to look after all three of them. She was really one for hard work. She did everything for them: bought the weekly groceries, cooked the meals, did the dishes, washed and ironed their clothes, and cleaned up the house. Above and beyond all that, she still made the time to go out with one of them every other day to the pub. None of them had any worries: she took care of their every need.

Mary's appearance had also changed a good deal. Her health improved and she began to fill out. She dressed up regularly before going out. But she still had those rings around her eyes. They didn't look so bad underneath all that makeup she put on to hide them, but they really stuck out in the morning when she got up and washed her face. Changes slowly began working their way into the house. Our socializing had ended ever since the tension began mounting on our floor. Ghulam Muhammad's life was, of course, set. He came home from work, ate and went to sleep. After dinner, I was the only one who wandered down to the second floor to chat from time to time.

Sherbaz, the Hafizabadi, couldn't stop lamenting over the situation. He said that as long as the matter remained between Husain Shah and Irshad, it was okay. The two of them would have worked things out. After all, Mary was beholden to Husain Shah, and Irshad had a legal hold over her. It was Saqib jumping into the act which was the root of all the evil. First of all, he wasn't related to them. Secondly, he was just a kid—totally inexperienced—and he was likely to get burned. We, of course, couldn't agree with Sherbaz more.

The hookers were back in the house again, pursuing their business on the first floor. We were unaware of it the first couple of times they came, but the news slowly leaked out. So far it was only the two Bengalis and a Hafizabadi from the second floor who were in on the deal. But deep inside we all knew it was only a matter of time before everyone else jumped in. After all, one picks up ideas from others. And yet, it would never be the same for us, we knew that, too. Ghulam Muhammad and I started playing around with the idea too. But as luck would have it, we never got the chance to act on it. Fate plays games with us all. The house was bound for destruction sooner or later, and the day had arrived.

Now that I think about it, I can scarcely believe that an incident of such magnitude—it blasted in our home like a bomb, flinging us all over the place—could have been over and done within the space of one minute! Although my room was right next to theirs, I hadn't even a clue as to what was happening. I had just returned from work and had laid down to rest a little. I did hear some voices coming from Mary's room, but that was nothing new. Anyway I didn't think anything of it. Suddenly, someone was shouting. I strained my ears and recognized Husain Shah's voice. He was furious, swearing his head off. Then silence all at once, followed immediately by a groaning "Agh!" Then there was a big thump on the floor. Another sound. I sat bolt upright. A few strange noises burst forth and subsided just as quickly. Then there was screaming—as though some terrible tragedy had occurred. Mary was screaming for her life.

People came bounding up the stairs. I kicked open the door to Mary's room. I was met with a horrifying sight: Husain Shah lay sprawled, flat on the floor as if he'd dropped dead. Half his shirt, from his underarm to the belt of his pants, was drenched in dark blood. Irshad was slumped against the wall on the floor, knees drawn up to his chest, absolutely motionless. One of his hands was on the ground, palm upturned, and the other was hugged to his chest, blood gushing out from between his fingers. The blood was so fresh and bright—I remember that there was a moment when I was surprised to find Irshad so lifeless, with his head slunk over his chest.

Saqib stood between the two of them holding Mary's butcher's knife, dripping with blood. He was staring at the two slain men, but his eyes weren't registering anything. Mary was screaming like she was never going to stop, clutching the child against her chest. We stood aghast in the doorway, gaping at the grisly scene inside. No one even had enough courage to step in the room and hush Mary up, or take the knife from Saqib's hands. Suddenly, somebody stole out of the back of the crowd and scrambled down the stairs. Then someones else's voice rang out, "Quick! Run for your lives! Or you'll be arrested!"

And then it was like stampeding cattle. Those of us who happened to be in the house at the time got a chance to grab our things; the rest who were out just took off. I shoved my money into my pocket, threw a change of clothing and a pair of shoes into a trunk and was out the door within two minutes.

It was already dark outside. The front door of the house was opening and closing like a swinging door. All of my housemates were fleeing from the scene one by one. I was three blocks away from the house when a police car went screeching by me with its siren blaring. I thanked God.

I've never even so much as looked at that house since that day, but I remember the scene of our departure vividly. I kept glancing back at the house until I left the street. Light streamed out as the door opened, and someone would go leaping out; darkness ascended as the door slammed shut behind him, and his form blended into the night. That was the last time I ever saw my housemates of two years. God only knows how many of them got away, how many were apprehended, how many are still in this country, or how many got deported. It's been so long now that if I ran into any one of them, who knows whether I'd still be able to recognize him? But one thing is certain; even now, I know they remember me just the way I remember them. It was the nature of the time—as though we were soldiers fighting in a war. Many people die in a war, and the survivors? Well, time virtually stops for them. After that, anything that happens looks ordinary, terribly commonplace and routine by comparison.

The way I travelled undercover, ended up in Scotland, and everything that happened to me there is another story again. I got work in a small, obscure factory. To alter my appearance, I grew a beard and began a life of anonymity. I'd been living in Glasgow for a few years when on a walk around town one day a familiar face in a café caught my eye. I stopped. Peering at him through the glass door, I remembered the man: he lived in the house next door in Birmingham. His name was Gul Muhammad. He was sitting alone at a table drinking tea. I went in and sat across from him. He looked at me, but he didn't recognize me. After I introduced myself, he remembered that time.

He had also been living in Glasgow for some time. We began talking of old times, and Gul Muhammad gave me the whole story of what happened after I left Birmingham. He was home when the disastrous incident occurred. He saw the police come to the house. Everyone except the Bengalis had already taken off. The Bengalis were at the door when the police went trooping in and they arrested both of them.

A crowd was gathered at the house until quite late. Saqib was placed under arrest. The landlord rushed to the scene. The whole place was crawling with police cars. Finally, after a lengthy investigation, Mary, Saqib and the two Bengalis were whisked into three separate cars. An ambulance carted the two corpses off to the morgue.

The authorities sealed off the house and a bobby was put on guard outside. The guard was removed later, but the house stayed locked up. The house remained uninhabited for as long as Gul Muhammad lived next door. The neighborhood kids threw rocks at the windows and smashed the glass panes. Birds started nesting inside the house, and cats bounded in and out after them. The landlord never once came to check the place. An air of desolation gripped the house.

Gul Muhammad left the city a year later. The court case concerning this incident gained quite a notoriety and its development was covered by all the newspapers. Gul Muhammad said that he bought the paper just to keep up with the case. He told me that the two Bengalis were granted immunity for giving all the names and addresses of the house residents, plus the names of all their relatives in the country, to the police. They were also given temporary legal residence for six months to produce evidence of regular work and start the required paperwork for permanent settlement. That was how all of our names got entered into the police record.

Mary was also called in to testify. She told the whole story as she knew it, but she didn't implicate Saqib. Saqib, however, pleaded guilty, whereupon the court ordered a psychiatric evaluation. He was found mentally incompetent. And so he was put into an institution for the criminally insane. I've seen this sort of place only in this country. It is both a jail and hospital, where only the criminally insane are kept. Gul Muhammad somehow found out that Saqib was put into one such institution near London. I asked him for the address, scribbled it on a piece of paper and slipped it into my wallet. Gul Muhammad and I parted with the promise to get together again. But Glasgow is a very large city. You can go on for years without running into someone from another neighborhood. I never saw Gul Muhammad again after that day.

All your deeds—both good and bad—stay with you. One of my own people exposed me to the authorities and I was arrested. I rotted in jail for three months fighting the charges. But luck was on my side, and I beat it in the end: the immigration laws changed and all of us were granted resident status. By that time, whatever money I'd managed to save had been eaten up by legal expenses, but those who leave their homelands to toil in a foreign country never lose their ability for hard work. I got out of Scotland as soon as I could. The winters there had made life miserable for me. After wandering around, I eventually ended up in this small city, near London. The weather is good here. This is a coastal town—a big vacation spot during the summer. I got a job in the local post office. It's hard work all right, but it's a steady job, and you can make good money working overtime. I worked day and night. Within a year I was able to buy my own house and begin the process of bringing my wife and kids over.

Once, idling about in my house on my day off, I suddenly thought of Saqib. I opened my wallet. The piece of paper with the address was still there. The place wasn't very far. I decided then and there that I would go to see Saqib. A fortnight later on my next day off, I finished my housework early in the morning and got on a bus to go see him.

The institution was a sprawling building enclosed by a low fence. When I got to the entrance and explained my business, I realized that visiting Saqib wasn't going to be as easy as I'd thought. The guard led me into a small office. I spent quite some time waiting there. Then an officer came in, called my name and asked me to follow him. He took me into another office and grilled me with questions: Who was I? What did I do? Where was I from? How did I know Saqib? Why did I want to see him? Was I aware of his present condition? And so on. I not only told him everything he wanted to know as clearly as I could, but I also showed him the papers stating that I was a legal resident and government employee.

The officer politely explained that this was all routine and required, and he said he hoped I wouldn't mind. Later, when he had finished the interview, he told me: "We are very happy that you have come to see Saqib. Until today, no one at all has come to visit him. Who knows—your visit might do him a lot of good." Then he told me I could leave and that I'd be contacted by mail soon. I thanked him and left.

A month passed by without any word. I'd almost given up all hope about the matter when a letter arrived. My request to see Saqib had been approved, and I could visit him for an hour on any of the three listed dates. But, the letter went on, it was very important that I inform them by letter well in advance of my visit. The letter bore the signature of the prison director. I had time off on one of the given dates, so I sent off the letter informing them that I'd be there at eleven o'clock that day. And so I waited for the day to come.

I've heard that you are separated by bars when visiting someone in jail. But this institution was different. I was shown into a small, furnished, carpeted room—it could have easily been somebody's living room. I waited there alone for about five minutes. Then the door opened and in walked Saqib, escorted by an attendant. The man turned to Saqib and said, "Saqib, this is your friend. He's come to visit you."

Saqib nodded and extended his hand. I shook it.

The attendant spoke again, "Okay Saqib? I can go now?"

"Yes," Saqib said, nodding.

"Okay," said the man, "I'll be off now. You stay here and talk with your friend."

The man left the room, closing the door behind him gently.

Many years had passed since I last saw Saqib. His appearance had changed considerably. He was wearing a suit and tie and shining dress shoes. His oiled hair was well groomed. He looked as if he were dressed up to go out somewhere. He had become quite fat. He couldn't have been more than twenty-six or twenty-seven at the time, but he looked considerably older. Putting on weight had given his face a firm, adult look.

"Saqib," I said, "do you remember me?"

"Yes," he replied, nodding. But his face didn't show a trace of recognition.

"How are you?" I asked.

"I'm fine now," he replied.

He seemed happy. He was talking in English—it seemed as if he didn't speak anything else. I began talking in English also.

"What were you doing?" I asked.

"We were watching a football game."

"Watching a game?"

"Yes," he said. " We have a color TV."

"Do you read magazines?" I asked.

"Yes," he answered. " I work in carpentry."

"Oh really? What do you make?"

"Everything," he said. "Tables, chairs..."

Our conversation came to a halt. We sat silent for a while. Saqib was giving me a glazed look; his eyes were vacant—empty, as if fixed on a single spot. I wanted to talk about old times with him to make him remember, but couldn't find the courage. Finally, I managed to say, "Saqib, do you remember Birmingham?"

Saqib nodded happily. "Oh yes," he said, and drifted off into silence. A little while later he suddenly said, " We went to London."

"What for?"

"We went in a bus," he said. "Just to go around."

He lapsed into silence once again, his eyes still fixed on me blankly.

I was feeling quite odd—torn apart between sparing him the painful memories and, at the same time, dying to remind him of anything that might penetrate through the numbness that surrounded him like a formidable wall. His expressionless face was beginning to depress me. "Saqib," I said, "do you remember Mary?" I gave him a probing look, searching for even the slightest flicker in his eyes. But his face remained as vacant as before, although he did answer me right away.

"Yes."

He began looking around the room. His eyes wandered along the walls, over a picture of some shirtless laborers digging a ditch.

"Wrestling comes after lunch," he blurted out.

"Where?"

"On TV," he replied cheerfully. "We're having fish for lunch."

When the time was up, the same attendant came in the room. When I stood up, Saqib rose quickly and extended his hand. Then, shaking my hand, he asked, "Are you coming back again tomorrow?"

"Not tomorrow," I answered, "but I'll be back soon."

"Wonderful," he said. "Just wonderful."

I took another bus to go home. It was a gorgeous day. There wasn't a wisp of cloud in the sky. Bright sunshine poured down on deep emerald fields and dark asphalted streets. Sunny days are rare in this country, and when they do come along, the memory of their brilliance etches itself onto your soul. God knows I'm not a fainthearted person, but all I wanted to do on that bus was simply cry my heart out. Saqib's world was so small, and completely sealed off from anything else: he was its only inhabitant.

I couldn't stop thinking about the time when he'd first come to this country and lived with us in that Birmingham house. He was so bright and quick! So fond of reading and learning! He never wasted his time in our small talk; he'd always be stretched out in his attic, poring over his literary journals. He used to tell us about our famous intellectuals who had come to London in times past, and about how they wrote marvelous stories and brilliant articles. He was completely wrapped up in that world. He'd tell us he'd get to London one of these days. It wasn't our world, but hearing him talk with such fervor made us forget whatever was weighing us down. Youth has its own special charm that way.

But the Saqib I saw today wasn't the Saqib who lived through that difficult time with us. One question troubled me again and again: What did Saqib do to deserve this? My heart contracted every time I thought of it. Finally I said to myself: For God's sake, man, keep your faith! You can't go on living grieving over somebody forever! The thought gave me some solace. I thought, why am I letting such a useless question bother me so? A question which has no answer? What's the point in even asking a question like that? I decided that henceforth I'd never let myself even think about visiting him again. The Saqib I knew was gone; the man I saw that day was a nameless, faceless nobody. I vowed to forget him.

It's said that there is quite a difference between words and actions. How true! No matter how hard I tried, I couldn't forget Saqib. I couldn't get the image of his pudgy face, his glazed eyes, and his immobile body out of my mind. So I ended up sending another letter to the institution six months later, requesting permission to see him again. The request was granted, and I went to visit him.

This has become routine now. I go to see him once or twice a year. Every visit is the same; his condition remains unchanged. I don't expect much either. I just listen to him and talk about the same things he always does.

Sometimes I think about what makes me keep going back there. I do not understand it. It's all very strange. Sometimes when I'm visiting him I can't help thinking: this man is dead, his life is as good as finished. He cannot think or feel. There is no difference between him and a vegetable. He has nothing to do with me. But the minute I leave him and he's out of my sight, a different image of the man springs to mind: exuberant, vibrant with life. And that's the image that stays with me. The same thing happens every time. This image of him is charged with such magnetism that I feel involuntarily drawn to it. I just don't understand it all. But maybe that is the reason I keep going back to see him all the time.

Perhaps the key to this riddle can be found in the incident Mary described to me last year. I met Mary again by sheer accident. Who would have imagined that I'd ever see her again? And the way we met! We literally bumped into each other. You can go years on end without seeing your own friends in the same city, and then suddenly you'll run into a forgotten acquaintance in the middle of nowhere. I tell you, life has no rhyme or reason; it's just a long chain of coincidences—growing larger link by link. Leaving my country, seeing Mary again—all of it simply adds up to chance. Spotting Mary's face among a crowd of hundreds was another such strange instance.

Every Sunday a big flea market is set up in East London where you can get new and used things very cheap. I had been planning to go there for several weeks, hoping to find a bargain. These kinds of markets are set up in many places here. I go to them on my days off. If I find something I like I buy it, otherwise I just have a look and return home.

One Sunday I rode down to this flea market in my car. It was springtime. In the winter when it snows, an eerie stillness hangs everywhere. It's as if the earth stops breathing, and lies motionless like a corpse under a shroud of snow. Many weeks pass by without a blade of green to be seen anywhere. One feels as though it will never be warm again, and not a grain of food will ever grow. No matter where you look, it's the same bland, depressing grey.

But when March, April, and May roll around, the earth miraculously transforms. Mist lifts off the ground and the sky turns a translucent blue. The spring air has a character all its own—you feel like you are swinging high on a swing with the air whooshing around you. You can only experience it with your eyes closed.

I had lived in this country for twelve years, but this was the first time I ever noticed the change of season. The climate of your own country is ingrained in your blood; you don't have to open your eyes to it. But when you come to live in a foreign country, you're so caught up in the business of finding your place that you scarcely have the time to look around and see what the country itself is like. And so it was for me. I had spent twelve years here, but in a sort of darkness. This was the first time I went out with no cares in my heart and took the time to look outside. There are many of us here, who carry this darkness around inside ourselves. But I say, the land sees some drought now and again, but nothing ever stops or lapses behind. Life always pushes on.

During spring in this country, the flowers and leaves burst forth at once in such a dazzling array of colors that it leaves you stunned. I stopped the car along the way, captivated by the sight of a particular meadow. The only thing growing there was grass, or perhaps it was hay, but the green was so intense that I couldn't take my eyes off it. There was something magical about the sun that day, or maybe it was just the spring, or perhaps the green itself was just new—whatever it was, I never saw anything like it before, growing wild or cultivated. I've seen plenty of birds and insects, and colorful fish in the water, but that luminescent green was clearly out of this world. Each verdant blade of grass pulsated with warm, gushing life; it seemed that green was the color of life itself. And if one were to step on it, all of that life would be squeezed out of it, leaving behind only a pile of crumpled, dry straw.

When one finally emerges from a seemingly interminable darkness, a desire is born—the desire for sparkling colors and soft, smooth-surfaced objects, for silk clothes, gold jewelry, and finely-crafted tools. All this simply betrays a feeling of exile. Who can quarrel about that? But no one has the right to look down upon those things, or take them lightly. This yearning is what keeps a man alive and hopeful. Such thoughts streamed through my mind as I stood gazing at that bright meadow that day.

At the market, a deluge of stalls—which people had set up by placing planks of wood on the sidewalks, or some on top of pushcarts—stretched easily a mile down the street. I browsed through a number of them. Everyone was shouting their wares into the street. It was just like markets back home. You couldn't hear a thing over the din. The tight space on the sidewalk made for a lot of pushing and shoving. I got bumped from behind and turned around. An older woman smiled and said, "Sorry." I returned her smile. When I turned back to move on, Mary was standing right in front of me.

It took a while for us to place each other. After all, it had been a long time. We stood there staring at each other for a moment or two. When I was sure it was her, I cried, "Mary!" I must say one thing for her, never mind what kind of woman she was, she was always very nice to me.

We got away from the crowd. Mary had four kids with her. She was pushing the youngest one, only a few months old, in a baby carriage. A three or four year old was clinging to her legs. The next one was near six or seven. The eldest was Michael, whom I recognized right away. He had grown to be a rather handsome lad. I figured him to be about eleven or twelve, but he looked like he was in his late teens. His hair was black and kinky, but his complexion was fair. He had the tall, strapping build of his Jamaican father. I patted him on the head as I said hello, and then I told him that he wasn't even a year old when I last saw him. He said hello back, smiling pleasantly like Mary. His eyes resembled his mother's. The six or seven year old also looked like he was of mixed race. The two little ones resembled each other, and they seemed to belong to a white guy.

Mary told me she lived close by. She had come to the market to buy some clothes for the children, and she got them for a very good price. Then she asked me with some hesitation if I'd like to come along with her for a little while and have a cup of tea. I looked at her for a few moments. The passage of time has a way of taking the bitterness out of even the worst memories. I bore Mary no grudges now. I thanked her and accepted her invitation.

Mary's two-bedroom flat had been allotted by the council. There were only the basic necessities inside: beds, tables, chairs, and a few miscellaneous items kept in built-in shelves. The floor was bare. A few toys were strewn around. Soon upon entering the house, the three-year-old boy named David picked up a big, yellow plastic elephant. After telling Michael to keep an eye on the younger ones, Mary led me into her small kitchen, where there was a table and two chairs set up in one corner. I sat down in one of the chairs while Mary stood by the stove making tea.

Dirty dishes were scattered all over the place. I remembered the old days when Mary wouldn't leave a single dish lying around even for a moment, and when everything in her room appeared very neat and clean. But then, she was no longer the same Mary. The intervening twelve or so years had changed her appearance as well. She must have been about forty by then. Her face was withered and those dark circles around her eyes had become permanent. There was a big bruise near one of her eyes, as if she'd been hit there. She touched it every now and then as she talked. She was still very skinny, and whatever flesh she did have hung loosely on her body. She shuffled around, dragging her feet as if she were dead tired. I felt the urge to talk to her about old times, when she was young and her face was fresh, when there was a spring to her gait. But she was talking of things closer to her heart as she made the tea.

There was one thing about her that hadn't changed at all. That natural cheerfulness still colored her personality. She told me she was living with an Irishman now. He was a construction worker. Back in Ireland he had a wife and kids. He worked hard and earned good money. But there was one flaw: he was a hard drinker as well. He'd get into a brawl when drunk, becoming quite violent. She went on:

"He's at the pub right now, otherwise I wouldn't have dared invite you home. He's the jealous sort, you know." She looked at me and chuckled. "Don't worry, he'll be out for at least another hour. I know him well. He doesn't leave the pub until closing time."

Mary set two cups of tea on the table and sat down across from me. When she was adding the sugar, she asked, "Still the same amount of sugar as you used to?"

I was stunned. "You remember after all this time?" I asked.

"I've always had a good memory," she smiled. "Okay, enough about me. Now let's hear about you. What are you doing nowadays?"

I gave her a quick description of my life during the last dozen or so years. She was very happy to hear that I'd obtained legal resident status. She smiled cheerfully and said, "You know, your life and mine are so similar: the same struggle! The same bumping around from place to place! Thank God you've found some comfort and ease at last."

Seeing her again made me feel nostalgic, and I asked, "Mary, things were pretty good in Birminham, weren't they?"

"Yes," she answered. "You're right."

"Mary, may God give you comfort and ease also. I pray for this in my heart."

She smiled cheerfully again, and then said, "My life goes on, whether good or bad. That doesn't much worry me."

"What do you mean?" I asked. "Everyone worries about comfort. I pray with all my heart that your burdens are eased and you live comfortably."

"You are very kind," she said and fell silent. After thinking for a little while, she said, "Let me tell you something, for you may not know about it. I have a brother, a year older than myself. When we were little, we used to play together. Whenever a guest came to our house, my father would tell my brother to show him his football kick. When my brother kicked the ball, it sailed across the street, prompting the guest to slap my brother on the back and say 'Bravo!' Then it was my turn. My mother dressed me up in pretty clothes and presented me to the guest, remarking, 'This is my daughter. See how pretty she is?' The guest would look at me and praise my beauty. Then he'd call me over, cuddle me in his lap, and feel happy."

Mary suddenly stopped and looked at me with her eyes wide open. Then she said, "Well that's it. That's just how girls are brought up. I know that I don't have to do anything. My job is simply to make a man happy. Women develop a certain cleverness. I've never worried about the future. I've this in-born confidence that I'll get by wherever I go. But yes, you're right about one thing. We really had a good time in Birmingham. I was very happy there. In fact, I have never been as happy anywhere else. You people were all exiles, and so was I. I felt at home with you, and became part of you."

Mary's son David came crying into the kitchen. He had had a fight with his older brother. Mary took him in her lap and tried to soothe him. Through all this I couldn't help remembering Saqib. I finally brought him up, as I couldn't hold it in any longer. I told her where Saqib was, and how I went to visit him now and then. Mary became quiet for a few minutes, twirling her spoon around in the empty tea cup and looking at it intently. Then, lifting her head gently, she said, "Saqib made a big mistake. There was no reason for what he did. They would have finished each other off by themselves."

I didn't understand what she meant by that. When I asked her to explain, she said, "You mean you don't know what happened?" I shook my head.

"How strange!" she said. "Right up until now I was sure that you had seen the whole thing."

"So what did happen?" I asked her.

She leaned on her elbow looking at me, as if trying hard to remember, or perhaps searching for a way to describe it.

"They had been fighting over money," she started. "Irshad had grown lax about his payments to Husain Shah. Finally, Irshad just grabbed a knife off the table and thrust it into Husain Shah's stomach. Husain Shah yanked the knife out and then he went at Irshad with it. They were both fatally wounded and were convulsing and gasping on the floor. When Saqib picked up the knife, I begged and pleaded with him to drop it and get out of the room, that nothing would happen to him. But God knows what got into his head. He fell on the two of them, looking at me again and again as he ripped them apart with the knife; it was as if he were performing some feat. He was so foolish.... And now he's paying for it."

I couldn't believe my ears. I was absolutely stunned. Why did Saqib do that? What was he trying to prove, anyway? "Did you tell all this to the police?" I asked.

"I told everything in my testimony," she said. "But it didn't make any difference."

I was feeling pretty lousy. I don't blame Mary for the whole thing, but all I wanted to do right then was end the conversation and get out of there. Luckily, just at that moment, Mary's youngest child began bawling in the other room. Mary started getting his bottle ready, giving me the excuse to get up.

The intervening period had changed none of her cordiality and warmth. She said goodbye to me in the same pleasant manner as always, and stood at the door waving until I had turned the corner. There was a lot of strength, a lot of resilience still left in her.

On the way back I couldn't stop thinking about Saqib. The whole thing weighed on my mind for days. I felt quite tense and on edge. The effect gradually faded away though.

It's been just a few days now since I visited Saqib. That turned out to be our last meeting. I vaguely remember some talk of him being sent back home on a previous visit, but I seemed to have forgotten all about it by the time I got there the other day. When I arrived at the institution I found out that there were only a few days left before Saqib's departure.

Before I saw Saqib, an officer took me into his room and told me it was time for Saqib to go home. Saqib's original sentencing required him to be kept in this institution and treated for at least ten years and promptly deported thereafter. The officer told me that it had already been over ten years. Saqib's stay could be extended for further treatment if there were any hope of improvement, but in the opinion of the doctors this was not likely to happen. So the government had ordered the institution to make arrangements for the journey back.

The officer reassured me, however, that the government would bear all the expenses of his return trip. The money Saqib had earned working in the institution's carpentry had been put away in his name and would be remitted to him in full, along with the accumulated interest. Moreover, the authorities had finally been able to locate Saqib's next of kin back home. Saqib's mother had been dead for some time, but one of his uncles, who had accepted the responsibility of guardianship, would receive him. Saqib's financial records had been sent to this uncle. Finally, he said that all these measures were being taken in Saqib's best interest. Still, all of this couldn't fail to make me feel terribly sad.

I found Saqib in high spirits that day. "I'm going home." He beamed.

There was some cash in his pocket. He kept shoving his hand inside his pocket and taking it out to look at it.

"You're wearing a new suit today," I said, starting the conversation.

"Yes," he said. "I got two suits, a pair of boots and socks."

He kept chatting away happily for a while about his forthcoming departure. Something stabbed at my heart as I sat there watching him. I couldn't stay there very long. I quickly said my last goodbye to Saqib, hugged him, and left.

I arrived home immersed in this feeling of sadness when the accident happened which put me into the hospital. Accident is just the right word for it, in fact, because it was something quite out of the ordinary. Well, what happened was that I came home exhausted and my wife began yapping away at me. I was still terribly upset over Saqib. My wife was yelling at me about something and I just slapped her. That was all—it's happened many times, the matter resolves itself. But God only knows what got into her that day. It was a snap reaction: she picked up a glass jug and threw it at me. I sat there looking at her like an idiot. I didn't even have enough sense to stop the blood flow coming from my head. Then she started screaming.

I've been lying here since that day. The doctors say that there is a hairline crack in my skull, and it will take some time to heal. They keep on taking x-rays. They've wrapped my head in plaster. My young son keeps joking with me. "Daddy," he says, "you're cracked!" And oh boy—what an investigation there was! Even the police showed up. I told them a thousand times, well, it's just a family matter. There's no need for outsiders to get involved. But they wouldn't leave until they'd completed their work.

Anyway, my wife comes and visits me everyday. She sits beside me and cries her eyes out in regret. I just comfort her: Look, I tell her, it really wasn't your fault. It was only an accident. It had to happen, and it did. It's as simple as that. But the poor thing, she just keeps on crying.

I've no complaints about my wife. She treats me like a king. But I don't know what's eating her away. She has been unhappy since the day she set foot in this country. She has all the comforts anyone can ask for: her own house, a car, a TV that she watches all day long. Why, we have plenty. She has a life of ease. The kids are in school. And yet, there's never been a glimmer of happiness on her face. I ask her, "Don't you like it here?" And she tells me that it is nothing to her; she's happy wherever I am. Now what kind of an answer is that? What I can't figure out is, what is it that makes her unhappy? Sometimes I remember what Mary said. I think she's right. Perhaps women too live in an exile all their own. The thought brings back faces of my mother and sister.

Well, I say, whether men or women, everyone is just trying to strike their roots in this world somehow. We planted a sapling here. We're just little people, but it is *our* heads that roll in the dust, whether it is a war or a protest rally. And life goes on. Sometimes it seems like everything is just a dream; like time coming to a complete stop, disappearing down a big, black hole in the ground. God knows what this feeling is. All I want now is to get out of this hospital as fast as I can and get home, get some peace of mind. But other than that, everything is just fine.